Book 8 in the SEEIN

PLAYING

JESUS

A NOVEL

Jeffrey McClain Jones

PLAYING JESUS

Copyright © 2022 by Jeffrey McClain Jones

John 14:12 Publications

www.jeffreymcclainjones.com

Cover Photo from Adobe.com

For the faithful readers who keep this series going with your enthusiastic support.

Playing Jesus

Chapter 1

A Solitary Saturday Back in His Hometown

Paul Bailey stretched one arm beyond the edge of his new mattress. He opened one eye to check the pale blue LED display on his bedside clock. Not much past six. Not time to wake up on a Saturday. He faded back into oblivion.

When he woke again, he exhaled long and slow, blinking both eyes this time. His Monday through Friday work schedule had snuck into the weekend, but that was okay. Better than sleeping through an alarm during the work week. He was not only adjusting to coffee shop hours, he was adjusting to living two time zones away from his apartment on the West Coast. Waking up at six on weekday mornings was workmanlike. Subtracting those two hours made it farmer-like.

Rolling to his side, Paul knew he wasn't going to stay in bed much longer. That would make it harder when Monday came calling again. And, even if he wanted to, he couldn't stay under his new sheets long enough to make up for the hours the time zones had robbed.

These chronological considerations dispersed before an aromatic interruption. Did his new mattress smell funny? Not a harsh chemical smell. More organic. Almost like cereal. Actually, the thing was advertised as organic. Organic and from California. Like Paul, these days.

He snorted at his own silly diversion. He had always wanted to be a Californian, especially since he began acting in high school. Did six years in LA make him a Californian now? His mom and his hometown in the lower Midwest still tried to claim him as their own.

He sighed through his nose, recalling his mom's obvious disappointment just after the funeral. *"Flying out here and back to LA like it was some business trip was very insensitive, Paul."* That exchange had represented early progress. Progress beyond fits of crying and refusing to even talk about it. A half a year later, his mom didn't mention the hurt he put on her back then. Maybe moving back had made the difference. Even if the move was temporary.

Paul sat up briskly, his head wobbly for a couple seconds. He noted that wheaty odor again, more comfortable focusing on that aromatic oddity than on his sins against his mother.

Did it really matter that his mattress was organic? It wasn't like he was going to eat it. Though maybe it would come in handy as an emergency food source in some post-apocalyptic dystopia. Was there a label anywhere that said, "Do not eat this mattress, even in a post-apocalyptic food shortage"? Such a warning would be like those little desiccant packets that came in vitamin bottles. He hadn't ever thought of eating the tiny bags of plastic included with his vitamin C until the label suggested it.

His head shaking like a sudden spasm, he dropped his feet off the edge of the bed. Settling his eyes on the nightstand, he could imagine his mom insisting he take his sister's mattress too. Her bed didn't come home with her other things, did it? He couldn't recall that particular decision about what to discard back there in Chicago.

The nightstand he was staring at had been his sister's, exhumed from Mom and Bob's garage when Paul moved back here. Him accepting that medium-brown Shaker-style table seemed important to his mom. Paul had turned off his own filters over things like that in favor of pleasing Mom. He owed her that much.

Bouncing off his bed as if he had discovered a spider under the covers, he barely avoided barking his shins on the storage bench crowded close in the small bedroom. His mom had insisted on him taking that too. Maybe he should have insisted right back. But at least that piece of furniture didn't remind him of his sister. Except that now, staggering into the hallway, he was thinking about how it didn't remind him of his sister.

He managed to get into the bathroom without knocking against the doorframe this time. This apartment was laid out similarly to his place back in LA, but the bathroom was on the left instead of the right as he exited the bedroom. The similar architectural styles, modern and sparse, enhanced the mirror effect of the bathroom location.

Hesitating in front of the actual mirror above the sink in his current bathroom, Paul confirmed that he was, in fact, grown up and no longer fully subject to the will of his mother. Still, to be real about it, he owed her a lot. For one thing, his mom was the biggest fan of his acting. She was the only family member who consistently watched the soap opera he had been in. She didn't even insist he tell her which days he was going to be on. Unlike Theresa. But his sister had been a busy nurse. She apparently didn't have time to watch all the episodes he had found recorded on her DVR when they cleaned her house.

He sighed heavily and took care of his morning business in the bathroom, his mind wandering back to questions about this move to his hometown for his mother's sake. The temporary move had probably helped to fix their scratched and dented relationship. At least minor repairs. But it was costing him a lot. Giving up the role on that soap opera, as small as it was, was a heavy loss. And not just in dollars.

He paused at the mirror again and evaluated what he thought of now as his Jesus look. He guessed the beard was still too short and well trimmed to match the real Jesus. But no one at church had complained. He surely looked the part more than anyone else in his mother's big congregation. At least anyone who could act.

"Well, I've met Jesus, and you're definitely not him." Paul couldn't recall who he was misquoting, which robbed him of the small chuckle he had queued up. But, as he dried his hands, he could imagine someone else laughing at his little joke. He imagined it so thoroughly that he could almost hear it. Sort of.

He was definitely not awake yet. Even on days when he worked at the coffee shop, he resisted genuine wakefulness until he tied on his apron and forced his first customer-facing smile. Now he was hearing laughter where he wished there was laughter. Someone to laugh at his jokes. Someone to share his space. This new space in an old town. This new situation in a life he had been working hard to establish two time zones west.

The laughter he imagined was like a part in a scene, probably on stage, not on camera. A laugh at his clever reference, though he still couldn't remember who he was referencing. While practicing a scene, he often had to imagine the contribution of absent others. A reply. A rebuff. A laugh.

In his little kitchen now, staring blankly at the brown marble countertop, Paul wondered what Jesus would think of his part in the passion play. Would Jesus mind Paul imitating him on stage? Acting on stage in church strained a childhood sense of what was allowed in such a holy setting. There would be shouting in this play. There would be cruel accusations. Even a torturous death. All that in a place devoted to peace and order. Was it appropriate for Paul to dress up as Jesus? Pretend to be him?

He scuffed the soles of his dry feet over the pale faux-oak floor and stood in front of his espresso machine, one of the few items he had brought with him from California. He was a barista again these days. Surely it was appropriate for him to have this shining metal appliance shipped back here.

The coffee shop job was at least reliable. Acting and modeling work was hard to find. And questionable in lots of ways. He shivered at the photo shoot he did just days after moving home. The cover of a romance novel. As awkward as it was, it was probably fortunate for him the female model couldn't show up to the shoot. Embracing that mannequin covered in green cloth with lust in his eyes was as cringe-worthy as it was laughable. At least it wasn't tempting. Not like holding the living female model who would be later edited into the scene. Whether he had constructed a convincing pose with his mute romantic partner was another question. He hadn't told his mom the details of that modeling job. She hadn't asked.

Pushing the power button on the espresso machine, the smell of fresh beans ushered him back to the present. Paul tried to remember whether he had seen his favorite coffee mug since moving into the new place. There might still be a box or two at his mom and stepdad's house. His mom had been loath to let him take his own apartment. Maybe she was holding on to a cardboard box as proxy for her only remaining child.

He retreated from worrying about his mother again as he pulled cupboards and drawers open. He was still unaccustomed to the new kitchen and compensated by opening everything. That approach would surely help him in the future. It was like reviewing for a test. Which reminded him of reviewing his lines before play rehearsal this afternoon. It was his only serious commitment for the day.

Would that set designer be at rehearsal today? What was her name? She was interesting. Not just beautiful. There was something about her. Something deep. What was her name? It was a strange name. Not one he had heard on a young woman before. Not Brittany or Tiffany or Crystal. Listing the names she was not called wasn't helping him remember. Thinking about her wasn't helping him get his latte ready either. He had opened the drawer next to the silverware three times now.

When he stood looking at the actual silverware drawer, his eyes fell on the tiny teaspoons his mother had probably accidentally included in the stuff she sent over. He would never use those delicate teaspoons for anything. His buddy Roger had called them coke spoons when he helped him move. Paul hadn't laughed. His brother, Peter, had died of a cocaine overdose ten years ago.

A robin chirping loudly on the railing of his little balcony broke Paul out of the heavy stare he was locked in. Coming back to live in his hometown, even for half a year as his lease implied, would not heal his mother. It would not heal him. He and his mother were like the scraps of wood left over from the stage construction at church. Made of the same stuff as the scenery, but looking a lot like discarded bits. Remnants. And that would never change.

Paul thought about going back to bed. His stumbling thoughts were tiring him. Then he heard a small sound. A human sound. Something like, "Mm-hmm." Of course he was imagining that voice, but *who* was he imagining behind it? Who would be agreeing with him? Agreeing with his weary assessment of where his life had landed.

If he wasn't going back to bed, he wished he were good at praying. This seemed like a good time to pray. "A little help here, Lord." That was the best he could muster.

Chapter 2

You Mean, Like, the Real, Original Jesus?

Eventually, Paul did make that latte. He was better at that than praying. He had lots of experience, of course. Not every dollar he earned in LA had come from a soap opera. Most of his paychecks came from a coffee shop west of the city. Though most of the dollars came from one studio or another.

He shook the french vanilla syrup bottle where the pump barely reached the liquid now. Setting the bottle back on the dark marble counter, he poured the steamed milk into the strong, sweet coffee. Caffeine usually woke him up. He clearly needed that, given his rambling thoughts. Not to mention hearing voices.

The voices were just in his imagination, of course.

Holding his mug now, he noted the play script in the middle of the butcher-block kitchen table. That table was a contribution from his stepdad. *"A guy needs a kitchen table. It's basically the center of the house."* Bob was a practical guy. He would know about things like that.

Paul had savings. He could buy furniture for himself. His nest egg would get him through the six months of his lease even if he bought a bit of furniture. But the short time horizon for this stay made big purchases seem wasteful. He bent and ran a hand over the butcher block. It looked like he should be able to feel the seams between the boards, but it was smooth. Sanded perfectly, maybe mechanically.

His eyes landed on the exposed page of his script. "He's just a carpenter from Nazareth." That was the line of some guy named Herschel. Not the character, the actor. The character was *Pharisee Two*. No proper name provided for him.

Apparently Herschel was one of the guys who had tried out for the Jesus role after their original Jesus had bailed. That unnamed guy had taken a job at some Jesus theme park somewhere south.

Reading for the part of Jesus in the church production had been one of the more satisfying experiences in Paul's return home. He wasn't the most sought-after talent in Hollywood, but he outclassed the church drama crew by a few miles. The stunned gaze on the director's face was worth a lot, though maybe not worth enduring six months in his old hometown and giving up his role as the handsome young bartender in that soap opera.

"Handsome, huh?"

A startled slosh stopped Paul in the middle of sipping his foamy drink. He instinctively licked at his mustache even as he turned to scan the apartment. Did someone really just say *handsome*? He looked at the digital hockey puck that he asked things like, "What's the weather today?" But it only answered in a woman's voice. The question about him being handsome had come in a deeper tone.

The soap opera role had been sold to him as "handsome young bartender." It was even on his original contract that way. Only after he appeared on a fifth episode and got a new contract did they give him a name—Derek. The character had a name, but the role was still "handsome young bartender." Someone else was in that role now, though his name was Rusty. Not Derek. A redhead. Paul didn't watch that soap opera now that he wasn't in it.

He stood like a robot powered off between the kitchen and living room. Had he actually heard a voice, or was he just imagining what someone would say? Who was he imagining? Not his stepdad. Bob was okay for a stepdad, but Paul didn't spend much time thinking about him. Pete, his big brother, came to mind next. Was his big brother speaking to him from beyond the grave? Metaphorically, of course.

Not his dad. Not his actual birth dad. Where was that guy, even? Did Paul even care where he was, let alone what his absent dad thought about Paul playing the handsome bartender? Well, maybe he did. Clearly he was thinking about it right now. But that voice didn't sound like his dad's voice. He had heard his dad last when the old man called to congratulate Paul on the TV role. And to ask for a loan.

Paul wandered into the living room. Sitting on the couch and crossing one leg, he held his cup to his lips without drinking. He didn't know where his father was. That was normal. It wasn't significant that Dad hadn't contacted him since Theresa's funeral. Was the old man depressed over the death of his daughter? Was he drinking again? Was he alone? Had he run out of gullible women to exploit?

Paul huffed at his ungenerous thoughts.

"You are not your dad."

Another of those audible thoughts. The coffee wasn't taking effect yet. Paul took a bigger sip. That he was hearing voices in his apartment wasn't unusual. The neighbors played hip-hop music at high volume at least half the day. Thankfully, it was the polite half of the day. Generally not this early. But what he was hearing now was a speaking voice. A voice speaking things that made a lot of sense, actually. Except that he was alone.

Maybe a shower. He should get a shower and decide what to eat. That would make his waking official. It would distract him from all these dark musings. And a shower would postpone the question of why his imagination had gone audiobook on him.

The temperature today was supposed to be in the upper fifties. Springish. It wasn't official yet, but this far south, he could expect spring to do a dress rehearsal or two. He pulled jeans and a gray T-shirt from his dresser drawers. He could wear that to rehearsal later. Jesus in jeans wasn't a problem while they waited for the costumes to be finished.

Was the set designer also doing the costumes? Paul stepped over the side of the tub and ducked under the steady rain from the wide shower head. What was her name? Something not really fitting was what he could remember. She was sharp and feminine.

Confident and beautiful. The name was something … something not like all that.

He hummed a song he had sung in a high school musical as he tried to remember her name. He could remember the way she laughed when he made that joke about turning to check if people were talking to him when they used Jesus's name as a curse. An irreverent joke. She laughed. Not particularly reverent, as it turned out. Did she have a boyfriend? Whatever her name was.

The water off, a fresh towel in hand, he looked across the narrow bathroom at the big mirror over the sink. It was a mirror made for an actor. Or at least someone who spent a lot of time getting ready in the morning.

The fog on the mirror seemed to be conspiring with his thoughts about playing Jesus in the passion play. It sort of looked like he was wearing a Jesus costume. The towel was medium brown, but the Jesus outfit in the mirror was mostly white, a dash of blue. Maybe the stress of everything was warping his eyesight.

Paul had known it would be stressful to come back to live near his mom as she recovered from Theresa's death. There was his mom's broken heart. There was him leaving his West Coast life. There was the stepdad he had never deeply connected with. And there were the memories of Pete's death. A death neither he nor Mom had gotten over yet. Being his mom's only remaining child was a lot of pressure.

"The only begotten son."

Paul stopped breathing. That was just like a real voice. A male voice. Not the voice of his digital assistant. Not the rap rhythm of the neighbor's thumping music. Words. A voice saying something. And it was something that tracked with his thoughts.

There seemed to be an extra set of eyes looking back at him from the mirror now. Paul glanced around. He wasn't looking for someone else in the bathroom. Of course there was no one else here. But he needed to find what it was in the gray-and-white room that made it look like there was a second person in the mirror.

His knees quaked feebly as he stepped out of the shower. Paul suddenly grew self-conscious about his state of undress and quickly pulled on his boxer shorts as he laid his towel on the edge of the sink. He stared at the mirror. A cold wetness on his neck prompted him to lift the towel again and dab at the places he had missed, places where his long hair was dampening his neck.

Now, as he looked more closely, the towel resting on one shoulder, he couldn't see anything unusual in the mirror. He had seen ads for digital mirrors that worked as screens for fitness training or things like that. He tried to recall if the real estate agent had mentioned that when she was reciting the merits of this apartment. He reached up and pulled at the mirror. There was no medicine cabinet behind it, nor any evidence of electronics attached.

When he stopped exploring and concentrated again on the mirror, a grunt jolted out of him. He grabbed the edge of the sink to keep from falling over.

"Hi, Paul. You seem surprised to see me." There was a man in his mirror. Another man. Another man with long dark hair and a beard. It was like there were two of him.

Paul had finally cracked. Now he was suffering from a split personality.

Then the other guy in the mirror was out in the real world. Standing next to him.

They looked at each other. The other guy smiled.

"I'll meet you in the living room once you get dressed." The guy was wearing a long robe. Really, it looked like a well-designed Jesus costume. Surely a better one than the team at church would put together for him.

Paul nodded as the other guy turned and left the bathroom. He huffed a sigh. It was extremely uncomfortable being so close to some strange guy standing in his bathroom. He looked down at his blue boxers. Grabbing his T-shirt, he pulled it on over his still-damp shoulders. His hair was mostly dry. How long had he been out of the shower? Had he forgotten to wash his hair? Clearly the numerous varieties of craziness he was experiencing would fill an entire grocery store aisle—an aisle in a big American store.

He took a long, deep breath once he had his jeans buttoned. Then he noticed he had forgotten his zipper. Rectifying that oversight, he looked in the mirror again. Was there anyone else in there?

That other guy said he was going to the living room. Which meant the living room was the last place Paul wanted to go. If the guy wasn't there, then it would prove his imagination had malfunctioned and he needed to see a doctor as soon as possible. If the guy *was* there, Paul would have to call the cops. Or something. Either way, it would ruin a perfectly good Saturday.

"You didn't have much planned for today anyway." That guy was still there. The voice, and presumably the guy in the Jesus costume, were still there. And they were responding to Paul's thoughts.

Unless his brain was totally broken, and he was hearing things no one was saying. And responding to things he didn't realize he had spoken aloud. That would explain ... probably ... nothing.

His hands were shaking as he wavered on unreliable legs toward his date with insanity.

His hallucination was there on the couch, his leg crossed just like Paul had done a few minutes before. The guy was wearing sandals. Very authentic. Nice costume. A very convincing Jesus costume. No denying it. The guy was dressed as Jesus. He was, what? Playing Jesus?

"No, that's your role. I'm just him."

Chapter 3

What Am I Supposed to Do Now?

Paul stood in his living room with his mouth hanging open. He knew he was doing it. He knew it looked stupid. But he kept doing it anyway.

"You're not capable of looking stupid, Paul. That's why they hired you to be the handsome young bartender for the TV show." The man on the sofa was smiling. His smile was natural and intelligent. He was not gaping like Paul. And he was talking to Paul as if he knew quite a lot about him.

"I know everything about you, Paul. I am who I appear to be. Not an actor." The guy not only knew him well, he seemed to be reading his thoughts.

The need to call the police was standing in line behind a fascination about such accurate mindreading. Was this guy some kind of superhero who could control people's minds? What if they put a special helmet made of rare metals on him?

The man on the couch laughed loudly. Then he shook his head. "Breathe, Paul. Just breathe and let *your* mind settle into what is real and obvious."

"My mind?" It was the first thing he had actually spoken to the uninvited guest.

"Ah. But you did invite me, in a way. You prayed."

Doing a fast rewind, Paul found a point that morning when he wished he was good at praying. Had he actually said any kind of prayer? Maybe he had.

"You said, 'A little help here, Lord.' Back when you were worrying about your relationship with your mother and the loss of so much of your family."

Paul was nodding now, but it was an automatic reaction. Like what he did when one of those uninhibited old guys came into the coffee shop and tried to tell him everything about his life. Nod and smile. Eventually they'll go away.

"But *I'll* never go away."

Stopping the automatic nodding and probably his breathing, Paul confronted a wall of fear. "Never?" This guy would *never* go away? Of course he was just saying that. But would he really try to stick around well past his welcome? That would wreck this Saturday even if the *never* part was an exaggeration.

"You haven't accepted who I am yet. That will make a difference. You don't really want *me* to go away. I'm not a crazy old guy buying coffee just so he can find someone to talk to." The tone with which the man on the couch said that part seemed to imply Paul wasn't taking those lonely old customers seriously enough. They had no one else to talk to. Shouldn't he care about that?

"I care. I care about them. And I care about you. And I'm here to bring the help you were asking for."

"Help? Help with what?" A flicker through his head suggested Paul should know what he needed help with, but he was feeling like he was in the studio audience instead of on stage in his own life just now.

"Well, at least I could help you run your lines for the play." The man grinned generously. A generous joke.

Paul's addled brain met this odd proposal with a level of acceptance. Clearly this guy was a professional Jesus actor. That made him well qualified to help Paul play the part of Jesus in the annual passion play at his mother's church. Maybe his mother had sent this guy over.

"She doesn't know about this visit, Paul. It's just you and me and a whole Saturday to enjoy it."

"Enjoy it?"

"You're not used to associating me with enjoyment, I know."

"You're ..." Paul skidded to a stop, refusing to follow that thought. Refusing to grant it the dignity of even launching the question. He adjusted. "You're staying in character." That notion, he could understand. It had kept him up one night, in fact.

Thinking about what it meant to stay in character when the person he was playing was the Son of God.

"I am in character. Visiting with my friends is part of my character. Helping those in need is who I am. I am always here."

Paul was pretty sure he and the guy on the couch were not talking about the same thing. Not really getting each other.

"Oh, I get you Paul. I had a hand in making you. I get you. But you're still fighting the obvious."

This was the second time the guy had said something about "the obvious." He sounded pretty sure of himself. Confident. Authoritative. Which was, of course, perfectly in character if he was playing Jesus.

"Have a seat, Paul. Before you fall down."

He was swaying. Paul had just noticed that. The room wasn't rocking, but he was.

"Or we could go for a walk. It's still a bit chilly, but not many people are out yet."

"Not many people?"

"Yes. Not many who will see you talking to an invisible man walking next to you."

"Invisible?"

"Yes. This is how it will work for us, Paul. I will appear to you today, and only to you. I will accompany you, visibly and audibly, wherever you go. That way we can talk about what's troubling you and what you can do about it. Most importantly, we can talk about what *I* can do about it."

The Jesus impersonator sounded very helpful. Pretty generous, really. Generous with his time. The whole day. He was offering the whole day to ... to deal with Paul's problems. Could they solve them all in one day?

"It's amazing what we can do in a day."

"We?"

"My Father and I."

"But who is your father?" Paul was seated in the old rocking chair his mother had loaned him. It had belonged to her father.

23

Grandpa Jenkins. Paul was rocking again, but this time he was doing it while seated. And he was saying lines from his play to a man who looked a lot like Jesus might look in a really high-quality production.

"The production at Faith Community is going to be high quality. The set designer is a friend of mine. She's very good. And Arabella knows me well. She's well qualified to direct you in playing your part. But I suppose you can also learn some things about playing me by spending today with ... me." He lifted his hands as if to present himself. "But that's not really the help I came to offer you. Not primarily."

"Playing you?"

"Jesus. Formerly Jesus of Nazareth. Jesus of heaven these days."

Paul stopped. He adopted a statue freeze in place of the nervous rocking. "You're him? The real ... him?"

"I am he." Another line from the play.

Another round of nervous rocking. What was Paul supposed to do with this?

Chapter 4

Because Easter Falls on April Fool's Day

When Paul got the part in the passion play at the large church his mother attended, he noted that Easter landed on April first this year. April Fool's Day. An unholy juxtaposition if ever there was one.

Now it occurred to him that someone was playing a joke on him. Roger? He was the only one of Paul's old friends still in town who would think of doing something like this. Roger must have arranged for this guy who played Jesus to come to his apartment and prank him. A professional Jesus, probably. Even more professional than Paul. Pretty funny, really.

But Paul wasn't laughing. Mostly because he didn't believe his own explanation. Even if Roger had hidden a camera in the apartment when he helped Paul move in, Roger couldn't read Paul's thoughts. Roger could barely read his *own* mind most of the time. But this guy on the couch had responded to a half-dozen thoughts Paul had not spoken to anyone. Ever.

"It may take you a while to accept this. I'm not worried about that." The Jesus guy on the couch didn't need to say he wasn't worried. Everything about him said that already. He didn't shift around. He didn't fiddle.

Paul was fiddling with his beard, twisting a small clump of whiskers beneath his chin. It was a thinking thing. A worrying thing. He was worried. And he was wondering whether the whole holiday around April Fool's Day was part of a bigger tradition. He was trying to recall if he had heard anything like that. Like the way Halloween was linked to some ancient religious ... something. Or was April Fool's sort of like a Groundhog Day thing?

"You're overthinking this, Paul." It was easy to link this guy on the couch with a voice that lived in Paul's head. His clarity was familiar. His familiarity was convincing. His conviction was ...

Around and around, Paul's thoughts spun. Dropping his fiddling hand to the arm of the chair, he started rocking again. He stared at the Jesus on the couch. "Are you real?"

The Jesus on the couch nodded.

"If you weren't real, would you tell me?"

Jesus smiled broadly. "That's a problem. Hallucinations are pretty unreliable witnesses, especially regarding their own origin."

"So you're a hallucination?"

"No, Paul. I am the one you're talking to when you pray. I am the one who has lived inside you since you asked me into your heart back in youth group. I am the one. I am." He didn't say any of that in a booming God voice. Still calm. Still unworried. Friendly, actually.

"I must be totally out of my mind." Paul wasn't shouting either. More like thinking out loud. "That's the only explanation. I've lost my mind. All the stress. All the ... everything."

Jesus nodded. His smile had turned meek and sympathetic. "It *has* been hard. You've been knocked around quite a bit. And doing it on your own, mostly."

"Doing what?"

"Life. Grieving. Searching. Working. Hoping. Wondering."

Those words each lit a scene in Paul's head. It was like seeing his life as a montage. He'd been living on his own since he broke up with Stefany. He hadn't admitted to his mom that he had a live-in girlfriend, so the scale of the breakup was as secret as the relationship had been. His other associations were just that—associations. Not like family. And not like having someone smile at him the way this stranger on the sofa was doing.

And the other things too. Grieving. Both of his siblings were gone now. He had been shocked numb when he heard Theresa's strange ailment had ended her life. He wasn't there when his mom decided to pull the plug on the respirator. If he had been there, he probably would have been as mummified at her side as he had been in his apartment on the coast.

Only when his emotions started to fray after the funeral did he go see a counselor. And that was like watching a guy talk to a mannequin. Paul was the mannequin in that scene. His pain insisted he needed it to stay hidden inside. But coming back home for several months would surely compound the pain. The counselor didn't really help him decide whether to do it.

His mother's calls for help had decided it. "Please come home, Paul. I need you here. I need you with me now."

He did come home, of course. Finally. But too late to prevent the knotting of the ties with his only accessible relative.

Paul scowled at the man on the couch. He was ticked at himself for doing all this introspection just because of a hallucination. "What ...?" He stopped when he considered the foolishness of asking a hallucination what was wrong with him.

"Being on your own is all that's wrong. It's a problem that goes in lots of directions."

Of course a hallucination could read his mind. Paul didn't even have to ask silly questions for the hallucination to answer him. That was kind of handy. As if he could talk to himself with half the effort. Now he was shaking his head. His brain was clearly melting down.

"Maybe we should go for a walk." The man on the couch waited a second and then edited his proposal. "Maybe you and your internal dialogue should take a walk. To clear your head."

Paul was out of the rocker on the next forward beat. "Yes. That's a good idea." He faltered on the word *idea*, given where that idea had apparently originated.

The man on the couch stood as well. Did he have to come too? Well, he was in Paul's head, so he would go wherever Paul went, obviously. That slowed his progress toward the bedroom where he planned to get socks. He was at least cogent enough to think of socks. Not a lofty achievement, maybe, but a positive step.

The stranger hung back as Paul pulled on running shoes and a button-up pink cotton shirt he had owned since college. The man was waiting by the front door with Paul's jacket in hand. Paul had forgotten about the temperature. Even in LA in March, he might wear a light jacket this early in the day.

As he took the jacket from his visitor's hand, Paul's brain twisted and strained. *Wait a minute. Did a hallucination just hand me my jacket?* His lips buzzed in the way they had when he broke his leg in high school. The same fuzzy feeling he got just before he passed out at the sight of a bone fragment poking through his skin.

"Nope. Don't do that." The man in the Jesus outfit grabbed Paul's shoulder and sort of injected a steadying calm.

The buzzing diminished. Paul's head stopped twirling, and he took a deep breath. "Thanks, man."

Then he lost it. This was so absurd. He started to laugh and laugh and cackle and slurp. Paul laughed harder than he could remember laughing in a long time. And he didn't sound like himself at all. It was like he was playing a part, being someone else.

During what was surely another stage in Paul's mental breakdown, the man who had grabbed his shoulder continued to hold him. Still steadying him. Not in a hurry to go anywhere.

Before he could drain all his delirium, Paul tried to talk. The sympathy in the stranger's eyes disabled his resistance. "What's happening to me?"

"Right now you're releasing a lot of emotional tension about your life, your losses, and what it all means for you. What it means for your future and even for eternity."

The sweeping scope of that answer added drag that subdued Paul's unhinged laughter. *All that?* He didn't say it aloud. It seemed unnecessary. The eyes of the man who looked like Jesus had linked into Paul's brain like he was reading his thoughts in real time, not just waiting for words to be said. Maybe not even waiting for Paul to form those thoughts.

Paul tried speaking again. "You're waiting for me to—to do something?"

"I'm waiting *with* you. You will have to decide. You will have to act. But for now we wait together."

"Wait for what?"

"For you to accept me first. Accept my presence. Accept that I am real and that I am available to you."

"Jesus?"

"Yes, Paul. I am him."

As if someone pushed him from behind, Paul tipped forward and wrapped his arms around the man in front of him. Whoever he was. Paul simply could not resist any longer. And he started to cry.

Strangely, the tears seemed to come from the same channel that was streaming laughter a moment before. And the tears activated that montage he was seeing before. The scenes of his recent life, waiting for life to make sense. Make sense to someone. Hopefully someone who would eventually share what they discovered with him.

Paul's head filled with images. His mom's reluctant forgiveness granted with hardened eyes and sharp little lines around her lips. His sister's house where he had seen her alive last spring. His brother's face. His father's eyes. Regrets seemed to waft up from some hidden storage area in his heart, some room he had not seen or was not allowed to access.

He was on his own. Yes. It was true. It was something he thought about as he lay awake at night. He had separated himself, really. To protect himself.

His life with Stefany had been part of that. He had to separate himself from the faith of his youth in order to live with her and to keep the secret from his mother.

Separated. Maybe even separated from himself. That would be a problem, wouldn't it?

"You wanna walk?" The man hugging him next to the front door shifted easily when Paul released him. No hesitation of clinging regret.

Nothing like his mom. But his mom believed in Jesus. Since she was a little girl in the Catholic church, she had believed. And she was Paul's connection to the evangelical faith of his teen years. Jesus was probably real. Paul had hoped his mom was right about that. This guy in front of him was not like his mom, but maybe he wasn't even like the Jesus Paul had imagined.

"Let's walk." Even this more direct attempt came with easy equanimity. Which made it persuasive.

Nodding, Paul opened the front door.

Jesus handed him his keys.

Looking at the keys now in his hand, Paul's heart leapt and then came down hard. This was impossible. A terrible April Fool's joke. And an early one at that.

Chapter 5

I'll Never Leave You nor Forsake You

During the walk down the freshly polished wooden stairs to the front door, Paul focused on breathing. It seemed as difficult as it was important. What was playing in his head was something he witnessed freshman year of college. One of his fellow students had a panic attack before opening night of a school production. A young woman, whose name he couldn't recall now, said she couldn't breathe. The professor directing the play had talked her down from some sort of emotional ledge. A ledge the professor seemed familiar with.

"You've never had a panic attack before. No reason to start now." The Jesus guy was right behind him. Close enough to catch him if Paul passed out on the stairs.

"Like I have a choice?" Paul reached for the front door and glanced back, but his attention was immediately called outside. One of his neighbors was following her dog toward the building. The middle-aged woman, at least forty by his guess, was contesting with the wind in her hair as she clung to the leash of her little gray mutt. It was breezier out than Paul had realized.

"Hello," the woman blurted through the interrupting wind as Paul held the door for her. "Thanks. Quite a wind. But not too cold."

Paul would normally have returned a benign, weather-related reply. But he was distracted by the little poodle mix sniffing at Jesus's feet. The main distraction was the whole hallucination question. And there was even something his hallucination had said about being invisible to other people. Which, of course, a figment of Paul's imagination would always be. That jumble of thoughts kept him from responding at all.

His neighbor didn't seem particularly disturbed by his silence. She was focused on the dog as well. "What are you so interested in there, Muffin?"

Muffin was the dog's name. That was clear. The woman was not calling Jesus *Muffin*. But, then, she couldn't possibly see Jesus waiting to go out the door, smiling down at Muffin. The dog. Not the neighbor. What was the woman's name? Paul was terrible with names.

He tripped over the metal strip along the threshold of the front door, something he used to be able to clear without any conscious effort. Until this morning. This was a hard morning. When he looked back through the big glass door from outside, his neighbor was scowling at him and then at her dog. She might have shrugged. Paul had to turn his head to keep from stumbling into the low hedge next to the sidewalk.

"She can't see me, but Muffin doesn't rely solely on sight."

"Huh?" Paul righted himself and took a right turn onto the sidewalk, headed toward work. His light blue jacket was flapping in the breeze, so he gathered the ends of the zipper and tried to connect them as he walked. A difficult maneuver this morning, as it turned out.

"Erin. Your neighbor. She couldn't see me, but I let Muffin know I was there."

Hearing Jesus say *Muffin* stopped Paul from his struggle with the zipper. What was already the weirdest experience of his life had gotten a little weirder. But why? Jesus was telling him something about the dog—was that so weird? Well, yes. But all of it was strange. Insane, really.

Erin. His neighbor's name was Erin. That didn't sound familiar. Had she told him her name before? She had seemed nervous the other two or three times they'd crossed paths.

"She seemed intimidated by you the last time."

"Who? Uh, Erin? Is that her name?"

"She didn't tell you her name before. You observed her discomfort the last time you met her. It happens with women and you."

"What happens?" He kind of knew what Jesus was talking about but was curious why he was saying it aloud. It was one of those things Paul kept to himself.

"It's your looks. Your romance-novel looks. Women see those pictures of men who look like you embracing women who look different than they do, and they're intimidated by you. Intimidated by all of it, really."

"But that's not my fault, right?"

"You didn't invent the system, the culture."

"But I did those photo shoots."

"Three of them if you include the mannequin one."

Paul stopped walking and finally got his zipper connected and zipped halfway. He laughed. "They could use those shots for some kind of psycho zombie novel or something if they wanted." He had introduced a version of that joke to himself but hadn't formed it into a complete thought until now.

Jesus laughed. "Yes. And it will occur to more than one person that the contract you signed will allow them some latitude in how they use your image."

Paul had just started to walk again. Now he slowed considerably. "Wait. What?"

"The contract said they could alter the photo to include other visual elements including other models. That was what you signed."

"And they're ... they're gonna take advantage of that?"

"Of course they are, as you expected. But they will consider taking *unfair* advantage as well."

Going for a walk had sounded like a good way to clear this hallucination out of Paul's head. Or maybe a way to ditch the crazy guy in the Jesus costume. But actually walking was proving as difficult as zipping his jacket. "So they'll use my green mannequin photo with me and that model they showed me. But they might use it for something more ...?"

"Someone is still deciding. I'm only telling you where it stands now."

"But can't I prevent them? Is there something in the contract ...?" He stopped talking when he noted he was seeking legal advice from a hallucination of Jesus in full biblical costume. It seemed a dubious solution at the very least. But he was distracted from this critical self-evaluation when he noticed a man and his dog make an obvious detour to cross the street instead of passing Paul on the sidewalk.

Jesus turned and watched the man and his dog. He waved at the dog, which barked in reply. The man sped his escape a bit, his old loafers slapping pavement over the sound of the wind.

"The man can't see me. You appear to be talking to yourself. You could pretend you have an earbud in, but it's too late for that now." Jesus continued to watch the man and the dog as if concerned about them making their way onto the opposite sidewalk. A white van had slowed to allow them to get across the street.

"Wait a minute." But it was Paul who waited, ceasing the folly of talking to this Jesus who was clearly not real. He needed to cease being a delusional homeless man talking to an invisible companion. That role would be against type, the opposite of the handsome young bartender role, certainly.

"You're more than just a pretty face, Paul. You have talent. You just have to let it out. To explore the possibilities."

They weren't going anywhere. Paul was no longer talking to the invisible person who was visible to him, but he *was* staring at that man. And he wasn't walking. Like a person with a bad wooden leg, Paul swung one foot forward. Maybe he could gather some pendulum-like momentum. Momentum to go where and do what, he hadn't figured out yet.

"I know it's an adjustment, but you should try to communicate with me through your thoughts. You've already noticed me reading your mind."

Okay, so there was that. A solution. But not the big solution Paul was hoping for. Now he had a reliable way to communicate with the person who had hatched out of his imagination. Maybe the guy had spawned out of rehearsing for the play. But the communication option wasn't a path toward freeing himself from this sudden-onset insanity.

"Actually, this isn't new. Not sudden. At least my presence isn't. The part that's new is the way you perceive me. The interface, you might call it."

"Interface?" Paul didn't say that aloud. For one thing, he was getting tired of repeating fragments of the strange things this guy was saying. For another, he knew exactly what the guy was talking about. But what would Jesus know about interfaces? No computers, phones, or tablets back in his day.

"The concept of an interface is more organic than that, in fact. Face-to-face interaction is the most basic form of interface. You just heard the term first in reference to communicating with an inanimate object." Jesus paused as if waiting for Paul to acknowledge the sense of what he was saying. But he didn't wait very long. "But you don't really care about that, do you? You really want to know how to get your sanity back, right?"

Paul glanced at Jesus as they turned the corner, then looked away when a young woman carrying a paper bag hustled past. The bag was from the coffee shop where Paul worked. For a moment, he considered seeking refuge there. Maybe Jesus would go away. Go back to being normal. Back to his normal interface. Quiet and invisible. To everyone.

"Not everyone."

Looking at him after checking that no one was watching, Paul forced himself to beam his thoughts instead of speaking. *"Are. You. Saying. Some. People. See. You. All. The. Time. Question mark."*

Jesus grinned playfully. "You just have to think. No beaming required." He was walking normally, not glitching like Paul. "I wouldn't say anyone sees me all the time. The only people who see me all the time are those who have joined me in heaven. But here on earth, I have appeared to many people in various circumstances."

"Really?" That was a simple thought. Not a spoken word. Not a beamed idea.

"First, you might recall the man for whom you were named. Though he was known as Saul at the time I first appeared to him."

"But that's someone in the Bible. Not a ... not a modern person."

"I haven't changed. Even if I do know something about interfaces now." He encored his joking grin.

Paul almost laughed. He was conscious of a joke or two from this guy that he had not found funny before. But wasn't Paul just telling himself jokes, really? How funny could they be?

"Let's go to the coffee shop, and I'll show you that I'm real."

Paul stopped in his tracks again. He stared at Jesus for a second and then resorted to looking in the storefront window behind Jesus. It was a daycare center with a carpeted play area surrounded by tiny, brightly colored furniture. It was closed on this Saturday. He hadn't noticed it before.

Back to what Jesus had just said. "You're gonna appear to the people at my coffee shop? I mean, where I work?"

"Remember, you don't want to speak aloud to me. But no, I don't plan to appear to anyone in the shop the way I'm appearing to you. I just want you to tell Irma something. And you will see that I know things you couldn't know. That will show you that I cannot be merely a product of your imagination."

"Wait, wait, wait." He stopped talking. *"Let me get this straight. You're gonna show me some trick so I'll believe you're real?"*

"I wouldn't call it a trick. I want you to tell Irma that the diagnosis is nothing to worry about. She doesn't have cancer. She'll get good news on the phone later today. They're calling her on a Saturday because it's that important."

"What?"

36

Irma was one of the older employees at the shop. Normally she wouldn't be there on a Saturday, but she worked six days a week when she could. That would be the first trick—finding her there this Saturday morning. Then there was another question. Was Jesus telling him some private info about one of his coworkers? Paul caught his reflection in the storefront window. He was gaping and staring again. Definitely not a good look for him.

"Come on. Let me show you. And you can try that new pecan ripple syrup like you were planning."

Hearing—or perceiving, or whatever you called it—this Jesus projection say, "pecan ripple" was like hearing him say "muffin."

"You could get a banana muffin too. You skipped breakfast, remember?"

This time Paul laughed. He laughed aloud. His imaginary Jesus was way funnier than he would have ... imagined. His phone buzzed in his jeans pocket. He was glad to discover he had remembered to put it in there. He pulled it out and saw a text from Arabella.

"No need to come to practice early for the fitting. Costume not ready yet."

Paul wondered if Arabella was upset about the late costumes. He would be. But she was mellow. And she had experience working with volunteers. Amateurs.

He answered. **"Okay. No problem."**

"See ya."

"It'll be almost as good as *my* costume." Jesus looked down at what he was wearing. This Jesus who dressed for the part. This Jesus who could read texts from a yard away. Or who could read the mind of the guy reading the texts. Or whatever.

Paul shook his head and let his autopilot lead him into the aroma of coffee coming from the shop. He noticed he was grinning. Hallucinatory jokes were getting to him. He was softening up, probably. Well, a latte and a muffin would help. Another latte. Had he finished the one he made at home?

Jesus shook his head at that.

"*Ah. No wonder.*"

"Oh, I am neither the product of too much caffeine nor a problem that can be cured by more coffee."

"*Did you have caffeine in your day?*"

"There was no coffee or tea the way you know it. There were no sources of significant quantities of caffeine until after the fall of Rome, according to most experts."

"*That doesn't sound like a sort of all-knowing answer. It sounds like you read it.*"

"Googled it."

Paul stopped half a block short of the coffee shop. He looked at Jesus, then away and back again. Essentially shaking his head. Then he resumed his trek.

This had to get better. More believable.

Chapter 6

How Could You Possibly Know about That?

Irma Hudgens worked the cash register Monday through Friday. She was part of the same crew as Paul. She was about fifty, he guessed. Short and stout. Her hair was dark and cut collar-length, probably colored, a few wrinkles around her eyes and mouth. Smile lines, mostly. Her posture was generally hunkered. Paul recalled that she had seemed distracted this week. He stood in line looking at her.

The first hurdle in this Jesus test was cleared. Irma was here. But Paul knew something about hurdles. He had broken his leg running hurdles when he was sixteen. That was when his prospects for a track career vanished and drama became his main thing. But he still knew the race wasn't over until he cleared the last hurdle.

Jesus stood close to Paul, bumping shoulders with him as they shuffled forward in line. He had smiled at Irma when she gave Paul a little wave earlier. She was waving at him, not Jesus, as far as Paul could tell.

"Don't worry. Just say you had this crazy idea come into your head and you thought it might be important, so you're gonna take a chance. Then tell her the call will come later today, and it will be good news." Jesus did this in a low tone befitting an assistant director feeding him lines before Paul went on camera.

Paul did his line as soon as he got to the register. At least he tried. "Uh, good to see you here Irma." He leaned over the register to get a little privacy. "I guess I … Uh, well, I have this … idea I should tell you this thing. And it's crazy. But it might be important. So … here goes." The rest he did more adroitly, with Jesus prompting him twice.

Irma stared at Paul. She seemed to swallow hard. "How could you possibly know about that?" She halted for a few seconds as if checking her system for information leaks.

Jesus reminded Paul of his coffee and muffin order, and Paul repeated it verbatim.

After another hesitation, Irma entered the order on the register.

"You believe in Jesus?" This was not in the script, but Paul felt he owed Irma an explanation. *Some* kind of explanation.

"I do. I go to church every week. Especially since I found out about the lump."

"Oh. Uh, I sorta ... I sorta feel like it was Jesus who told me to tell you that." He paused. "But I'll deny that if you tell anyone else." Paul laughed uncomfortably. He wasn't sure if he was kidding.

Irma's shoulders relaxed, and she tilted her head to the side. "Well, we'll know if it was him who told you if I get that call later. It would be weird to get a call from the doctor's office on Saturday."

"But it would be an important call." Paul dutifully slid toward the pickup counter as a couple pushed up to the register next.

Punching buttons and asking questions, Irma snuck a few peeks at Paul even as she took the next order. She seemed to be looking at both Paul and Jesus, actually.

In fact, just then, Paul felt like he wasn't alone. This other guy who played Jesus was actually here. And he was a ringer for the part. He had even done something miraculous. It reminded Paul of the story of the woman at the well. Which made him grateful Jesus hadn't told him anything about Irma's love life, considering that biblical example.

Jesus chuckled close to Paul's ear.

When Paul picked up his pecan ripple latte and his banana muffin, there was a break in the line in front of the register.

Irma leaned forward with her hands on the counter. "Give me your number so I can text you when I get the call."

Paul noticed a *when* where he would have put an *if* as he pulled out his phone and entered her number to send an introductory text. "Thanks. I'm really anxious to know." He said that thinking about his need for confirmation that seeing Jesus wasn't a symptom of a mental breakdown. Then he realized he was also anxious to know Irma was all right. She was the kind of person no one would wish any kind of sickness upon.

"Well, thank you. I feel lighter already." She stood up straighter and waited on the next customer as a muted buzz in one of her pockets confirmed Paul's text.

Paul wasn't supposed to eat in the dining area when he was on a work break, but he didn't want to do so on his day off either. Going to work on his day off seemed a bad habit to get into. It would look like his coworkers were his only social network. Which they weren't. They were less than half his social network of live human beings these days.

Out on the sidewalk, Jesus seemed content to walk silently next to Paul. Paul suspected he was waiting for an apology. Too cool for an "I told you so."

Jesus chuckled, his laugh jogging his shoulders slightly.

"I don't think I can play you this way. I mean, the passion play is solemn and serious. No jokes." Paul said that without thinking first, including forgetting to send it silently. He put his hand to the ear opposite the woman who was leading her toddler past, pretending he was talking on a wireless earbud. Jesus had taught him that trick.

Jesus laughed loudly at this thought. "I wasn't advocating deception. But I have observed a few of my friends resorting to that before."

"So you do this a lot? You show up like this?"

"As I said, it's not common. This is something of an intervention."

"Oh. Am I really getting that bad?" He touched his ear again at the approach of an older man with a dog. The sidewalk was flowing with Saturday morning traffic, much of which would probably go to the coffee shop over a block behind them now. "Or is it an intervention for someone else? For Irma?" He felt like a secret service agent, touching his ear so much.

A teenage boy walked by on the side where Paul was pretending to have an earbud. The kid, wearing the uniform of a fast-food place farther down the street, scowled briefly.

Paul dropped his hand and the pretense.

"What you did for Irma was very valuable. She not only has more peace now, but she will see evidence that I'm watching over her when she gets the good news."

"Hmm." Paul could say that much without acting like a secret service agent. He would have to get a haircut and put on some weight to get a role like that anyway.

"This is a good look for you." Jesus was grinning again.

Paul could see them both in the reflection of the last store window before they turned the corner. A pretty reasonable similarity. "Not a lot of call for Jesus roles these days."

"No. Not outside of church passion plays. A lot of those this time of year."

"Maybe I should have shopped around to see if I could earn some cash at it."

Jesus shook his head. "I'm glad you didn't. Your mother really is grateful. And there are a few people I want you to help over there at Faith Community." He clearly knew more than the name of the neighbor's dog and the newest flavor at the coffee shop. He knew churches too.

Jesus laughed merrily at that thought.

Something about that laugh brought Paul back to what had happened at the coffee shop. *"That sure was weird, telling Irma stuff I could never have known."*

"Unless I told you." Jesus held the door for Paul.

Paul evaluated Jesus as doorman. What would other people think if they saw that? They would see the door opening on its own, wouldn't they? Maybe he could pretend to hit a remote or something. But did he really want to hide that Jesus was hanging out with him?

"When we get inside, you can relax and stop touching your ear." Jesus spoke close to Paul's ear.

That was when he realized he was hearing Jesus like a real person. He may have even noticed a little warmth from his breath.

"I have my tricks. But right now you probably don't want to talk aloud to me because Mrs. Childress is listening at her door. You don't want her to think you're sneaking a woman into your place."

Another funny joke, but one sandwiched inside the revelation that the neighbor directly below his apartment was spying on him. That triggered some guilt about Paul's relationship with Stefany, who had lived at his place in LA. Paul had concealed her residency from his landlord to keep from having his rent raised. He had a similar deal here. He was supposed to report any additional regular residents of his apartment.

Did Jesus count?

Jesus laughed at that one all the way through the apartment door.

Chapter 7

So Tell Me How This Works Again

It felt like Paul was watching himself play a role. The setting was his apartment. This wasn't a bit part like so many of his roles. Not the young tech guy he played in that movie about the aliens invading. Not the handsome young bartender. It was a major role. A starring role.

"You need to be the star of your own life, Paul. Or at least my costar."

Paul gripped the paper bag containing one banana muffin, his hand sweaty as if it were the middle of July. His latte was still hot as July, gripped more loosely in his other hand. When he noticed the coffee, he took a sip. "Hmm. Pecan ripple is pretty good."

"Good thing I reminded you."

"Yeah, you're like my personal assistant. And legal adviser." He wondered again about that contract he had signed. "Is that gonna come back to bite me?"

"There's not much you can do about it now other than pray."

"Huh, pray. Yeah."

Jesus took up his place on the couch. From there he would be able to see Paul seated at the kitchen table.

Paul sat with his back to the kitchen. It would feel rude to face away from his ... guest in the living room. Uninvited guest? He stared at Jesus. "Are you really here? Is this real? I mean, not a dream?"

"Take a bite of your muffin."

Paul considered that for a moment. It was an unusual commandment, but it was one he could keep. The banana muffins were his favorite. This one didn't disappoint. The bakery was pro, of course. When he swallowed the first bite, he raised his eyebrows at Jesus. But he knew what had happened before the answer to his nonverbal question arrived.

The bite of muffin was real. Not a dream. He had never tasted anything in a dream. He ran his hand over the smooth butcher-block surface of the table again. That was real too. None of it was a dream.

A man was sitting on his couch dressed as Jesus. And that man had told him about Irma's diagnosis before Paul knew there was anything that needed diagnosing.

"Holy ..." He stopped himself from swearing.

"Yes, Paul. This is real. I am real. I am really visible in your apartment right now. I am also really present with you all the time. Me. The real me." Jesus chuckled as if he knew how funny he sounded.

Well, the man on the couch actually sounded totally sane. Paul was the one who had lost his mind. He paused, then took another bite of muffin as if it were an antidote, a cure for insanity. But maybe it was just a clarification of the definition of sanity. Wasn't that the purpose of Jesus's instruction to take a bite?

Something occurred to him. "If I jump up and run out of here, will you follow me? I mean, no matter how hard I try to get away from you, will you come after me?"

The smile Jesus adopted was sympathetic and reassuring. He probably knew Paul wasn't going to jump up and run away. And maybe he knew he could catch him if he tried. "I am visible to you today. That does not mean I go away tomorrow. I'll just return to being invisible. That's how it works."

"Yeah, that's what I was wondering. How this thing works." But he was wondering a lot more than that. "You said it's an in-tervention. Like, am I an addict?" He tried to fit this visit into the interventions he had seen portrayed in movies. He had never been part of a real intervention. When Peter was spiraling down, his mom talked about getting people together. But you have to find someone in order to intervene. Find them before they're dead, that is.

"You are not your brother. Many people require an intervention who don't have one of the widely recognized addictions."

"So I do have an addiction?" He sipped his latte and hoped Jesus wouldn't tell him to renounce his caffeine habit.

"I wouldn't call it that, but you do have a habit or two that don't serve you well."

"Like what?" Paul was thinking of his top five sins list.

"Like assuming I'm not real. And assuming I'm not really with you."

Those were not on his top five list. At least not before this.

"Sin is falling short. Missing the mark. Without condemnation we can look squarely at the ways you fall short. Imperfection is inevitable but not unavoidable."

"Huh?" Repeating the strange things this Jesus said was getting to be embarrassing. Paul's latest dull reply was a step down from that, perhaps.

"Imperfection in any given area need not be a permanent state." Jesus arrowed his eyes at him as Paul nibbled a corner of the muffin half remaining. "You can fall short and then get up and try again."

That sounded easy. Too easy. It sounded like nothing Paul had heard before. But maybe he was mixing some things up. The people he hung out with in LA were not church people. And what they said about God always seemed a little off. He rarely paused to figure out just how far off. But the simple description of falling down and getting up didn't fit with what he had heard in church either.

"Go ahead and finish your muffin. Breakfast is the most important meal of the day."

Paul snorted at Jesus as dietary adviser. It felt good to let himself laugh. Not that crazy laugh where it felt like his brains were evaporating and a padded room with a little window in the door was waiting for him. He sobered a little. "Do I need my breakfast because you're about to say something really hard to me?"

"I've already said the hardest part."

"My sins? Like basically ignoring you?"

Jesus nodded in a waiting manner, and Paul remembered to keep eating. It was hard to focus on such mundane things as even a really good muffin while he was edging toward believing the Son of God was sitting in his living room. He took a deep breath while chewing the last of the muffin.

Another text message arrived on his phone. That was when he realized he was still wearing his jacket. Rolling his eyes at himself, he reached for his phone.

"You don't carry a phone?" Glancing up at Jesus, Paul felt compelled to try to keep up with the joking.

"No. I couldn't find a plan that fit my particular needs."

Right back at him.

The text was from Paul's mom. Just checking in. What was he doing today?

Well, what *was* he doing today?

"Whatever you want to do, Paul. But I'm offering to be visible and audible to you for the whole day."

"Like, up till midnight?"

"Yes, Cinderella. Right up until midnight."

For a moment, Paul paused to note how much he enjoyed this joking Jesus. Pretty clever. And way more interesting than the pale and distracted Jesus he had imagined. Where had that other version come from? And where had he gone?

"Are you going to tell her what you're doing today?"

"You mean the part about spending the day with Jesus? She'd think she texted the wrong guy if I said something like that."

Nodding knowingly, Jesus sighed just audibly. "Pleasing everyone in the audience is very difficult. Beyond even your skills."

Paul's thumbs seemed destined to hover over his phone forever. "Uh, what do you mean by audience?"

"Isn't your mother part of the little audience you take with you everywhere? Always expecting you to perform, to please them?"

"Dang." His breathing suspended for a few seconds, Paul absorbed that description of his life. "That's heavy stuff. It's like you live inside my head or something." He didn't mean that as a joke, though it sounded like one when he listened to himself.

"Go ahead. Don't let me hold you up. Let her know your plans."

By that, Paul assumed Jesus meant the generic itinerary for his day, which was pretty open. Laundry. Sweeping. Sorting a week's worth of mail. Some golf on TV possibly, and then play rehearsal. Supper with the crew after that, most likely. And back to his apartment. A small fantasy about drinks with that stage designer peeked out from behind the curtain, but he shooed that away, considering the guy watching him from the living room.

He texted a dull, generic summary of a boring, maybe even restful, Saturday. Play rehearsal was the obvious highlight.

"How is the play going?"

"Good. Good director. Good people."

He noted how he used the word *good* three times without a lot of weight behind any one of them.

"It's such a blessing you could do that. I know people will really benefit from having such a talented Jesus."

Paul looked up at the Jesus sitting on his couch. "You're pretty talented, I guess."

"I have my skills." Jesus grinned at him, his chin nearly resting on his chest.

Paul diverted back to the conversation with his mom. **"Okay. What are you up to?"**

His mom filled him in on her to-do list, including hosting dinner for some friends from church. Then she asked a question. **"You're not available for dinner?"**

Had she been working toward that invitation all along? Play rehearsal would probably run too late. That was a good excuse. A ready escape from his mother parading him in front of her friends.

"No. Have rehearsal. Might get a bite with crew after."

They ended with goodbyes and a small assortment of emojis. His mother had just started using those recently, and not always appropriately. He guessed she didn't always have her glasses on when she selected those little yellow characters to stand in for her emotional state. She was a bit vain about how she looked in glasses, and allergies kept her from wearing contacts comfortably.

Maybe Paul could get a good part in a real play, or in a movie even, and pay for laser surgery for his mom. He could always dream.

Chapter 8

I Was Afraid This Was about That

Paul returned from a trip to the bathroom, which happened a predictable number of minutes after finishing his latte. Jesus still appeared to be sitting on the couch, but Paul turned his head to the left and right to test whether it was really so. He recalled seeing their reflections together in store windows and in the morning mirror. A hallucination couldn't be so three-dimensional as this.

"You had your eyes checked before you left LA." Jesus's tone was reassuring. A simple reminder not to worry.

Shaking his head at how silly it was to try to solve this new religious problem as if it were strictly optical, Paul slumped into the rocking chair again. There was a sort of pressure at the top of his stomach that didn't usually come after eating a banana muffin. A rising ... something.

"A question, maybe?" Of course even a hallucinatory Jesus would have access to Paul's thoughts if he came from in there. "Maybe wondering what I know and what I think about it?"

"What you know?"

"The answer, if you asked it that way, would be everything. Omniscience is what the theologians call it."

"You know ... everything." Paul had learned this in Sunday school as a teen, of course. But the plastic packaging in which it had been sold to him was off now, peeled away and discarded in the recycle bin.

Jesus was nodding. The real Jesus. The Jesus who knew everything about everything. Including about Paul. And what Paul did on Thursday night.

Then Jesus said, "You haven't called her. Did you really mean to call her?"

"Uh ... at least ... a text." Paul looked away, feeling himself sliding with the world he thought he knew. It was like he was swimming in a vat of coffee beans, trying to get a footing, trying to escape.

"What are you afraid of?" Jesus's voice did not escalate, but he was clearly raising the stakes.

It was a question. Paul didn't want to answer.

"I'll still know about it even if we don't talk about it." Jesus gave half a shrug. "And we can still talk about it after I go invisible again."

Invisible? Was Jesus really invisible? Was it like that old Kevin Bacon movie? Paul knew someone who knew Kevin Bacon. Only one degree of separation. But that was a distraction. Resorting to distractions was very tempting.

"I understand." Answering his thoughts had started to become the norm for Jesus.

Maybe Paul would never have to say anything about anything. But could he control his thoughts? Don't think about pink elephants.

Don't think about bringing Amber Yu home with him on Thursday evening after work and dinner out. It was just yesterday morning that she left. Just over twenty-four hours. And now here was Jesus on his couch instead of the pretty college student.

"You said this was an intervention." Paul couldn't stop himself from saying that out loud.

Jesus was nodding again. "You need some help."

"Don't you mean some ... correction? Like, as in, confrontation?"

Raising his eyebrows, Jesus tilted his head just slightly. He uncrossed his legs and leaned forward, elbows on his knees. "You remember the story of the woman caught in adultery?"

Paul blinked for a few seconds. Why would Jesus ask if he remembered something? Didn't he know? He might even remember ... well, he probably did ... definitely *did* know when Paul first heard that story.

"Campus fellowship, March 3ʳᵈ your freshman year." Jesus cast a glance toward the corner of the room as if accessing a memory from over there. "It was a Tuesday."

"I don't remember. I mean, I don't know ... I guess those meetings were on Tuesdays. March 3ʳᵈ? I suppose it might ..."

"But that's not the point, Paul. Just another distraction."

"What if I don't wanna talk about it?"

"That's allowed. There are no mandatory conversations set for today. Which is no different than any other day, as far as that goes."

Paul puckered as the churning in his gut swelled. He excused himself and headed back to the bathroom. He suspected the problem was not digestive in nature. On the other hand, he did need to digest what Jesus was offering.

He leaned on the sink and stared at the guy in the mirror. Just him this time. Jesus seemed to be waiting in the living room. But was he really there? Just there? Only there? And not right here?

"I am wherever you are, Paul. I am with you. I am even inside you. All the time." The voice might have come out of the mirror. Or maybe out of Paul's own ears. How did that work?

No answer to that question. No more betraying the eavesdropping this Jesus manifestation seemed to be constantly doing. What was Paul supposed to do about that?

"Hmm." A humming in his ears. A very human humming. A voice. That sound did not come from an *idea* of a person. It was a real human voice. And not far away at all.

Jesus. Here.

Paul ran water in the sink and splashed some on his face. Images of Amber flickered between the rivulets of water. Her laughter harmonized with the rush of the tap. Her voice was deep for one so slender and so young. "*Augh!*" He stood up sharply and grabbed the thick terry towel from the edge of the sink.

A trio of voices seemed to be swirling in and around him. Amber's was one of them. The twenty-year-old had only worked afternoons and evenings at the coffee shop for a couple months. Not much longer than Paul had been there. That was part of their bond. That and obvious animal attraction. She had smiled slyly and made her own humming sound when Karen introduced them to each other.

Karen flirted with Paul too, but she was his boss during the afternoon shift. Harmless flirting. Was Amber less harmless?

It wasn't like the flirting had only gone in one direction. Paul had teased her about the way her ponytail stuck out of her hat, not quite long enough to look dignified. A friendly slap at the tuft of hair might have been innocent enough. She came back at him about his own hair, a bit longer than hers.

Her voice was sexy. That's what he had told himself. Internally. No one listening. He had assumed no one was listening at the time, anyway.

Stumbling out of the bathroom, he could hear the metallic drum of dish against sink in the kitchen. Jesus was doing dishes.

"You don't have to do that." Paul heard an echo of his mother's voice when he said those words. He and Mom were constantly going back and forth over whether Paul was a guest at her house. Guests had fewer cleaning responsibilities than residents, in her mind. Was Jesus a guest or a resident of this apartment?

"I suppose that depends on you. And the analogy of your mother's house is a good place to start." Jesus dried the plate on which Paul had eaten his muffin. A cup and two glasses from the previous day were already in the drainer. One of those glasses Amber had used for water early on Friday.

Paul's heart dove. Something about Amber and Jesus both touching that glass was unseemly.

"You think I don't know Amber? That I don't have access to her in that off-campus house? Access to her thoughts?"

Up to that point, Jesus's visible presence had been a problem, a shock, a crack in Paul's sanity. But it hadn't been creepy. "You're watching? Like, everyone?"

Jesus dried his hands and faced Paul squarely. "You're seeing me as if I were a regular guy. A guy in an ancient costume, perhaps, but a mortal human being. Visible the way humans are. And I do have a human body, though it doesn't have the limits I had before my resurrection." His pause seemed like just that. Not the end of what he was saying. The pause allowed Paul's mind to access the resurrection scene from the passion play. *His* resurrection scene.

"The way you're seeing me is fit to your abilities to perceive and comprehend. But I am also united with my Father, who is the God of the universe. With him I am not just a man, limited in how I can watch someone. Or limited to appearing in one place at a time."

Paul startled and nearly fell over. A second Jesus projection appeared in the living room. Two Jesuses. What the ...

"Yes." Both of them spoke in perfect unison. Stereo Jesus. "But I'm not here to creep you out, Paul, or impress you." The two Jesuses met at the door between the dining table and the kitchen. They merged into one.

Paul swore. He started to apologize, but his guttural exclamation seemed fully justified. And he wasn't sure what all was happening to him. Did he even want to complain? Or apologize? Or respond to the tricks his eyes and his ears were playing on him?

Jesus returned to the sink. He pulled a glass from the dish drainer and opened the fridge. He pulled the filtered water pitcher from the top shelf and poured a full cup. Replacing the pitcher, he turned to Paul and offered him the glass. "Take, drink ..." He smiled. Still doing lines from the play.

Examining the glass poised before him, Paul would have preferred the water be turned to wine first, though it was really early in the day for that. On the other hand, today seemed to be an exception in a lot of ways.

Jesus laughed. Again.

Chapter 9

What If Others Knew What You Know?

They were back in the living room, but this time Jesus took the rocker and Paul the couch. He set the tumbler of water on the glass surface of the coffee table. That table was easier to reach from the couch than from the rocking chair. Had Jesus calculated that when he switched to the rocking chair? Paul looked at his guest idly rocking and knew it was so.

"I guess you would make a really good roommate."

"I would." Jesus smiled. "I do."

"Better than Stefany. Is that what you were thinking?"

"Clearly you are thinking about her. This time, though, you're not just missing her. You're regretting your relationship with her."

Paul puffed his lips. "Really? Is that it?" He let that stand for a few seconds. "I guess it isn't like I'm missing her. Not like I want her back or wanna start over with her when I go back to LA."

"So, what do you regret?"

"Uh, well ... not really ... Well, I guess right now I'm worried that you're gonna somehow tell my mom that I was living with Stefany. Or maybe tell the people at church. I don't think they would let me do the play if they knew about that."

Jesus puffed his lips too. "That's a reasonable conjecture, but not a reasonable fear. I can reveal your sins to others if it's beneficial to you, but you don't have to worry about that now. I have your attention already."

"So you would, like, reveal my sin to someone to get my attention?"

"It has happened, but usually in a more subtle form. Such as someone at church coming up to you and saying they felt like they should pray for you this week. 'I had a strange thought about Amber. Is that an amber alert or something?'"

Paul shook his head sharply and sorted through the possibilities. The scenarios. The scenes. He could imagine himself playing dumb in that scene. *"I don't know what that could be about. Amber? Hmm. Well, thanks for praying for me."* Of course he would then wonder if that person knew he was lying. And around it would go.

Jesus was smiling. Was he joking again? "You have a good imagination. An actor's imagination."

"Hmm." Paul felt Jesus's words as a real compliment, but worried he was being manipulated. "You can come up with a way to do that subtle messaging thing with the name Amber, but what about Stefany?"

"Oh, something like, 'Does the name Stephany mean anything to you? Or is it with an *f* instead of *ph*?'"

His brain boggling about the spelling angle, Paul almost laughed. Jesus was talking to him about what the church would clearly consider a sin, but he was joking.

"Yes." Jesus seemed to be answering an unspoken question. As he had done before. But had Paul asked a question, even in his head?

"It was implied."

"An implied question?"

"Whether I consider your relationships sinful."

"Oh. Yeah. I guess so."

"Sin is falling short of the glory of God, as I said. Did those relationships fall short of glorifying God?"

Paul huffed out a big breath. How could he answer that? How would he know the answer?

"You know what glory is." Jesus stepped into Paul's thoughts again, and he stopped rocking. "You've felt it on the stage. People applauding. Standing. Even shouting. For you. Giving you glory."

Whoa. That was *not* the way Paul wanted to think about the applause at the end of a scene or the end of a play. A stage production in LA, in which he played a Vietnam War veteran with PTSD, came to mind. The reviews from that play had opened the way for the job on the soap opera. Ironic, given the limited emotional range of his character behind that fake bar on TV.

Paul was drifting. What were they talking about?

"Glory." Jesus was good for reminders as well as other things, clearly.

"Yes. Glory. So ..." Paul wasn't just being difficult, as his mother often accused him of being. He had lost track. "Oh, yeah. Glory and Amber. Or was it Stefany?"

"Sin is falling short of glory."

"Falling short of ... applause ... for God."

"A standing ovation." Jesus stood and clapped and even hooted as Paul had heard audiences do at the end of some of his best scenes.

It had started in high school. *Les Misérables*. Enjolras, the revolutionary. The tragic martyr. Paul had brought down the house. He still got chills thinking of it. The faculty director, Mrs. Evinrude, had actually cried during a dress rehearsal. Paul was that good. And he had looked the part too. His dark hair was on the way from clean cut to his current long locks. The tousled mop halfway in between was perfect for the disheveled radical.

Jesus, seated again, started to sing. "Have you asked yourself what's the price you might pay?" And he held that last note longer than Paul had done back in high school.

Inhaling in order to join Jesus in the song, Paul's breath caught in his throat. Instead of a note, a sob burst out of him. Jesus was doing to him what Paul had done to the director in high school. Breaking him down. *Such a performance.*

Paul gripped his face in both hands. Jesus's astonishingly good voice diminished gradually over several seconds.

Why was Paul crying? Not because of Jesus's rendition of that song, nor the beauty of that memory. Was it sadness? Loss? Loss of his dream. His dream of stardom. Of glory. Or loss of something else? Like innocence.

He slowed his breathing and grabbed a stray napkin, which was all that remained of his latte and muffin order. He didn't remember bringing it to the living room. But the recycled paper napkin offered assistance and another distraction. Paul could see how readily his mind ran away from the things Jesus was saying.

"This is intense." Paul sniffled and blew his nose. Then he laughed at the less-than-intense moment.

Jesus smiled and started rocking slowly again.

Paul watched him for a few seconds. "You're not worried?"

"About what?"

"That you won't be able to fix me in just one day?"

"Are you inviting me to stay longer?"

Paul wiped at his mustache and sat up straighter to get a better angle on the man in the rocker. "Is it up to me, if this is an intervention?"

Half squinting one eye, Jesus eased out his answer. "I don't strictly adhere to the rules about a lot of things, including interventions. I consider myself exceptional regarding even some of the best rules."

"Rules like a guy shouldn't be able to decide how long his own intervention takes?" Paul had done research for a TV series role he didn't get, and a couple of his friends had taken part in an addiction intervention.

"I'm not calling this an addiction intervention. It's an intervention in the broader sense. For a friend to come over and visit when you're lonely is an intervention. So is inviting a young woman to stay the night with you. A self-intervention against loneliness."

"Self-intervention. That sounds very ... American." Paul thought of Pete, his big brother. He was always criticizing American culture.

"You miss Pete." Jesus stood up and walked to the white built-in shelves under the front windows. There was a photo of Paul and Pete and Theresa as kids on a camping trip with their dad. One of the last times they did anything with the old man.

The memory of that camping trip was sullied by a general sense that things didn't go well and didn't end well.

"You came home early. Your dad forgot to pack a few things and was embarrassed."

"He was embarrassed? I don't remember it that way. I remember he was pissed off."

"Mostly at himself."

"Oh." Paul stood and joined Jesus in front of the shelf. The day was clouding over, but the clouds were white and nonthreatening. He turned to look at Jesus, right there next to him. He was surprisingly nonthreatening as well.

Paul lowered his gaze to that overexposed color photo and focused on Pete, who was a little out of focus.

Jesus started narrating Paul's feelings. "Losing Peter was not the beginning. The losses seemed to start after that camping trip. First your dad left, then your mom had to give up the house. Then Theresa went to Chicago right out of high school. Pete left home early and never really came back. You had to move again when your mother remarried. That, too, was a loss."

"Jeez. That's a lot of depressing reminders."

"Jeez?"

"Sorry. I didn't mean it that way."

"An old habit, I know."

"Yeah." The day was starting to weigh on Paul. He couldn't even remember what he had intended to do with this morning. It was getting loaded up like a rented trailer for moving stuff to storage. It was a lot of stuff he would be glad to stow away somewhere.

"You already had it stowed away. I just pulled some of it out." Jesus followed Paul back toward the couch. This time they both sat on it, one guy with long dark hair and a beard at each end of the newish sofa.

As if Jesus's words had been sifting down into his heart during their transition, Paul felt a vacuum expanding inside. Too much. That's what it was. Too much.

Jesus pursed his lips. "Yes. All those losses. It was too much. And still is."

Paul blinked hard at Jesus, his breathing close and tense. He was about to protest that it was Jesus who was loading on all those losses. But he inhaled sharply and let his shoulders slump. Complaining about what Jesus was saying would imply that Paul's life had been fine and satisfying before this visit.

No. It hadn't been any of that.

Chapter 10

Seeing Much More than He Ever Imagined

According to Jesus, Paul's night with Amber had been about rescuing himself. Self-intervention. At least an attempt at self-rescue. Amber cooperated. She was the one who suggested dinner, though Paul was the one who invited her to his place afterward. Then the movie he chose was probably too sexy for an innocent date. Had he ever intended it to be an innocent date?

Any introspective pause he might have taken during that evening with her would have surely yielded reassurance. Just dinner. Just a movie. Just talking. Just company for two lonely souls. Just ... justification.

He really did enjoy Amber's company. She was funny and energetic. And she was something of a fan. She binged about a dozen episodes of his appearances on the soap. She might have been on her way to being his first real groupie. That could be innocent enough. Possibly.

Now, in the company of a visible Jesus, evaluating each decision that led deeper down the labyrinth on Thursday only yielded guilt and regret. After rehearsing all that inside his head, Paul looked up and saw something in Jesus's eyes. Recognition, not regret. And anticipation, not anger.

"But you *are* disappointed in me ... I mean ... for spending the night with her."

"I think people play the disappointment card too heavily sometimes. Doesn't that kind of disappointment feel like giving up on you? 'I'm disappointed in you' turns easily into 'You *are* a disappointment.'" Jesus lowered his voice a little. "You are not a disappointment, Paul. I'm happy with you. Glad I know you. And glad you are who you have grown up to be."

Giant stone breakers stood in the way of those waves of fresh affirmation. "But ..."

"But what? But you made a mistake? You followed your need past where it was healthy and constructive?" Jesus arched his eyebrows. "Yes. You did that. But you are not that."

"You're saying I can do better? That sounds like the same thing as saying I'm a disappointment."

Jesus looked past him. "It's a beautiful day. How about another walk?"

That sounded good until Paul pictured himself touching his ear, pretending he was talking on his phone.

"You could just put the earbuds in. I can still reach you." Jesus clearly knew quite a bit about phone technology. And his own technology.

"But isn't that, like, deceptive?"

"A trick. Not a lie. There is a difference."

"What if we just went up to the roof?" It wasn't warm enough yet for morning sunbathers, and the gardens on the roof weren't getting a lot of attention yet as far as Paul had seen. The view of the city from up there wasn't a tourist attraction. But it was pretty good, and the air was mostly fresh.

Jesus nodded his agreement and raised himself off the couch with little effort. Paul did too. He wondered if Jesus did as many ab exercises as he did.

"You think tight abs were one of the requirements for playing the Christ?" Jesus followed Paul to the closet where he was reaching for his jacket again.

That question was probably a joke, but something about it lodged in Paul's head like a bag of snacks stuck in a vending machine. That was officially the name of the role. *The Christ.* It had bothered Paul at first, but he got used to it. Was Jesus endorsing that as the title of the role, as his own title? Or was he making fun of it? Paul cocked an eyebrow at his guest.

"I only say it that way because I know it bothered you."

"Should it bother me?" Paul asked that aloud as he opened his front door, only stopping to check if he should fake a phone call after the door was open. No one in the hallway. He turned right, leading Jesus to the stairs up.

"I understand why it bothered you. It made the role seem stiff and lofty. I mean, any guy whose name starts with *The* is pretty stiff, right?"

Paul snorted a laugh and checked for anyone in the stairwell above or below. It occurred to him then that he had often been caught running over his lines, essentially talking to himself, as he walked along. Why should this be any different?

"Hey, we could run your lines together later, right? I could give you some pointers."

Paul snorted again. This guy wasn't stiff, but was he really *the* Christ? "I don't know." Arriving at the top, Paul unlocked the roof door with his key and stepped into the daylight. "I may not be able to go on playing you after this. My head is really messed up about you now. I can't see that getting better before Easter."

"Messed up by meeting the person you're playing in a stage production?"

"Way more than that, man. Way more than that." Paul led the way to the railing on the west edge of the roof. Five stories above the street, it was one of the highest perches for a mile in that direction. The view wasn't the Grand Canyon or the Pacific coast, but it was bright and airy and the best place for Paul to catch his breath without leaving the building.

Jesus took a deep draft of air and smiled as the wind pushed his hair away from his ears. And something about seeing Jesus's ears twisted a tangle of feelings in Paul. He had never imagined Jesus's ears. He had seen pictures of him all his life. Some probably included glimpses of Jesus's ears. But standing there in the broad daylight looking at an apparently real, apparently human person so close to him shot panic through Paul and splashed him with elation in the same instant.

"I'm real, my friend. Always was. Even before I showed myself to you like this."

"In the sunshine. For real." The clouds had parted. Probably not a miracle. Paul was staring.

Not shying from Paul's stare, Jesus seemed to pose there next to the railing, the morning sun highlighting his dark hair and dark eyes. His skin so real.

"I never imagined this. I never could have ... This has to be more than just ..." As if it had all finally added up to an overload, Paul's knees buckled. He gripped the square metal railing and kept himself from crumpling onto the gravel rooftop. He remained on his feet, though squatted deeply.

There was a hand on his shoulder helping to prop him. Jesus's hand. Paul focused on those fingers gripping his light blue jacket. Then he fell the rest of the way, his butt landing on the sharp gravel.

And that Jesus, that real Jesus, knelt next to him, still gripping his shoulder. Maybe this guy was invested in Paul not fully laying out on the roof. Maybe he was just plain fully invested in Paul. His glistening eyes and ready smile seemed to communicate that possibility.

"What am I supposed to do now?" Paul searched the penetrating brown eyes just above his. "How can I go back to ... to my life ... after this?"

"Do you really want to? Was it really so great? Too precious to give up?"

"My life? Give up my life?"

"Take up your cross. There is a crucifixion and resurrection waiting for all of us."

"Us?"

"I went through mine. I'm here to help you survive yours."

"Oh." Paul focused on Jesus's hand on his shoulder again. Fingernails. Jesus had fingernails. Something Paul might have also seen in Sunday school illustrations. Actors playing Jesus in the movies were real in this same way, this same level of human detail. Focusing on that detail seemed to weaken his battle against insanity. It wasn't a well-planned battle. "I wasn't prepared." Was it an excuse? Perhaps a plea for help.

"Prepared to be crucified and raised? Or prepared for a real savior who can actually touch you?"

"You have ... fingernails." Paul shook his head in embarrassment.

Jesus laughed hard, and he stood up straight. He curled his fingers to examine his nails. "Yes. I have fingernails." His laughter diminishing, Jesus looked more closely at Paul, on the ground next to him. "I am here in my body that looks like yours, but my body is not limited in the ways yours is." As he spoke, he seemed to be sliding away, like he was on a tracking camera pulling out for a wider shot.

The track Jesus appeared to be rolling on went right off the edge of the roof. He slid right through the railing as if it were a hologram. That painted metal now seemed unreal. And Jesus seemed more real. Except now he was hanging in the air over the sidewalk far below. No visible means of suspension.

Laughing, as if at Paul's thoughts or maybe at the look on his face, Jesus reeled himself back in through the railing, arriving on the gravel next to Paul again. And he stopped laughing, adopting a more serious set to his eyes, his smile reduced to the minimum grin he always seemed to wear.

"I showed you this to make it clear, Paul. I am real, and I am more real than the world around you. I have my eternal body. I am eternally present. The things you see around you will all pass away sooner or later. Your body will pass away. But I will remain."

Paul realized his hands were shaking but suspected that hadn't just started. Maybe he was getting back in touch with his own body after drifting away from solid reality for some moments. Moments when an apparently real person hung in midair. Why? To prove a point?

"The point is that I am real, but I am not merely human. That is important for what I have to offer you. I offer more than mere human companionship. I am not offering to accompany you like Roger or Amber. I am offering to live inside you in a way that you know is real, a way that makes a difference."

"But ... weren't you already ...?"

Jesus reached his hand, and Paul took hold of it. He explained as Paul rose unsteadily to his feet. "I have been present, but you haven't noticed my presence most of the time. Not even enough to be creeped out by me."

Paul coughed a laugh that came from both surprise and disapproval. Jesus would never say "creeped out." At least his Jesus. His former Jesus. The Jesus in the script for the passion play would never say that.

"In the days you portray in the passion play, I didn't speak English at all. Not even King James English." Jesus tipped his head in parallel with the tilt he was putting on Paul's world. Yet another tilt.

Paul let that commonsense reminder about language push him forward. He might just be rolling away from life as he once knew it. Rolling on those same rails that carried Jesus into miraculous defiance of gravity itself.

Chapter 11

A Living Invitation to Death and Resurrection

Since his earliest days in youth group and Sunday school, Paul had accepted the concept that Jesus died and rose again. He didn't hear much about Jesus calling his followers to do the same until college. But, even then, it seemed like an advanced topic reserved for upperclassmen or graduate students of God and the Bible.

More recently, Paul had begun to act out the death and resurrection of Jesus. He was acting. He was acting out the suffering and triumph of someone he considered a real historical figure. But it had not been his own death. He had not owned the death. So, of course, it was not his own resurrection either. He acted out both the suffering and the triumph, but they were not his.

As soon as they got back to Paul's apartment, he slid the balcony door open. Remaining on the roof had become vulnerable. It felt risky somehow. Maybe that was just about Jesus's floating trick. Or Paul collapsing onto the gravel. At least inside the apartment, Paul could collapse onto the rug.

He stood looking out at the apartment building across the street without actually going out to the balcony. Going from the roof to his balcony seemed awkward and anticlimactic. Not nearly as great a view down here.

"So, what do you really mean by death and resurrection?" So much of Paul's faith was based on metaphor. He assumed that also lay beneath these words from Jesus.

"You're right. You are not called to literally be executed for me. That is not your place in history. But the death I call you to can be more profound and impactful."

"More impactful than execution?"

67

"Death is finite when it is only physical. Surrendering to my will is everlasting."

Having a guy look soberly at him and say Paul should surrender to his will brought back the creep factor, but only for a moment. If anyone could say things like that, it was Jesus. This Jesus.

"Thanks. I'm glad you recognize that. It is my uniqueness that is crucial, no pun intended."

Paul winced and turned away from his balcony door. "Usually when people say 'no pun intended,' they're actually pointing out that they just made a pun."

Jesus grinned shamelessly. "Good observation, but I meant the cross reference quite seriously. No joke."

"Dying on a cross is no joke."

"Right. Even if it is metaphoric."

Paul scratched his head with one hand, and the other joined in. He followed an urge to dig in with his own real fingernails. Maybe it was a way to make some space for his brain, to dig a vent to release the impending explosion. The result of his manic scratching was hair hanging over his eyes and a relieved scalp. He probably did forget to wash his hair.

"Feel better?" Jesus carefully lifted locks and strands of hair away from Paul's face. Yet another intimacy only this man would be allowed.

Paul nodded and glanced at the clock on the kitchen wall. It was after ten in the morning. Was that surprisingly late or surprisingly early? He couldn't decide.

"Just like your cross. You might ask yourself, 'Is it too late to consider taking it up, or too early?'"

Paul immediately recognized an assumption he had never articulated, not even to himself. *Someday he would get serious about his faith.* Someday when he was ... ready. And certainly when he was older. But that was probably wrong. "It's not too early?"

Taking Paul's arm and leading him back to the couch, Jesus bowed slightly. "No. And not too late either."

"I haven't totally blown it ... yet?"

"No. Not totally."

That response raised Paul's eyes for a check on whether this jokey Jesus was being serious. Maybe it was half and half. The glisten in his eyes was friendly and playful, but his smile was subdued and patient. That patience was obviously required by Paul's endless hesitations, his endless postponements when it came to investing in his spirituality.

"Don't worry about that right now." Jesus settled at the other end of the couch again. "I'm not here to tell you to get your ... *stuff* together." He winked. "The thing about a cross is that you don't get to choose it. You just get to choose whether to willingly embrace it."

Paul scowled at his visitor. His mind was so fatigued. Right now he was embracing the fact that he didn't have to say everything. But embracing a cross?

"You have lost so much. You can embrace what that has done to you, or you can ignore it, resist it. You have the opportunity to let your great losses be instruments for tearing down false salvations—the self-interventions. And, in that, you will make way for resurrection."

Pausing before even collecting words in his head, Paul sensed the gravity of the offer. This was transformational stuff. But, of course, if this was really Jesus, it would be, right?

Jesus was smiling again when Paul registered his face just three feet away. That smile seemed like yet another distraction, however. Paul noted how he retreated each time he sensed a vital truth landing on his addled brain.

"It's a lot to take in, I know. I put it out there to help you understand the stakes. Both what you have to gain and what you have to lose. That's what I'm offering."

"You're offering both loss and gain?"

"Both death and resurrection."

"The cross has to do with ... losses."

"I know you felt burdened when I listed those losses earlier, but that was not me adding burdens to your soul. That was me explaining the burdens under which you've been laboring all your adult life."

"And even before that."

Jesus nodded. "It started before that, but a child is prepared to wait for the adults to provide him what he needs. An adult expects, and is generally expected, to make his own provision. Carrying the weighty luggage inherited from your family became a profound problem only when you became a man, responsible for carrying it yourself."

"But I thought *you* were responsible for my life." Maybe Paul was looking for an escape clause. The bolts and latches clacking shut behind Jesus's description of adulthood escalated his need to flee.

"Escape has been a theme with you for a long time."

"I'm not that old."

"No, but the length of time is expanded by the weight of the burdens you carry."

"So I'm responsible for my life."

"I will not take it away from you, but I will gladly receive it if you offer it to me."

"That's the cross."

"That's part of the crucifixion process. Handing me your life is not the same as the death imposed by the world. The cross is an instrument of torture invented by the fallen world. Being willing to ride that cross into eternal freedom is my twist on the problem."

"Twist?"

"You could call it redemption."

"I could?"

Jesus smiled, but it faded to an inquisitive look. "Are you going to see Amber today?"

"Amber? Today? Uh, no plans." Another soup of emotions bubbled in Paul. Why was Jesus mentioning Amber in any context other than repentance? And why would he ask about something as if he didn't know the answer already?

While Paul was stirring all that, his phone buzzed in his pocket. He stretched his leg and extracted the slender new device.

Amber. A text. **"Hey. What r u doin fr lunch?"**

"Lunch?" Paul looked at Jesus for an answer. And not just to Amber's question. He was looking for confirmation that this was what Jesus had in mind when he mentioned her just now.

Jesus gave a deep nod.

Paul looked at the clock and then texted back, **"What about brunch?"**

"R u really that old?"

"What?"

"Just kidding." [Smiley emoji].

Paul looked at Jesus again. "Am I supposed to be too young for brunch?"

Jesus shrugged. "Wait, I'll check what's trending." And he sat up as if reaching for his own cell phone. But he stopped, confirming that it was a bluff.

Bluffing Jesus. Just when jokey Jesus was getting to be the standard.

Paul rolled his eyes at Jesus for the first time. Then he answered. **"That place a block east of the coffee shop. 10:45?"**

"Which way's east?"

"Are you really that young?"

"LOL"

She finished with, **"See ya there."** [Heart emoji].

"Heart emoji." Jesus was too far away to be spying on the exchange.

"Yeah ..."

"I'm glad you're getting together with her."

"Really?"

"For brunch."

Paul knew it was only for brunch, obviously. Not like he was going to send Jesus away while he and Amber snuck back to the apartment after omelets and orange juice.

Jesus looked a little somber when Paul settled his eyes on him. What was that about, exactly?

For once, Jesus seemed to ignore Paul's thoughts. No answer to that question. Which left Paul to create his own answer. And it had something to do with that cross and that death.

Chapter 12

Something I Want You to Tell Her

"I want you to tell Amber something for me." Jesus was standing by the front door waiting for Paul to find his good leather shoes.

Paul's first response to Jesus's news was, *"Why can't you tell her yourself?"* But he didn't let that stand long and didn't say it aloud. Bent over in his closet, he wasn't sure Jesus would hear him from there.

His next response to Jesus's proposed message was recalling what had happened that morning with Irma. But that had just been to show Paul that Jesus was real, hadn't it? It wasn't like Jesus asked people to give other people messages from him. At least not people like Paul.

"Are you so sure about that?"

"That you don't give messages that way?"

"And that I only asked you to deliver that message to Irma so I could prove I'm real?"

"Oh. Yeah, I guess it did help Irma relax a bit, probably, to hear that she had good news coming. Although now that I think of it, she's gonna start to think I'm, like, her psychic friend or something."

"She won't think that. Neither will Amber. If the message comes directly from me, it will become the point, the focus. You don't have to say much about how you know. The message is reason enough. You'll see."

They arrived at the restaurant a couple minutes early. Amber was already there. The flush to her cheeks and rapid respiration implied she had run to get there. Paul wasn't sure how far away she lived, so he didn't know if she had run a 5K or a sprint.

She pushed her golden-red bangs out of her eyes and stood to give him a hug. A surprise hug. Paul wasn't sure they were on a hugging basis, but he was also discovering a possible generation gap spanning their eight years of age difference.

She leaned forward. "Hey, there. How's your weekend?"

"Good. Not working today, so that's good. What about you?" Paul pulled out a chair and sat across from her at the small square table.

Perhaps that seat choice delayed her response. She watched him sit down. "I get the late shift tonight. Three to ten."

"Not till eleven?"

"No, I don't have to stay after closing. Past my curfew, probably."

"Curfew?"

"Brice treats me like I'm a little kid. He does that with all the college girls."

Paul didn't want to get into punching holes in the character of the general manager of the coffee shop. Nor into defending Brice. He was distracted by Jesus in the chair to his left, filling the space Amber might have intended for Paul. "So no one under twenty-one does brunch? Is that it?"

She laughed, leaning her thin elbows on the table as if trying to get closer to him. Those elbows were covered in magenta, a stretchy sweater. "I was just remembering my stepdad and his business brunches at the country club. But, yeah. I mean, none of my friends ever invite me to brunch."

"No brunch in the student center?"

"Well, they serve breakfast until, like, eleven. So that could be called brunch, if any of us ever thought to call it that. At the student center country club."

"I was never part of the country club set." Paul didn't mean to douse the conversation with that, but he apparently did.

After lowering her head toward the table, Amber revived. "I saw that sci-fi movie you were in. Last night, after I got home from the library."

"Yeah? How long did it take you to find me?"

"Oh, you described it well enough. I just waited for those scenes in the command center or control center, or whatever, and looked for the hot guy in the fake glasses."

"They did look pretty fake, didn't they?"

"Not an obvious prop." She did a brief eye roll.

"So you saw some compelling acting, did you?"

"Really. It was good. You were convincing. I just know you and know those weren't your glasses. But you were, like, all into being the tech guy and all. It was crazy good."

"Well, I got paid for nine days, anyway. And better than I get paid for foaming milk."

"And rightfully so." Amber batted her eyelids and grinned. She probably really was a groupie now. Maybe the only one he would ever have.

Paul checked in with Jesus without being obvious. He knew how to look *through* someone like he was acting on a green-screen set. He registered the usual happy grin and attentive eyes that were familiar on his Jesus.

Amber reached across the table and took his hand, interrupting Paul's surreptitious check-in with his invisible companion. "I was thinking we might have some time after we eat." She raised an eyebrow suggestively.

"Ask her about her stepdad." Jesus was interrupting now, but he had warned Paul about some kind of agenda he was bringing to the table.

Embarrassed by Amber's seduction attempt in front of Jesus, Paul followed his directions immediately. "So tell me about this country club family of yours."

Her smooth young brow flexed for a second, and Amber released his hand. She leaned back and cast her eyes around the restaurant. She wore at least three tops in layers from darker to lighter magenta. Her stiff posture implied she might suspect something was off between them.

Paul tried smiling in a friendly, not seductive way, to keep the meal as pleasant as possible.

"Oh, you know. The usual. My stepdad, not my real dad. He's this exec in a big Taiwanese company with, like, regional headquarters in Ohio. Don't know why Ohio. But anyway, he schmoozes clients and such at the country club and plays golf once in a while there too. Some Jack Nicholson golf course or something."

Paul suspected she was getting some of the details wrong, noticing now how young she really was. He just nodded to encourage her to go on. He hoped this counted as following Jesus's directions. The stepdad character had been confirmed and had entered the story.

"So boring. My mom likes him *because* he's boring, I think." She hesitated in a way that reminded Paul of a video glitch, an obvious cut in a film that had been spliced together. He really wanted to ask Jesus what that was about.

"Just listen. She's coming to the part I want to address." Jesus was talking inside Paul's head. At least Jesus didn't have to put his hand up to his ear to pretend he was listening over earbuds.

"Yeah. And I made sure to go far enough away for school to not have to see him more than the bare minimum. I make my own money as much as possible." Her eyes drifted toward the waitress who approached their table.

As they each ordered juice and main dishes, Paul only devoted half his attention to the menu. Fortunately he had eaten at this place once with Roger. He ordered the Italian skillet his friend had eaten that time. The other half of his head was trying to get Jesus to give him more specific instructions.

"Just wait. I'll tell you when the time comes." Jesus was sitting right there. He could have talked and presumably no one else would hear, but he was still sending his voice inside Paul's head.

"That's to remind you not to talk to me aloud." Jesus smiled. "And stop looking at me." He raised his eyebrows in correction.

Paul did his best easy fade away from staring at the invisible man in the seat next to him. He was acting a part. Again. Maybe he always was. That distracting thought apparently made his drift obvious.

"You still with me?" Amber scowled at him much more seriously than usual. Her scowls before this morning had all been mock. Lacking real tension. Other than the sexual kind.

Paul cleared his throat and tried not to think about sex. Or pink elephants. "Uh, I'm with you ... still. Uh ... I guess your relationship with your stepdad reminds me of my stepdad."

"I hope not." She grimaced with horror-movie eyes for half a second. Then her face and her tone changed. "So we're not going to your place after ... brunch?"

Taking a deep breath and glancing at Jesus, Paul nodded. "I shouldn't have invited you over the other night. I don't do that. I shouldn't do that."

"But we connected. And you seemed to have a pretty good time." She leaned forward again but didn't reach out this time.

"Of course. You're beautiful and amazing. But I just ..."

"Are too old." She finished his sentence for him.

Paul shrugged, then flipped back in the conversation. "Why did you do that freaky face when I said our stepdads sounded about the same?"

Amber returned to that serious scowl. A sincere scowl. Then her face softened, and she looked more squarely at him. "It's funny. I get this feeling that you ... that you know what it was like for me. Though I'm pretty sure it's not the same as your stepdad."

"How long has yours been around?"

"Since I was six."

"Oh. 'Cause you talk about him like he's a stranger."

"Strange, yes. And I wish he was more of a stranger." She took an unsteady breath and did a shiver-shrug.

That was when Paul knew what she was not saying. It was his turn to shiver. "Oh. Huh. I guess I do kinda know what you're talking about." He tried to slow his breathing, glancing quickly at

Jesus. "Maybe it's just the bad rep that stepdads get in general, but ..." He didn't know how much to say. He also wondered when Jesus would jump in to help. Paul resisted another visual check-in, but not being able to read Jesus's face was a serious disadvantage. Visual cues were very important to him. Especially when he was acting.

"Focus on Amber." Jesus said that just as their juice glasses were delivered. Hers was melon orange, Paul's olive green.

Even as he sipped his custom juice concoction, Paul focused on Amber. She smacked her lips in a brisk and satisfied way, but she still seemed subdued.

"When did he start ... messing with you?" Paul may have been the most surprised person at the table when he released that dicey inquiry.

Amber leveled a look at him that might not have been lethal but it certainly hurt, especially a visual reader like Paul.

"Sorry. Maybe I should keep my mouth shut." Paul glanced at Jesus, looking for an exit strategy.

"Stay on her." Jesus sounded like that assistant director again.

Paul turned his focus back to the nervous girl across the table.

"It started when I was, like, seven or eight, I guess."

"Oh."

"Funny that you say 'messing with.' That's kinda what he called it."

"Have you seen a therapist or somebody?" He spun his juice glass where it sat on the varnished table, letting go when he realized he was doing it.

"Oh, yeah. The therapist tried to mess with me too."

Paul swore under his breath and resisted apologizing to Jesus in that same breath.

"Tell her you're sorry." Jesus was locked on Amber. He hummed those instructions, not limiting himself to the internal channel now.

"Amber, I'm so sorry you had all that trouble. But—" Paul stopped when Jesus raised his hand.

"Wait." Jesus was in Paul's head again.

Tipping her head toward him slightly, Amber almost seemed to be hearing that other voice. "I guess I've done some nasty stuff myself since then. Maybe I'm completely ruined."

"No way. No way are you ruined. You ..." Again, Paul aborted when Jesus signaled. That only annoyed him a little since he was resorting to his own lines, and he wasn't entirely sure of their value. Jesus's interruption was a relief, actually. Offending Amber seemed as likely as comforting her.

"Thanks. Thanks for saying that, Paul. I know it's awkward." She looked at him in that way he had noticed before. He realized then that her default look was a sort of three-quarters angle with one dark eye pointed at him. But this was two eyes square on. A real connection.

The urge to solve everything by getting her to a professional was still strong, but Jesus's two stop signs had slowed Paul's fixer reaction. He could see that was what he was trying to do. That revelation was reinforced by Amber's two-eyed connection.

And Paul had another revelation. "I have to work on some stuff of my own. That's why we can't ... you know ... again."

With those words their fledgling relationship ended, even before their brunch was delivered to the table.

79

Chapter 13

I Actually Do Believe He is Real

"I expected you to tell me some secret about her that would, like, crack her open. Like you did for Irma."

"Different situation, different need." Jesus was walking next to Paul, who forgot to communicate without his vocal cords and also forgot to touch his ear as if he were tightening an earbud.

"Amber seemed to be listening to you, sort of. Like she could almost hear you." He shook his head at himself, still speaking aloud.

"Almost. That's right."

"How does that work?" He tried not moving his lips too much.

"I created her. She belongs to me even if she doesn't know it. She wants to belong to someone in an ultimate way, but she hasn't accepted my invitation."

His phone buzzed. Probably a text. Paul pulled his device out and saw an unknown number. He looked at the message.

"Wow. I am totally blown away. Good news from my doc. No cancer. Jesus is real!"

He stared at it for several seconds. Reread it and literally scratched his head.

"It's Irma." Jesus was grinning, as usual.

"Oh." Paul stopped himself from saying more, standing on the corner near his apartment building. He reread the news again. Yes. Jesus is real.

"Yes, I am." His grin came with a side order of chuckles.

Paul texted her back. **"That's great. Thanks for sharing."** But that sounded lame. He backspaced and tried again. **"That's great. I really do believe he is real. And he's looking out for you."** [Smiley emoji.]

She responded, **"Actually looking forward to church tomorrow."**

Apparently that was different for her. Paul could relate.

He turned left at the corner toward his apartment. His stomach was full for the first time today. The muffin for breakfast had failed to satisfy the hunger Jesus was generating with his emotional calisthenics.

Jesus rested a hand on Paul's back as they approached the sidewalk in front of his building.

Before Paul could say anything about Irma, Mr. Warner, a guy who lived on one of the higher floors of the little building, caught his attention. He was approaching the front doors patting his pockets.

"You left it in your car." Jesus spoke while looking at the neighbor, and Paul took it as a line prompt.

When Paul repeated Jesus's line, Mr. Warner stopped patting and stared at Paul with his chin hanging. "Hey, you're right. How did you know that?"

"Psychic powers." That line came straight out of Paul. No prompt from the script assistant.

"Huh." His black eyebrows scooting closer to each other, Mr. Warner stared at Paul.

"Not psychic, really." Paul glanced at Jesus, who was now right next to Mr. Warner. "More of a divine assist, I guess."

That clearly did not put Mr. Warner's mind at ease. The older gent just nodded vaguely and turned away from the front door toward the sidewalk.

Paul headed for the door, shaking his head at himself. "You set me up for that."

"You're blaming me?"

"You knew I would just repeat the line."

Jesus puckered and nodded. "He may want to ask you a question about it again sometime."

"Will he wait until I actually have answers for him?"

"You can always avoid him." Jesus entered as Paul held the door. He hit the stairs first, treading lightly to the second floor.

Paul was following this time. Following footsteps and not dialogue prompts. He was thinking about Amber again. "Did I say what I was supposed to, to Amber though? I mean, I thought there would be more. And then my mouth just got away from me." He slid his key into the door lock. "But you stopped me those two times, right?"

"You were going to try and fix her, as you know. It's a natural instinct, but it generally doesn't work." Jesus followed Paul into the apartment.

"Will she get help?"

"I hope so."

"You don't know?"

"You want me to travel into the future and then come back and report?"

"Is that how it works?"

"I'm not telling you all my secrets." Jesus grinned and leaned on the kitchen counter as Paul retrieved his water glass from the sink.

"So you're, like, telling me to mind my own business?"

"Amber and I made it your business, but only to a limited extent. You could pray for her and leave the rest to me and my Father."

"Huh. Pray. Not something I do very much, as you know."

"Yes. Lots of room for improvement there."

As he gulped his water, Paul watched Jesus over the edge of the glass. After a hard exhale, he said, "I wish it could just be like this. Like, just me talking to you as a friend, sort of."

"Sort of?"

"You know what I mean. You're not like any friend I've ever had. And this is so easy. Talking to you isn't all stiff and tense like praying."

"Why does praying have to be tense?" Jesus turned and headed for the rocking chair.

"Well, speaking to God and all that. I ..." Paul stopped himself this time. What was he saying? He didn't know what he was talking about. "Maybe you could teach me how I should be praying." It occurred to him that this Jesus might have different expectations for prayer than the Jesus he had imagined. The Jesus of the Bible studies and the Christian rule books.

"When you see me, you see the Father. You can talk to him just the way you're talking to me. He's not against you. He's on your side. He's glad to hear from you. And he has some things to say to you as well."

Sitting on the couch, Paul had to squelch a clip of Morgan Freeman in his head. The God voice of his generation—or maybe his mom's generation. Thinking of God talking to him probably had nothing to do with Morgan Freeman. He pictured God zapping him with lightning and laughing like Morgan Freeman. Maybe a sort of demented Morgan Freeman. Was that from a movie?

"You mean God isn't gonna zap me with lightning?"

Jesus shook his head, his lips a straight line. No grin this time.

"I guess that's not funny to you. Seeing how there's that 'act of God' thing and all that." Again, Paul had no idea what he was talking about.

"It's built into your legal system. The idea of an 'act of God.' Disasters. They are assumed to be from God." Jesus shook his head, his feet crossed at the ankles, his elbows on the arms of the chair. "The 'act of God' clause in your culture was actually introduced by Satan."

He waited as Paul furrowed his brow and tried to follow where this was going.

"Your culture assumes every disaster is an act of God. The god they speak of is the god of this world. The deceiver. The destroyer. That's not my Father."

Digging deep into theology was not his thing. Paul used to stay on the sidelines in college as the Christians around him debated this and that. Paul couldn't even think of an example of something they had debated, let alone his position on it. But the things Jesus was saying seemed important. Even Paul could see that. Jesus's face had hardened, and his voice turned almost stern.

"Why do we do that? Blame God for bad things happening?"

"To escape responsibility. If every bad thing is automatically categorized as coming from God, no one has to investigate causes. And where humans are the source of their own pain, they can avoid all the hard work required for real solutions. Being made in my Father's image, in my image, includes taking responsibility for your part in your own life. Including the consequences of bad decisions."

That reminded Paul of something his mother had said to him recently. *"I don't know why God brought all these storms into my life. I just hope I'm learning what he wants me to."*

"She was talking about storms such as your dad leaving, Pete's death, and Theresa's too. Stealing, killing, and destroying. Those are the devil's signature moves. Blaming God for those things is what Satan has done from the beginning of human history." Jesus waited again.

Paul wasn't even tempted to interrupt. Absorbing a fraction of what Jesus had just said was enough, maybe for the rest of the day.

Jesus took a deep breath. "It's difficult to trace all the causes of any event. Impossible for humans to get it right all the time. If you or your mother wanted to figure out why all those bad things happened to your family, you might end up simply blaming yourselves. As simple as it is to blame God for trouble—or to blame the devil for that matter—it is also simple to just blame yourselves. The truth is usually much more complicated than any one of those explanations."

"'It's complicated' is a familiar answer. But I'm thinking you just said a lot more than that."

Jesus chuckled. "I didn't come to make you a theologian, Paul. Contrary to your namesake. But I did come to give you some comfort. And even some correction. It's too simple to blame God and too simple to blame yourself. The truth is usually braided—one cause with another, with another." He motioned with his hands like he was braiding a rope. "And you don't really need someone to blame. What you need is trust that my Father is always on your side. Fighting *for* you. If you find yourself in a storm, look for shelter. God is your refuge. God is not your storm. Unless you're actively running away from him. Then he might also send a very big fish."

"*Big Fish?*"

"I was thinking Jonah. Not Ewan McGregor."

"Ewan ... Oh." *Big Fish* was movie Paul had enjoyed a lot. It also included a very big storm. But he didn't expect Jesus was actually referencing that movie.

"I know all of them—the movies and the actors. Including Kevin Bacon. Zero degrees of separation." Jesus gave his winky smile.

Paul just shook his head.

Chapter 14

Time to Do Laundry with the Christ

A car horn sounded in front of the building. Someone shouted something that probably was not a compliment. Paul hoped everyone was okay.

"You could pray for them."

"For who?"

"Whoever just got honked at. Or maybe the one sounding the horn. He might need your prayers most of all."

"But I don't even know him."

"But you formed an opinion of him."

"I did?"

"I know it's an old habit. You don't do it consciously. Just a passing thought. But what if your passing thought was a blessing? A word of support or sympathy instead of judgment?"

"Would that work? Or help?"

"It wouldn't hurt the people you're praying for, even if your prayers feel generic. And it will certainly encourage your own sympathy for the needs of others."

"Sympathy? Do I need help with that?"

Jesus rocked forward and stood from the chair. "Let's do your laundry."

"Let's?" Instead of rocking forward, Paul leaned back. Knocked back, maybe. "You and me? You want to ... help me with my laundry?"

"Did you think I only washed feet?"

Some part of Paul's brain was rolling on the floor laughing, but it was an invisible part. His body was plastered to the back of his couch. That gave the rest of his brain time to process some fragment of what Jesus was saying. "Uh, okay."

Jesus was already across the room and turning down the hall toward Paul's bedroom. By the time Paul was standing in the kitchen, his drinking glass clutched in one hand, Jesus appeared in the hall next to the bathroom with the laundry basket. Another donation from his mother. Paul's mother, not Jesus's.

After setting the glass on the counter with a loud tap, Paul stepped close and reached for the basket. Then he withdrew the offer.

Jesus laughed and handed it over. "We're gonna see Destiny down there, so you'd better carry it."

Taking the basket mechanically, Paul contemplated the laundry soap bottle already in the basket, not sure where Jesus got that. And then he noted that Jesus knew his neighbor, Destiny. But of course he did. She sang worship songs while she did her laundry.

They only ever saw each other on Saturday mornings. Doing laundry. She had accused him, jokingly, of being a laundry-room stalker.

"We'd better hurry to catch her. She's almost done." Jesus pulled the front door open.

"Now you sound like *you're* stalking Destiny in the laundry room."

"I'm really not as creepy as you make me out to be." Jesus said that with a mock tone of offense.

But Paul's muddled thoughts didn't stay long on Jesus's teasing tone. He played instead with the idea of Jesus carrying the laundry basket. He pictured Destiny discovering that Jesus was with Paul. Guys hanging out together on a Saturday. Doing laundry. Not a pair of creepy stalkers.

Fortunately, Jesus knew the way to the laundry room. Paul just had to follow him down the stairs through the lobby to the door marked Laundry. God was giving Paul all the direction he needed, including a very clear sign.

As predicted, Destiny was in the laundry room. "Hello, laundry stalker. You almost missed me." The petite woman with glowing brown skin and loopy black curls greeted him in her usual ebullient voice.

Out of his muddle, Paul started to explain that Jesus had warned him to hurry to catch her. But stopping himself from that unguarded response blocked him from responding at all.

Jesus helped out by greeting her warmly. "Hello, my dear."

Actually, that didn't help. It was not a line Paul could repeat without getting himself into trouble. As attractive as the probably older woman was to him, he really wasn't pursuing her. He didn't know much about her outside the laundry room. Did she have a boyfriend? Did she even live alone?

When he set his laundry basket on the high table in the middle of the room, Paul found Jesus rolling his hand in the way a director might when a line was due. A line from Paul.

"Good think I hurried down here. Got a late start today." He wanted to go back and replace *think* with *thing*, but Paul was feeling awkward enough. Maybe Destiny didn't notice the glitch. A dryer was running, buffering all other sounds.

Destiny looked at Paul more directly than usual, probably oblivious to the little purple underwear she was folding as she examined him. "Huh."

Clearly Paul was not the only one tongue-tied.

"Ask her about church." Jesus, the script boy, helped out more directly.

"So I never asked you about church. You attending, uh, somewhere these days?" It was still awkward. Paul wasn't in character. What was his character? Handsome young laundry room guy?

Her head dodged an inch to one side. "Funny you should ask. I had a thought about church when you came in. Is that a strange thing for me to think?"

Paul shrugged and set his detergent bottle aside before checking for an available washer. "I go to church these days myself, though I haven't always been so faithful. At going to church, I mean."

88

"I've been pretty faithful. To church." She seemed to be studying him. Maybe she had done that when he wasn't looking during previous laundry encounters. She seemed as disoriented as Paul this time.

"I'm actually in the passion play over at Faith Community. My mom's church."

"Passion play? Oh, yeah." She grinned. "Who are you playing? Jesus?"

Jesus and Paul answered simultaneously. "I am."

"You are?" She chuckled. "Not really surprised. I guess you look the part. Though maybe a little too ..." Her smile curled playfully, and she chuckled some more.

"Too what? Too young? Too tall?" He laughed as he dumped his dirty clothes into one of the big washing machines. He paused to watch her.

"Nothing. I didn't ... I shouldn't have said anything."

"You're blushing."

She chortled some more. "I know. And now you're making it worse."

"Sorry. I'll pretend I didn't see anything."

Destiny shook her head and continued a breathy laugh. "Just like we have to pretend we haven't seen each other's underwear."

Now Paul was blushing. He looked at Jesus. He wasn't blushing, he was smiling. The purity of Jesus's smile colored Destiny's joke. In a good way. Without Jesus there, Paul would have assumed Destiny was flirting with him. But the simple humor Jesus clearly found in their exchange seemed to sort and sanitize the air. If that was even a thing.

Destiny had stopped laughing. She was still folding and stacking. "Huh. Funny that you would ask me about church." She snuck a peek at him. "When you came in here, I had this sorta sense of Jesus being with me." She laughed. "Must just be from you practicing your part for that play."

Paul's laugh was nervous. How much should he say? He knew he couldn't tell her everything, but it seemed like it might be helpful for her to know something. He looked at Jesus, a little afraid of what the third person in that noisy room might ask him to do.

Jesus nodded, and Paul knew he had permission. Maybe even encouragement to say something. But how much? He took a chance at extemporaneous lines. "Interesting that you would say that, though. Because I've been having a really ... amazing day. Like, it feels like ... well, like you said—like Jesus is right here with me. I've never felt that so clearly before."

No longer folding clothes, Destiny stared at him with her wrists resting on the edge of her wicker laundry basket. She shivered visibly. "Oh, my. Thank you, Lord. Wow."

Chills were crawling all over Paul's skin. He leaned one hand on the washing machine, alternating between looking at Destiny and watching Jesus. The look of love in Jesus's eyes raised tears in Paul's. "And I get this really clear image of him looking at you with so much love in his eyes."

Destiny clapped a hand over her mouth. Her eyes expanded and then scrunched shut. She let loose a gasp and took some deep breaths. "Thank you, Lord. Oh, thank you, Lord."

The washing machine was the only thing keeping Paul standing. His knees threatened to drop him to the floor like they did on the roof.

Though he didn't know what was supposed to happen next, Paul was surprised when Destiny grabbed her laundry basket and stepped toward the door.

"I gotta go. I ... thank you for ... for whatever. I just gotta go." And she did. She left. Leaving Paul and Jesus looking after her.

Chapter 15

Learning Sympathy from a Man Who Knows

Paul shook his head and clenched his brow as he adjusted the washing machine controls and poured in the detergent. When he hit the start button, he turned his eyes to Jesus, who was now seated on the sorting table, his sandaled feet dangling above the concrete floor. "That didn't feel right. I mean, her exit. It seemed like something else should have maybe happened. Did I blow it somehow?"

With a tight-lipped smile, Jesus simply shook his head. "No, my brother. You did well. And I'm very pleased with what happened here. Your relationship with Destiny will never be the same."

"Was that the point?"

"No, not the point. Just a necessary by-product."

"Necessary?"

"I wanted to remind her that she can feel my presence. And I wanted her to associate that presence with you. You'll be growing in awareness of me after this. She can help you grow if you want her to." Jesus raised his eyebrows but didn't wait for an answer to the implied question. "And your encounter with her was a way to show you something about sympathy. It's one of your gifts. But you avoid it in some areas of your life where it might feel threatening."

"Sympathy." Not a question. Just returning to his earlier questions. "So I was, like, feeling a lot with Destiny. Like, I could pretty much understand most of what was going on with her. Is that what you're talking about?"

"Yes. You have particularly sensitive receivers for emotional signals. It's one of the tools you use for acting. That skill helps you imagine what a character would be feeling in a situation, and it helps you respond to other actors in a scene. It's real. Not just for acting. You're gifted with sympathy."

"I thought it was called empathy."

"Empathy could be seen as another level beyond sympathy. It's good in many situations, but people can get tangled up in empathy. You are a separate individual and have your own separate emotions. Empathy implies that you take on the emotions of another. That's what your acting coaches tell you you need. And it works for acting. In your life, however, you need to be clear about the boundaries between you and others. Your emotions and those owned by others."

Paul worried that he was getting lost again, like with what Jesus said about blaming God. But he only had to scowl to get help.

"I don't expect you to solve the ongoing debate about sympathy versus empathy, Paul. That's not my purpose. But I do want you to offer yourself more sympathy. To call that *empathy* gets confusing. But lacking sympathy for yourself is a bit confusing, though entirely understandable."

"Wait. Sympathy for myself?"

"It's another way to say you need to feel your feelings more fully. Allow yourself to feel."

"This is about all those losses, then."

"Yes. That. And more than that. Your culture lacks both sympathy and empathy in many ways. It's a culture you've absorbed throughout your life. On the other hand, it's also possible to fill yourself with empathy for others while lacking sympathy for yourself." Jesus patted the table next to him, and Paul complied after checking that there was a supporting leg right beneath that spot.

"What people are really reacting to when they sharpen the distinction between sympathy and empathy is pity. I'm not asking you to have pity on yourself. Just some mercy. Some grace and some sensitivity. Feel your feelings, Paul. Go ahead."

"So, like, pitying myself wouldn't be so useful, but being willing to give myself a break would be good? Sympathy."

"Permission. Give yourself permission to feel."

As long as they were talking about definitions and acting tools, Paul was glad to thrash through it all. But he knew they were back to those losses. Had he not allowed himself to feel all those losses?

The door to the laundry room opened. Now Paul had to face the fact that he was sitting alone in the laundry room as if he had nothing better to do. Sitting with Jesus seemed a perfectly good thing to do. But his self-consciousness faded when he saw who it was.

Destiny looked at him sitting on the table as if assessing the sturdy furniture for weight-bearing capabilities. Paul wondered in that moment what she did for a living. Engineering?

"You're still down here." She adjusted her gaze to Paul's left and then his right. "Alone?"

Clearly he was alone, by all appearances. The fact that she was asking that implied something else. Paul allowed a crooked grin. "I was feeling like I was down here with Jesus, actually."

"You getting some pointers from him on how to do that play?" She said that as if only half her heart was in the joke. And maybe as if she had another question she was afraid to ask.

Paul could understand that hesitancy. Empathetic with her for sure. "Just listening. Learning."

"In the laundry room with Jesus?" She shook her head and then accelerated as if recalling why she had come back down. The dryer that had been running stopped as if triggered by her tread toward it.

Paul shrugged. "I guess so. He does more than just wash feet, apparently."

Destiny let out a cackle. Paul would not have thought her capable of that sound, but, again, he couldn't blame her. The scene was unhinged, the dialogue unexpected. They had gone where improvisation often led.

"You're not the person I thought you were." She stood next to the dryer, the door standing open now, the warm air wafting far enough for Paul to feel it and to smell the floral fabric softener.

93

He turned his head to look at Jesus. "I guess I'm not the person I thought I was either."

Grabbing a handful of maroon, blue, and yellow items—maybe sweaters—from the dryer, Destiny stood and looked at him, completely serious this time. "Well, blessings on that, I suppose."

"Thanks. You too. Blessings." Without thinking about it in advance, Paul lifted his hand as if he were the Pope blessing a crowd. Or Jesus sitting in the laundry room.

Jesus did exactly the same move.

Retreating again, Destiny cast a single glance over her shoulder when she reached the door. Again, Paul got the impression she was deciding what to say and what not to say. Maybe deciding what she thought of this new person Paul turned out to be. Or appeared to be.

Was he really changed? Would one day with Jesus change him completely? Permanently?

"It is possible." Jesus aimed an eye at Paul and nodded once.

Paul took a deep breath, resolved to accept the possibility.

Chapter 16

When You Look a Bit Too Closely

When the washing load was finished, Paul moved it to the dryer before they left the laundry room. Two other tenants arrived as Paul and Jesus squeezed past them in the hallway.

Paul tried talking to Jesus without vocalizing. *"So what you were saying about sympathy and empathy was really so you could get me to face all those losses."*

"Get you to face them? More like help you to face what you can't effectively avoid." Jesus opened his apartment door for him, magic none of the neighbors witnessed.

Paul took a deep breath. As dreadful as was the prospect of thinking about any of those painful events, everything Jesus had started had ended well. So far.

"Thanks. I think things are going very well." It was hard to tell whether Jesus was teasing him about hearing his thoughts—all his thoughts—or whether it was a simple affirmation.

Paul decided not to overthink it. He lifted his drinking glass off the kitchen counter and went to the fridge. "Can I get you something? Water? Anything?" He could tease right back.

"No, thanks. I'm still full from brunch."

Okay, Jesus was better at teasing than Paul was. But that tease raised a question. "If we eat here, you could have food with me, right? Your body is real? Like, physical?"

"It's the same body with which I ate the fish after my resurrection—to prove to my first disciples that I was really raised from the dead and not just a ghost."

"Huh. We don't do that part of the story in the play."

"No. That was after the climactic finale. A bit less dramatic than the stone rolling away and coming out of the tomb." Again it was not clear how much he was teasing.

Paul snickered anyway. "I assume you were joking about running lines with me, but I also assume you're coming to rehearsal with me today."

"I plan on it. Glad to be invited."

Paul contemplated the odd opportunity. Sitting in the auditorium would be the guy he was portraying on the stage. That would normally be an intimidating scenario, if he'd ever even imagined it before. But, as he set down his water glass, he looked at Jesus. Talk about sympathetic. And wise. And apparently without any kind of insecurity or resentment or anything. He couldn't ask for a better audience or even a better critic.

"Wait until you see my review in the morning."

Paul snorted at that before wondering about tomorrow morning. "You'll be gone tomorrow, right? I mean, invisible."

"Invisible. Not gone. Never gone."

"So this ..." He gestured to include the whole Jesus standing in front of him. "This is, like, the introduction to you being around all the time?"

"More of an awakening to the reality that has always been available to you."

"Available. You were always available?"

"Of course. Remember youth group? That first week, you invited me into your life. I haven't left since."

Paul drifted toward the living room while recalling his first week at youth group. His mom had dragged him and his brother to church with her. Pete didn't last long. Paul was too young to arrange an escape. He had suspected that Pete took the fast-food job just to get out of going to youth group. At fourteen, Paul couldn't follow his brother under that fence.

In Paul's mind, even at the time, it was too late for Pete. His big brother was a lost soul. Their father leaving and Theresa escaping to Chicago hit Pete hard. In fact, seeing the angry self-destruction glowing beneath the surface of his brother, like the precursor to a volcanic eruption, made church seem like a viable option to Paul.

And there was that guest speaker at youth group. He wasn't one of the straitlaced, buttoned-down people Paul couldn't hope to emulate. He was real. In recovery from one addiction or another. Paul couldn't recall the details now. Just that the guy's story seemed authentic, and the hope he offered was credible.

Actually, Paul's key thought had been, "May as well give it a try." Not the most inspiring commitment, but he had been sincere. More sincere than he himself expected. That visiting speaker put a hand on Paul's shoulder and prayed like he meant it. Paul had never bawled so much in front of strangers in his life.

At the time, he was guessing his tears were about more than just repentance. More than just religious fervor. He was letting something out. Letting out the pain. And that release seemed acceptable in the sweaty little gathering at the front of the youth room that summer evening.

"Words matter. And you meant what you said that night. You knew then that you couldn't be sure where it would lead you, but you were truly willing to give it a try. That was all the invitation I needed."

"Hmm." Paul's thoughts were still with that tight prayer circle in the basement of the church building that no longer existed. Being able to sense the genuineness of that guest speaker was part of what convinced him.

"Yes. You could tell he was real, not scamming you. Not surface deep. He was, and still is, an effective witness."

"Really? He's still going?"

"Still going strong."

"Oh. Cool. Good to know." He was tempted to ask Jesus to remind him of the guy's name. He could google him, but that was probably another distraction.

"You were sad about your dad leaving and Theresa leaving too. And you were already sad in anticipation of Pete moving on."

"That explains all those tears." Paul wiped at his nose and focused on the coffee table and his feet propped on it.

Jesus put one foot on the opposite side of that coffee table, tilting the rocking chair back a little. "I only needed you to open the door a little. And you could sense that it would be good to let some of your sadness out as you let me in. You cooperated. I took as much space as you gave me."

"Space inside me?"

Jesus nodded. "I still come knocking at doors now and again, checking whether you'll let me into another part of your house, your life."

"I guess this is one of those times, huh?"

"Yes, it is. A bit of a moon shot, really."

"A moon shot? Like, a last-ditch effort?"

"No. A moon shot, as in a big investment in order to accomplish a very big goal. An epic endeavor."

"Wow. No pressure, huh?"

"Ha. Yes. A little bit of pressure." They laughed together.

"So what's the goal?"

"Total domination."

"What?" Paul's voice squeaked.

"I want to completely rule your whole life. Total domination."

"You just upped the creep factor again." But Paul was laughing. He couldn't exactly explain what Jesus meant, but he knew there was a clause he had agreed to about turning his whole life over to God. He'd probably made that commitment first in youth group that late summer evening. And he had renewed something like it in the college fellowship group, and at the church he attended during school.

"Total domination." Paul smirked and nodded at Jesus. That phrase brought to mind Roger, who was an avid gamer, even making money by streaming his game play and having people subscribe to his video feed.

"I have to be careful who I say that to. Not everyone will be attracted to that prospect." Jesus looked at Paul contemplatively.

"Maybe Destiny would." Paul was just throwing darts.

"Yes. She is open to me and willing to accept all kinds of things, even meeting me in a new way in the laundry room."

Paul stopped smirking when he noticed Jesus arrowing his eyes at him. "What?"

"Why do you think your father left?"

"What? What do I think, or what did my mom tell me?"

"Why did he leave?"

"I think he was messed up. He was, like, this restless guy who never seemed to find enough of what he needed or wanted. Or maybe he couldn't tell which it was—want or need."

"Your counseling in college was pretty helpful, wasn't it?"

"I didn't stay with it, but it helped me know it wasn't about me, really. When he left."

"He didn't leave because of you. Not even because of what you couldn't offer him."

"What I couldn't offer? Like …" He dropped the argument he was prepping when he noticed something. It was like discovering a hidden piece after he thought he had cleaned everything up—the dishes or his bedroom.

Jesus was smiling meekly at him. "You've grasped with your head that it wasn't your fault your dad left, but you still cling to a long-shot possibility that if only you had been *more,* he might not have left."

"More what?" Paul was asking himself as much as Jesus.

"More entertaining. More interesting. More accomplished. He might have stuck around to see what you could make of yourself if you had just succeeded more at track or had gotten further with acting."

Sighing wearily, Paul let his chin sink to his chest. "Sounds familiar."

"Why did Pete leave?"

"He was like Dad. Restless. And dissatisfied."

"Nothing you could have done about that as a kid."

"No. I know that. I mean, of course that's true."

"And Theresa?"

"To get away from Mom. Mom was leaning on her too much. She was worried about all us kids and hoping Theresa could make everything better. I don't know if they ever cleared that up between them."

"Theresa had to move out to find her own way. It turned out to be a similar way to the one you and your mom found with me and with church. And they were fully reconciled, your mom and your sister, before the end."

"What was that guy's name? The guy Theresa was engaged to?"

"Phil. I call him Philly."

"Yeah. What?"

"Philly. It's a nickname his dad gave him."

"How's he doing?"

"Philly's having a hard time. He expected me to heal Theresa. It didn't happen."

"You couldn't heal her?"

"What I said about blaming God, and the causes of events being tangled, applies here. We have provided people with what they need to heal, but very few take up the calling, and fewer still persist when it's difficult."

"So it wasn't you who couldn't heal her, it was the doctors?"

"The doctors, and the people at her church praying for her, and at Philly's church. It's not always easy to heal people. And Theresa went quickly."

"I know. I was still debating whether to come home ... or to go to Chicago, I mean, to be with her. The news just got worse and worse so fast."

Jesus looked sad for the first time in Paul's experience.

Paul spoke again before Jesus did, for a change. "You're sad because the people who were supposed to heal Theresa didn't do it?"

"I'm not blaming them, but I am sad. Sad for them and for you and your mom. Your mother has lost much in this life."

So much of Paul's energy went to fending off his mother's attempts to manipulate his life that he seldom paused to pay attention to what she was going through. He wasn't always very sympathetic.

"But you came home. You did that for her."

"Yeah. I was worried about her. Bob just doesn't seem to be all there all the time. Like, distracted or absent. And I ... I guess I was afraid I would lose her too."

"So you came back for her and for you too."

"We're all that's left."

"Your father is still alive."

Paul looked hard at Jesus. "I know he is." He let his neck relax and allowed a slow nodding to begin. His dad had been at Theresa's funeral. Snuck in the back, apparently. Paul didn't see him, but he believed the people who said they had.

"You knew he would be there. That's part of your intuition—not so far from those sympathetic gifts I was talking about."

"Hmm. I wonder how sympathetic I am toward my dad. I might be willing to pity him, probably."

"He's had a hard time. You might pity him if you knew what he's gone through, his regrets and losses."

"But pity isn't what you want us to feel, right?"

"Pity isn't bad. Especially at a distance. The closer you get, however, the more you need to get beyond pity to sympathy. Or even empathy—closer still."

"Was he following my acting career all along?"

Jesus took a deep breath as if preparing himself for something. Though, more likely he was preparing Paul. "I'm not ready to tell you his story. I'm not here to give you specific information about your dad. That's not what you really need."

"What about him? What does he need?"

"He knows how to reach you if he wants. When he feels the need to talk to you, he can do it."

That wasn't the answer Paul was looking for, but maybe it was better. Did he even know *what* he was asking? What he wanted from his dad? In a way, the old man was dead to him already. Paul had given up on receiving anything from him. Knowing there was still a chance of ... *something* was a new idea. A bit of a relief, probably. Maybe that was enough.

"It's enough for now, Paul. Things change. People change."

Chapter 17

Time to Stop Waiting and Start Living

Paul returned from a trip to the bathroom, tugging idly at his mustache and wondering what Jesus had accomplished with him today. Was the moon shot on schedule?

"On course. No worries about schedule. It's not like a real moon shot."

Paul stood by the couch. "No. I think those folks worry a lot about schedules. Precision timing."

"Spoken like a young technician in a space command control room."

"Always playing a part."

"Why do you think that is?" Jesus stood from the rocker and stepped around the glass coffee table toward the balcony.

Paul followed him idly. "Why am I always playing a part? I don't know. You tell me."

"You're waiting. Waiting for real life to begin."

"*Ha.*" That was it. Jesus had just rewound time back to Paul's college days. Real life was what they were preparing for. What came after graduation. The great disappointment was that it didn't arrive after graduation. No neatly folded life was delivered to him that day. There was just Mom and Bob and Theresa, the women teary eyed. Mom clinging to his arm, insisting on one more picture in his cap and gown. Those were the early days of selfies. Maybe they didn't even call them that yet.

"When do you think it will start?"

"What? My real life?"

Jesus had two hands on the railing, standing shoulder to shoulder with Paul. "*Living* your real life."

"What do you mean?"

"It's here. You can live it now."

"Like, life to the fullest or something?"

"Something like that. Letting go of past losses will make it more satisfying, more complete. Like going up and down the stairs without the laundry basket."

"Dirty laundry?"

"I think the dryer is done now."

"You *think*?"

Jesus laughed and followed Paul in from the balcony toward the front door. They thumped down the stairs on two sets of feet, Paul's steps landing harder. Wearier. It was only one o'clock or so, but it had been a full day in lots of ways.

"Why can't you stay visible more than one day?"

"I can, but you'll do well to have a break from it for a while."

"So you'll come back? I mean, become visible again some other time?"

"It could happen."

"But ..." Paul stopped talking when they approached the laundry room door, which was swinging open. He probably blushed.

Mrs. Shukla nodded a greeting and then squeezed her laundry basket past him ... and Jesus.

Paul and Jesus exchanged a little smile inside the laundry room. No one else was there. The dryer Paul was using sat silent, but the clothes were still piping when he opened the door. He grabbed his basket and set it on the ground in front of the dryer. He extracted hot clothes in a dark and muted avalanche. Paul was still relying on his cool-weather wardrobe, maybe with an eye still toward mourning. He wasn't conscious of doing so most days, but the frequency of wearing black had ramped up after Theresa's funeral.

He recalled what he and Jesus had been talking about before his neighbor opened the laundry room door. "So you're saying I may get to see you like this again sometime later. After tomorrow."

"After tomorrow."

"Does that mean you'll need to do another intervention, or do you make appearances for other occasions?"

"Cameos? Definitely." Jesus grinned at Paul.

Paul stood up with his basket gripped in two hands. "That's good. Something to look forward to."

"Hmm. We were talking about living your life today. Not waiting."

Paul sniffed a laugh and rolled his eyes at the reminder. "Oh, yeah. I guess it's an old habit."

"A refuge from risk."

"Really?" As he followed Jesus, who opened the door for him again, Paul tried to figure out what he was avoiding. What was he not risking that he should be?

"You're not a failure at this, Paul. You do take risks. You put yourself out there. On stage. In front of the camera. But there are some internal chances you have avoided."

"Sympathy for myself?" Paul walked close behind Jesus, noting the sound of his visitor's rough, woven robe rubbing against the stucco wall.

"I'm talking about being your authentic self. Not just playing a safe version of yourself."

Paul leaned the plastic laundry basket against the wall as Jesus pushed his apartment door open. He considered just standing there a while as he figured out what Jesus was talking about, but he would probably get more clarity by following the man himself into the apartment.

"I don't do it consciously," he muttered as he waddled down the hall to his bedroom. He plopped his laundry basket on his bed. Pulling out socks, he piled them on one side of the basket to collect pairs. Shirts, pants, and underwear were each folded before being placed on the other side of the basket. "Just like I never consciously invented this system for folding clothes."

Jesus bent slightly and began pairing socks. "That's right. It just happened. No premeditation. And your habit of playing yourself like it's a part of someone else's life even predates your acting career."

"Really?" Paul couldn't think of any examples of that habit, even if he believed Jesus was telling the truth.

"Remember how you used to laugh at your grandfather's jokes even though you didn't understand them?"

"What?" But as soon as he uttered that spontaneous question, he recalled doing what Jesus described. Paul was probably eight or nine or so. He wanted the adults to think he was smart. They would think so if he knew what was so funny when they all laughed at what Grandpa said. Paul's dad was still around. His father also told jokes around the holiday table.

"You thought you had to be a bright kid with an adult sense of humor, though you couldn't have explained it that way at the time. You wanted them to appreciate you, and you believed that was more likely to happen if you laughed along." Jesus was finished with the socks. In record time.

Paul nodded, reliving a conglomeration of several holiday dinners.

"It's no fault of yours, Paul. The adults didn't seem to understand you, so you pretended to be someone they could understand. It was a reasonable desire and a fair attempt at getting what you wanted."

"Wow. This is deep stuff."

"It's a small example. Not a big event in itself, but it left a mark." Jesus touched Paul on the chest at a good place to start open heart surgery, probably.

Even as Paul continued to separate and fold clothes, his joints seemed to go mushy. A sort of vibration started at his core. He was having a hard time finding a thought, let alone words for a response. Finally he turned and looked at Jesus.

Jesus still had that finger on Paul's chest. It felt like it was going deep. Standing up became a struggle.

"You could sit down, if you like."

Sitting on the bed seemed a sensible option. Less risky than trying to remain standing. As he relaxed on the corner of his bed, Paul recalled some of the joking with Jesus. Clever and playful. That was Jesus and that was Paul, each of them being himself. He could be himself with Jesus.

That reminded him of his realization that he would enjoy having Jesus attend play rehearsal. Jesus was generous with his humor. No malice toward Paul at all.

Paul leaned forward and rested his elbows on his knees. He was still shaking.

Jesus put a hand on his shoulder. "I'm here to welcome you, Paul. To welcome you into your own life. A starring role. Just being yourself. Not playing a character."

A halting breath didn't end in sobs as Paul had assumed it would. Instead, he started to laugh from deep in his belly. A release. Like his heart was a restless dog finally being set free at the dog park.

Go ahead, boy. Go ahead and run.

Chapter 18

A Drive and a Stop with Jesus

They put away the laundry and straightened up the bedroom. Paul collected all the garbage in the house and consolidated it in the kitchen can. Perhaps the ordinariness of those tasks was a fitting response to Jesus's invitation for Paul to join his own life. To fully take part in the life he had been given certainly included the boring parts.

But there really were no boring parts today, not with Jesus present.

"Is this whole thing just to show me that I really need a best friend?" Paul didn't filter that question as he stood by his front door, getting his jacket on once again. He was idly checking his phone weather app, after the fact, to figure out if he needed the jacket. He found that it hadn't gotten much warmer outside. He could carry on.

"Perhaps you could see this as my audition to *be* that best friend." Jesus opened the door for him.

"Best friend, not just doorman?" Paul stepped through the door and instantly regretted making a joke about Jesus's suggestion. As much as he joked, Paul could tell when Jesus was being serious. In fact, even when he was joking, Jesus was obviously making a point.

"I guess the hard part is you being invisible after this." He kept his voice low with his chin near his chest, as if he wore a small microphone clipped to his shirt. He usually had something like that on stage. Paul focused on hitting each of the stairs instead of on whether his means of secret communication made any sense.

"That is a challenge for most people. But being aware of what you don't see is something you can learn. You can practice noticing the air around you, for example, instead of taking it for granted."

Paul stumbled on the hard rubber mat at the bottom of the stairs, caught between the demands of secret communication and imagining the air around him.

"You don't have to imagine it, Paul. It's real. You just have to be aware of it."

"I do?" He resorted to his interior voice automatically.

A neighbor he hadn't yet met was following his dog into the building. The older man nodded at Paul and touched the bill of his baseball cap.

Paul imitated that gesture, though he wore no cap.

"Well, the point isn't about being aware of the air you breathe. It's an analogy. I am as present as the air all around you. And as easy to ignore."

"Oh. That must be depressing."

Jesus lifted both hands briefly, bumping shoulders lightly with Paul on the sidewalk in front of the building. "Being ignored is something that leaves me longing for a connection. But I don't get depressed, of course."

"Of course." Paul paused to recall where he had parked the little blue car his mother and Bob had loaned him. He seldom drove it and had lost track of where he had left it a few times.

"Over on Haliburton Street." Jesus pointed his thumb to their left. Haliburton was the first cross street in that direction.

"Thanks. You're handy."

"Glad to help. Even an invisible friend can help you remember where you left your car."

"What about finding parking places? Do you have powers on the other end of the whole parking enterprise?"

"I can make suggestions."

Paul glanced at the young couple across the street who were sneaking furtive glimpses. He had been caught talking aloud to his invisible car locator, of course. He nodded at the couple and tried again at that internal dialogue. *"Are you saying that I can* have a conversation with you even when you're not visible like this?"

"Would you like to give it a try?" Even as he spoke, Jesus was fading. Until he was completely invisible.

The disappearance of his companion ignited a dozen small fires inside Paul. The most obvious blaze came from the feeling of being left alone. Abandoned.

"I'm still here." The voice was still there.

Could this actually work? Could Paul actually keep up a conversation with an invisible Jesus?

"I will never abandon you. The fact that others have gone out of your life does not prove that you are destined to be abandoned. People will inevitably let you down, but I will never do that. Just listen to me and shape your expectations according to who I really am." Jesus became visible again as they stopped next to the five-year-old compact car Paul was using while back in town. How long he would need to borrow it was as uncertain as everything else about his future.

"People let me down even though they don't mean to, right?" Paul unlocked the passenger door and opened it for Jesus. It was what he would do if he was driving somewhere with his best friend.

Jesus just grinned and slipped into the passenger seat, pulling the door closed as Paul stepped around the front of the car.

Seeing Jesus sitting in the car seemed to laminate the reality of this experience in some new way. Paul couldn't help staring as he walked around to the driver's side.

Jesus just smiled and stared right back through the windshield.

The concept of an invisible presence with him all the time seemed to fit with general Christian explanations of God and Jesus, even the Holy Spirit. But the future that Jesus described seemed like a different experience. At least different than what Paul had expected based on his previous twenty-eight years and on the lives of the people around him. He couldn't imagine anyone in his life who walked around with even an invisible Jesus accompanying them.

Maybe Nathan Berck had been like that. Maybe he saw Jesus with him. He was one of those religious fanatics who seemed to be way ahead of everyone else in the campus fellowship group. He went to a different church than Paul and his friends. Paul didn't know which one. But he had assumed in college that he wouldn't be totally comfortable wherever it was. Nathan's intense and literal faith was attractive in the way a big fresh pie in a bakery window is. It looked great, but Paul had no intention of buying it, let alone swallowing the whole thing.

"Interesting that you're thinking of Nathan now." Jesus responded to his thoughts as Paul checked for traffic on the tight side street.

"Interesting?"

"Yes. He did think of me accompanying him through his day when you were in college, but that doesn't mean you have to become like him to do the same."

"Huh." Paul fiddled with the gears, devoting only half his attention.

"Nathan has a particular personality. He has particular experiences and his own set of limitations. He's not like you in many ways. But you're tempted to assume that awareness of my presence will make you like him."

"I guess that's true. But was that really why I was thinking of Nathan just now?"

"You thought of him because he struck you as someone who saw things you didn't see. And he worried you. You're worried now what you will become if you accept my invitation to be aware of my presence when I'm not visible."

Paul had to set all that aside to get out of the tight parallel parking space without damaging any of the three vehicles involved. He drove a Jeep in LA, which elevated him above many cars and made maneuvers like this seem easier. He seldom had to get out of such a tight space in his California car though. His manager, Grayson, was keeping the Jeep at his place in Beverly Hills. Paul thought about selling it whenever he got anxious about his diminishing savings.

It probably took him longer than usual to get out of that space and start rolling on the secondary road toward the west side of town. Concentration on anything seemed fleeting and fragmented.

"You're doing fine. You'll be fine." Jesus wasn't a nervous passenger any more than he seemed anxious about anything else.

"I'll be fine, as in I won't hit anybody on the way to rehearsal? Or I'll be fine even if I imagine you with me when you're invisible?"

"You won't become Nathan Berck. And you won't become a crazy version of yourself. It's not insanity to be aware of what is actually true. In fact, one might consider ignoring me to be questionable behavior."

"One might?" He appreciated the diplomacy in Jesus's tone.

"I know people say seeing is believing. But that's been shaken lately, with fake photos on the internet, for example. You can't always believe your eyes. And there are things you cannot see that you do believe are real."

"Like the air?"

"A good example. Wish I had thought of that." Jesus grinned but kept his eyes straight ahead. "Remember to pick up toilet paper."

Paul had forgotten. He had left home early so he could stop at the discount grocery store on the way to the church. "Thanks for the reminder."

"You're welcome."

At a stoplight, Paul turned to consider his passenger.

Jesus turned toward him, all smiles, all peace. Fully visible.

"I could act like you're with me even if I can't see you or hear you. Will that work?"

"It wouldn't hurt. Sometimes you can get your mind and your spirit to follow your body. Your whole self will rarely unite. Leading with your imagination could work for you."

"Because I use my imagination for my acting?"

"Yes. You have practice with that. And you have discipline."

"Discipline in this one thing, at least."

"Go with your strength."

When they reached the grocery store, Paul signaled and turned left into the parking lot. It was mostly full. He coasted around until he found a spot near the far corner. No problem. He had about ten or fifteen minutes to pick up a couple items. On a Saturday, he hoped lots of registers would be open.

Striding toward the front door of the store, Paul glanced at Jesus, whose long hair streamed away from his face as they walked into the breeze. He seemed pleased. Pleased with a trip to the grocery store?

"Don't underestimate the importance of having plenty of toilet paper." Jesus raised his eyebrows and tipped his head instructively.

Paul laughed and forced himself to stop looking at the man no one else could see.

"And you never know who you might run into here." Something laced into Jesus's voice hinted that he wasn't just saying that.

"Am I gonna run into someone I know?" Paul congratulated himself for keeping the question internal.

Jesus nodded once, eyes forward, which drew Paul to look at the person on whom Jesus was focused. The guy looked familiar, but Paul could only see the back of his head now.

"Who is that?"

"Greg Swanson. You remember him."

That last phrase was not a question. Paul slowed a bit, as a skinny kid with dark circles around his eyes and crooked teeth climbed out of his childhood memories. "Greg?" He said the name aloud, but not to the man who had already passed through the automatic doors. "I didn't even know he was still around here ... or alive."

"His best friend, Mike, killed himself right after high school. Greg survived."

Paul remembered hearing the news about Mike Able. It shook him even though he and Mike hadn't been friends. Paul and Greg, on the other hand, had played sports together. Greg was a fast runner in those days. Almost as fast as Paul. Maybe the wrenching pain Paul had felt when he heard of Mike's suicide was sympathy for Greg. He was feeling it again, though Paul hadn't seen him since their high school days.

"Bailey." A man's voice and Paul's last name stopped him as his eyes adjusted to the light inside the store.

As a kid, Paul was used to being called by his last name. On the baseball field. On the basketball court. At track. But he rarely heard it as an adult. He swiveled his head to find the speaker, trying to imagine what Greg would look like now. The man with the long goatee was not what he pictured, but the eyes didn't lie.

"Swanson! I saw you come in. I thought that was you."

"Seriously? I'm surprised you recognized me."

Paul pumped the brakes for a beat. Was he being dishonest? He had recognized his old friend only with Jesus's help. "Actually, I was as surprised as you." That wasn't full disclosure, but he wasn't going to reveal more. Paul watched Jesus do that fading trick, observing only with his peripheral vision, but still distracted.

"So, how ya been? I heard you went to Hollywood. What're you doin' back here?"

Not calculating how it would land, Paul answered honestly. "My sister died last year. I came home to be with my mom and make sure she's okay."

Greg swore. "Sorry, man. That's terrible. Huh." His eyes drifted away, though he still leaned toward Paul, just two feet away. Other shoppers squeezed past them where the two men stood at the end of the candy and cookie aisle.

"Yeah. It's hard. But you know something about that too, right? I haven't talked to you since Mike Able died."

Closing his eyes as if suffering a sudden bout of indigestion, Greg flinched. "Yeah. Man, that was terrible." His face sank, and his voice with it.

Inside Paul's head, Jesus's voice hummed clearly. "He blames himself for not being there to stop Mike. Tell him what a good friend he was."

"Yeah. You guys were close. You were a good friend. I know he had a hard time with his family."

Greg just shook his head and looked at the grayish floor tiles.

"It's hard not to blame yourself, but we can't stop people from doing what they're determined to do." He was thinking about Pete now.

"You ...?" Greg looked up and tucked his eyebrows down in question.

"My big brother, Pete. You remember him?" Paul took a deeper breath. "Yeah. He killed himself. Maybe an accident, maybe not."

Greg swore again, more resigned this time.

"But it doesn't help to blame ourselves. Not at all." Paul was tempted to test himself right then. Was he acting? Did he believe his own words?

"Strange that you say that. I mean, I never told no one, but I really thought I could've stopped Mike if I'd known."

"Sure. We all think that. But they're taking their own life in their own hands. Making their own choices. You were a good friend, man. But you couldn't always know what he was thinking." Now Paul was wondering where all this was coming from. He wasn't exactly hearing Jesus say these things, but they felt like things Jesus would want him to say.

"Hmm. Yeah. Thanks. It's good to remember that." All the charge was out of Greg's batteries. He stood there tottering as if Paul could tip him over with one finger.

Paul worried that he had started a downward spiral for his old friend.

Jesus replied to that thought. "No. He's thinking about it. I'm not worried. It will help him to let go. At least a little."

Addressing Greg again with enough lift from Jesus to keep himself out of that same downward slide, Paul clapped him on the shoulder. "Good to see you, man."

"Yeah. Good to see you too. I should grab some stuff and get goin'."

"Mm-hmm. I gotta get to rehearsal."

"You in a ...?"

"Actually it's a church play for Easter week. Five shows. You should come check it out." He recalled now that Greg and Mike had been altar boys together. Greg probably wouldn't be totally shocked at an invite to church with Easter approaching. Paul told Greg the name of the church and the street it was on.

"Wait. So you came home to see your mom, but you got roped into a church play?"

"It's a really good production. And a great part."

"What, are you playing Jesus or something?"

"I am, in fact."

Greg swore again but apologized this time. "That might be worth seeing."

"Check it out. Five nights. You should be able to get in. And tickets aren't expensive."

"But they might be hard to get once people know who's playing Jesus." Greg flexed a sideways grin. "Okay. See ya around."

"Bye, Greg. Good to see you."

Without fading back into view, Jesus patted Paul on the shoulder. "Well done, Paul. Well done."

Chapter 19

Playing His Part for a Solo Audience

"You think I should try to get my costume to look like yours?" Paul was looking at Jesus. "I don't have time to grow my beard out that much. And I doubt they can do it with makeup." He reached for the handle of the tall glass door to the church entryway. As someone approached from his right, he realized he'd been speaking aloud again.

"Practicing your lines?" Mavis Williams reached for the handle of the next door to the left as Paul stepped inside.

He had to decide what to say. An uncomfortable laugh was all he managed initially. Telling a lie right across Jesus seemed impossible.

"Good call." Jesus grinned and turned toward Mavis. "I like her a lot."

Paul nearly crashed into the inside door as he lurched under the burden of what Jesus was saying and what he himself was not saying.

"You don't need to be embarrassed. I've been talking to myself every day, and I only have two lines." Mavis grinned at Paul, right past Jesus, who was still grinning at her.

"Uh, yeah. Well, they're crucial lines. You really set Peter up for his line with the way you say it."

Mavis was playing the young woman who spotted Peter next to the fire and accused him of being one of Jesus's followers. She was in other crowd scenes, but those two spoken lines were the height of her performance.

"Being convincing with those two lines makes that scene."

"Oh, you're just being nice."

"No way. I'm never being nice." As soon as he said it, he realized how funny it sounded. So Paul made a comical face to punctuate the joke, unintended as it was.

Mavis laughed and then waved at one of the other young women in the cast whom Paul couldn't name. The pale and slender woman ahead of them in the lobby didn't have any speaking parts that he knew of, but there were scenes when he was off the stage.

Mavis's scene was a split stage. Peter by the fire, stage right, with Jesus being questioned by the religious leaders, stage left. A spotlight stayed on Jesus as Peter denied him in the light around the artificial fire. The simultaneous staging added impact to Peter's repeated denials.

In the auditorium, Paul and the real Jesus found most of the cast already gathered in the first three rows of theater-style seats. The venue would seat about two thousand. Paul didn't expect they would fill it to capacity five nights in a row.

Jared, one of the assistant directors, was leaning his backside on the front of the stage, watching as Paul strode down the aisle. "Behold, the Lamb of God."

Everyone turned, and half of them laughed. Their laughter was probably prolonged by Paul's confused response. He stopped in the middle of pulling his script out of his pocket, thinking Jared might be seeing the real Jesus walking with him.

That Jesus patted Paul on the back. "It's a joke, Paul. Relax. I'm not going to make this hard for you. I'm just here to watch." Jesus's voice was right next to Paul's ear.

Paul restrained the urge to turn and make eye contact with Jesus. Instead, he settled for a peripheral check, while he more directly surveyed the eager faces of the cast and crew.

He assumed most of them had googled him by now, watching online snippets of his work in movies, plays, and TV. So far, no one had complained about Jesus being played by a handsome young bartender. Hopefully they would see it as an ironic twist and nothing more.

"Okay, folks, let's get it together." Arabella Gomez was a stout woman with short dark hair, heavy eyebrows, and riveting dark eyes. "Ken, will you open with a word of prayer?" She glanced at Paul but aimed her request at one of the church elders who was playing a Pharisee in the production.

Slipping into a seat next to one of the other Pharisees, Paul peeked at the older man's watch. He was exactly on time, but the culture nurtured by the director made on time feel late. Paul appreciated that, as he appreciated so many ways this production was being taken seriously and being given plenty of chances for success.

That serious effort included the two young men seated on the other side of that watch-wearing Pharisee. Those guys were both drama majors at the university, part of the large college group at the church. Paul wasn't the only real actor in the cast, though he surely had more clips on the internet than the others.

The older man who played James, the disciple, had been in professional stage productions when he was first out of college and usually starred in the plays produced by this church. He had gladly surrendered the role of Jesus to Paul, however, declaring himself too old to credibly play the carpenter who was in his thirties.

As the prayer ended, Paul looked around for Jesus. He found him sitting directly across the aisle. Settled in to observe, it appeared. Observe and inspire. Paul was supposed to look toward the audience at several points in the play. He knew where he would land his focus for at least part of those scenes.

Doing rehearsal with Jesus watching was bubbling giddy expectation in Paul's middle. He couldn't recall ever being this excited about a rehearsal. Maybe an opening night, but never a rehearsal.

"You look chipper. Got plenty of rest on your day off?" Arabella marched up the aisle with a fresh script in her hand. She held it back as if awaiting an answer first.

"It has been a great day off, I gotta say." Even as he stretched a silly grin, Paul wondered what he would say if she pursued the cause of his unusual cheeriness.

But she had business to do. "Here are those script changes we talked about. I think I included most of what you were suggesting. I hope you're comfortable with it."

"I trust you completely. You know what's best." As he accepted the new script, Paul knew he meant every word. But he also knew he hadn't been good at communicating those sentiments to Arabella before.

"Well, that's what I like to hear. Maybe I'll just take those changes back." She reached for the script but paused dramatically. Just a joke. After snickering at her own humor, she allowed her gaze to linger on Paul a little longer before she turned back to the stage.

If Paul had been acting, he would tell himself he had overdone his words of affirmation for the director. But it wasn't an act. It was what he really felt, and he spoke that praise with confidence.

One source of his confidence was Jesus smiling just beyond Arabella. He clearly agreed with Paul's assessment.

When he turned his attention to the stage, Paul saw the set designer he'd been thinking about this morning. Now that he saw her, he wondered at his reckless heart, turned so quickly away from Amber.

That self-recriminating introspection distracted Paul from the set designer and from Arabella calling together the first scene. After she caught his attention, he shed his jacket and left his old script with it, thumbing through the new one as he strode toward the stage.

Darren White was just ahead of Paul. He turned and smiled. His wry grin seemed filled with anticipation at having his sight restored by the miracle worker in the opening scene. It was a small part for the talented young man, another drama major from another college. But Darren's emotional response was so convincing that the healing scene launched the play with a resounding blast.

Paul was still paging through the script when he took his place. Arabella had highlighted changed lines. There were none in this opening scene, so he wedged the script into his back pocket. And he focused on Jesus as everyone settled in around him.

Maybe looking at Jesus was a mistake. As Paul was getting into character, into the scene, he let himself imagine the real Jesus restoring Darren's sight. His throat tightened, and his heart accelerated. To avoid collapsing into tears before reciting his first line, Paul diverted his attention from Jesus and bowed his head thoughtfully.

As he entered center stage, he felt the jostling of disciples on both sides, heard the rising cheers and exclamations of the waiting crowd. Darren was there with a young man in his teens kneeling next to him. In the play, the teen was a relative of the blind man, though the script didn't specify his relationship. Many of the characters were composites drawn from a variety of gospel accounts. Paul let his eyes rest on the young man, whose gaze was fixed on him as he approached.

When the boy said something to Darren, the blind man began his haunting cry. "Jesus, Son of David, have mercy on me." His face turned aimlessly as if trying to locate the healer with his ears. Darren was overmatched for this part, perfectly executing it every time since they began rehearsing in positions on the stage.

To Paul, Darren's role was strategic not just for the throat-clenching emotion of his reaction to being healed. He also set the tone for the rest of the rehearsal with his tight execution.

"Have mercy on me. Please, teacher. Have mercy on me." His voice tailed as a few of the disciples muscled in front of him.

"Be quiet, you."

"The master is busy."

"He has an important destination."

The knot of disciples slowed in front of the blind man. He had struggled to his feet with the help of the teenager. In reality, Darren was hardly more than a teen himself, but he would be made up as an older man during dress rehearsals.

"Rabbi, have mercy on me, please." He raised his hands and pleaded with the air around him. Then he stilled himself at the sound of Paul's voice.

"My friend, what would you have me do for you?" Not until he said it did Paul realize he had added the word "My" before "friend."

"Lord, I want to see." Darren, of course, did not miss a beat. But his reply seemed more tender, like the request of a real friend. A desperate friend. Not a desperate stranger.

"Bring him here." Paul spoke this to the boy who was grasping Darren's arm. The stage wasn't quite big enough for that line to make perfect sense, but Darren made it look like he approached from several steps away, emphasizing his disorientation amidst the obstructing crowd.

Disciples aimed resentful scowls as Darren pressed through them. Paul raised a hand and gestured to encourage the boy. This was another addition. Another unprepared enhancement. It was a natural extension of his authentic desire to see this man healed. That desire was accelerating Paul's breathing.

Paul grabbed Darren's hand and drew him close. Closer than they had stood in previous rehearsals. A gasp near his shoulder worried Paul a little. Maybe he was playing this too freely. He didn't want to lead the others astray. He carried an obligation as the star as well as one of the most experienced cast members. But his second-guessing didn't last.

With enough remaining external awareness to keep from turning away from the audience, Paul reached up and gently touched Darren's eyes. Previously it had been a mere pantomime of touching him. This time it was real. And Darren's reaction seemed real. He gripped Paul's wrist like a new convert about to be baptized in a muddy river.

"Eyes, be opened!" Paul declared it with conviction.

Darren recoiled as if shocked with power from that touch. He grunted inarticulately. More throaty than previous rehearsals.

Though Paul had never actually seen someone healed of blindness, Darren's reaction seemed real to him.

"What? What? What is happening?" Darren staggered back and flailed his hands at the air, his head back, eyes casting about. Then he landed those eyes on Paul.

There were tears in his eyes. And Paul couldn't resist. He smiled and laughed as tears filled his eyes too.

The little crowd of cast members burst into praise suited for a late-night prayer meeting, even if this church might not hold such meetings. When the rejoicing ended—including impromptu hugs—the scene had grown in length by almost a quarter.

"End scene!" Arabella's voice cracked.

Someone off stage shouted, "Thank you, Jesus."

The director was up out of her seat. She stopped with a foot on the first step at the front of the stage. No words came out, though she shaped and reshaped her mouth as if to speak, leaving Paul wondering what she was trying to say.

Finally Arabella exclaimed, "Where did that come from?"

Another "Thank you, Jesus" followed that question.

Darren shook his head and aimed a thumb at Paul. "It was all him."

Paul didn't hesitate. He pointed out to a seat occupied by a man in a Jesus robe. "No. It was all him." Then he realized what he had done. Quickly, he redirected his finger toward heaven. "Him."

That was a close one.

Chapter 20

Getting a Grip without Shutting It Down

The scene in the upper room, Jesus warning his friends of what lay ahead, choked Paul two or three times. The baffled and concerned looks on the faces of his disciples fit the scene. What was he saying? Why was he getting so emotional?

During a scene between Judas and the religious leaders, Arabella found Paul guzzling water backstage. "I see someone brought his A-game to rehearsal." She raised her eyebrows as if challenging him to deny it.

He wiped at drops escaping into his beard and grinned. "Is it okay? Not too much?"

"Well, I'd rather not weep in rehearsal, though I have been part of productions that evoked a different kind of tears." She rolled her eyes briefly. "But I'm not complaining. I just hope you can keep it up on opening night and beyond. Be sure to save something." Arabella was a high school English teacher who directed the major productions at her school. She was a professional, but also a volunteer, like Paul. She was, unlike Paul, a regular member of this church. He would rely on her to direct from that perspective as well as her theater experience.

Just as Paul was about to explain his improvement, he noticed Jesus standing behind Arabella. That altered what he was going to say. "I'm sure I'll adjust. It's just that I feel like I understand the part better. More empathy for the character." He flicked his eyes toward Jesus and back, checking for signs that he was misusing what Jesus had been teaching him.

"That's good. That's very good." She paused as one of the assistant directors shouted something that Paul didn't understand.

"I guess empathy with Jesus would be a pretty valuable lesson for any of us."

Paul grinned and nodded as Arabella turned to feel her way past the curtains to see what was brewing.

"Yes. Very valuable." Jesus nodded with raised eyebrows. Probably affirming and not joking. No bounce to those dark eyebrows.

Forcing himself to not answer aloud, Paul wiped at his beard again, though he found no more water there. *"I was about to take credit for that scene. For the change."*

"I'm not worried. Don't judge yourself too harshly. You deserve credit. I didn't force you to use what we've experienced together. That was your doing. I only provided the inspiration."

"More than that, though." He checked for listeners as soon as he heard his own voice in the sound-dampened surroundings.

"I created you. I have protected you, nurtured you. But you are still free to choose how you use all that. Well done, I say."

Affirming as were those words of Jesus, as well as the ones from Arabella, Paul worried. Could he sustain his intensity? An uneven performance would bother the audience almost as much as a lackluster portrayal.

"I can help you. I am constantly offering you inspiration. I never rest." Jesus turned his head toward where the next scene was being called.

Paul had more work to do. He would rest later. Now he was taking part in a dramatic production that felt experimental, if only for him. Actually, he was making it experimental for everyone when he got on stage.

The garden scene took a bit longer than usual to set in place. The foliage had been updated by the set designer, and she was supervising new placements. "Over there. We have to give Jesus room to kneel and stand up without knocking into these."

When she said that, Paul was gazing across a fake stone wall toward Jesus, who was back in his seat. There was one Jesus in that room, and it wasn't Paul.

"Excuse me, Paul, can I back you up a bit? Then we need you to test this spacing." The set designer was a tall woman with medium-brown skin. She had dark brown eyes and black braids highlighted subtly in gold and purple. She had always intimidated Paul with her confidence, but just now she showed considerable tenderness in maneuvering him around. He looked at her slender hand where it rested on his elbow.

"Sorry. I don't mean to push you around."

"No problem. Glad to let you do your job."

A young man with a jar-top haircut jumped onto the stage. "Hey, Tildy, I think that bush there has to be farther left, stage left, or some of the audience won't see him when he's on his knees."

"Tildy." That was the name Paul had been trying to recall. At least the nickname. During his struggles to recollect, he had been testing variants of Hilda and Helga and even Brunhilda. Hildy wasn't far from Tildy. She didn't look German, but that was an old-school thought. Germans came in all hues these days.

"Okay. Hey, Paul, you mind testing this? We need to see if you're still visible during the kneeling part."

"Let's hurry up, people. I wanna get more than halfway through today." Arabella was standing on the floor directly in front of the stage.

Paul stopped trying to remember Tildy's proper name and quickstepped around her to take the kneeling position of Jesus praying in the Garden of Gethsemane. He knelt mechanically, not really reenacting the scene.

Tildy supervised. "You're not going lower than that?"

Paul reconsidered and folded himself a bit more tightly. He caught a glimpse of Jesus through the little hedge next to him. The look on the Savior's face was new to Paul. Was he remembering? Returning to that night? Would he have lingering feelings from an experience nearly two thousand years ago?

"Paul. Hey, Paul."

"Uh, oh. Sorry."

Tildy had her arms crossed over her chest, standing on the outside of the hedge. "Where did you go?" She asked it like someone who knew something about zoning out.

"Oh. I was just thinking ... about Jesus." That honest answer escaped automatically.

"Well, I guess that's allowed in church." Her grin was elfish, her chin delicate and sharp. But her eyes impressed him the most. They seemed to be sorting him and not particularly frustrated by all that needed sorting.

All Paul could do was snort a laugh before Arabella took charge again and called the start of the garden scene. To begin, Paul would exit stage right and join his disciples, or at least seven of them. They had to economize with the space. Rarely was he on stage with all twelve at once.

Standing shoulder to shoulder with the men murmuring and whispering behind the curtain, Paul leaned forward just enough to get another look at Jesus. But he wasn't in that seat. And Paul noted an odd sense that Jesus had joined the little crowd of men.

When Paul turned to look at the guys around him, he couldn't see Jesus, but that didn't erase the feeling that he was right there. He checked again. Jason and another guy whose name Paul kept forgetting were closest. Something about their proximity reminded him of bumping shoulders with Jesus.

Arabella called the scene to begin, and a jostle behind him focused Paul into action. He glanced at Jesus's former seat again, then tried to pull himself into the very emotional scene. It began easily enough with him leaving four of the disciples in one spot, which might not be big enough given the new garden scenery. Then he left three more in another spot—actors playing James, John, and Peter.

Just looking at Casper, who played James, helped Paul get into character. The older actor cast his gaze about and hunkered as if fearing incoming arrows. He even looked longingly after Paul—Jesus—as if he wished he could stay close.

Someone was staying close. Paul snuck a glance to see if one of the disciples had forgotten his place and was rubbing elbows with him. No. No one there. No one visible. This solidified his suspicion that Jesus had gone invisible and snuck up to his side. That thought seemed to trigger Jesus becoming visible again. The real Jesus.

Jesus took up a position on the outside of the little hedge that served as a sort of privacy shield for Paul during the agonizing scene. Jesus knelt and locked his eyes on Paul.

At first, Paul resisted. But then he realized that Jesus had placed himself in a position that would allow Paul to watch him without appearing to stare into the audience. For this scene, the audience was to be as invisible as was this Jesus.

"The agony, Paul, was that humans had fallen so far that my crucifixion was the only solution." Jesus seemed to be speaking directly into Paul's ear even as he knelt five feet away.

As Paul delivered his lines, Jesus explained during the long pauses. "I knew what this would cost those who committed this crime. I knew the curse it would bring on them."

A swelling compassion replaced the self-pity Paul had tapped for his earlier attempts at portraying Jesus's agony. The self-pity he had used probably came from the loss of his own father, as Jesus cried out to *his* Father. But Jesus was transforming all that with his commentary.

During the next pause, Jesus added, "I came to save them all, but some would be condemned for the way they rejected me."

Paul could see agony on the face of the real Jesus. He tried to mirror that. The compassion in Jesus's eyes fueled Paul's monologue. It also overwhelmed him enough that he botched two of his lines. Arabella fed him a correction on one and let the other roll past.

He nearly forgot to go back to check on the three men posted nearby, but Jesus stood to walk him there, perhaps even making himself available to feed Paul lines.

Looking at the three actors playing disciples, Jesus explained. "They had no idea the magnitude of what was happening that night. Even less did they understand that I had equipped them for this trial. But they didn't receive all that I offered."

The consternation this explanation hatched in Paul probably served well for scowling at the three who were sleeping instead of praying. And then he returned to his secluded place and to crying out to God in heaven. Paul had to close his eyes and not look at Jesus for that final part. He didn't want to totally fall to pieces in front of the cast. It was only a rehearsal with more than a week until opening night.

When he finished his lines and looked up one last time toward heaven, Paul saw Jesus back in the theater seat along the aisle. He looked satisfied.

Lights were to drop to black at the end of that scene, but they weren't doing lights this afternoon, so Paul just stood up and looked at Arabella. It was a habit. Looking for approval, certainly, but also checking for guidance.

She wiped at a tear and shook her head.

Paul turned toward Jared, the assistant director. His eyes were wide, his head nodding slowly.

Casper, the veteran actor playing James, patted Paul on the back. But he didn't say anything either.

Chapter 21

Delivering a Message or Maybe Even Two

After a somewhat clumsy arrest scene, Jesus and his disciples bumping and mixing lines over one another, Paul got a break. He was backstage for the scene where the Jewish leaders stirred up a mob to call for Jesus's crucifixion and then received Judas's pieces of silver back.

That part of the play was supposed to switch quickly from scene to scene. Paul helped Tildy get some walls ready to roll out for the trial scene.

"Thanks. I'll have more help for the first dress rehearsal. I think having Jesus put the walls in place goes a bit too far."

"I get the feeling he's determined to go too far in every way he can." He didn't know exactly what he meant by that. Paul was caught between the temptation to flirt with Tildy and a desire to share with someone what Jesus had been doing to him all day. Though surely this woman would think he was nuts if he told her about that. Paul assessed her reaction under one lowered brow.

She stood up straight. "Wow, you're really getting into this part. Did something happen?"

Paul stared at her, though his focus was mostly internal. Could he tell her what was happening? That would be a weird way to get to know her. But it wasn't like this was really him. Today was a one-off.

No. That wasn't right.

He was delivered from giving her a cogent answer by Arabella signaling the start of the scene. Paul gave one rolling wall a push but held back so he could enter properly. That way he also avoided the curious expression still painted on Tildy's face.

Stepping to the edge of the curtain, Paul checked on Jesus again. His guest waved and smiled. Did he know what Paul had been saying to Tildy? Did he know what Paul had been thinking? Did his mindreading powers work over this distance? Were any of these questions reasonable ... at all?

The trial scene was the first one Paul felt he was doing entirely on his own, no inspiration from the real Jesus sitting in the fourth row. But the scene didn't really demand as much of him as some of the others. Stoic was how he saw Jesus in this situation. That was probably just the Jesus in his imagination. Or maybe in a movie or two. Was it right?

He caught himself scowling as he tried to figure it out. Not the right facial expression for the scene, but no one said anything. And he didn't forget any of his lines. Standing there in those aluminum chains, painted dark gray to appear to be iron, he started to feel weighed down by the day, not just the chains. He couldn't check the time very well while chained. The digital clock hanging on the front of the balcony was powered down. But it had to be suppertime soon.

"Okay, everyone. That was fantastic. Very good, Keith. You got the right tone this time, I think. And Paul, you were the best I've seen you. Thanks for bringing so much energy today."

"I think I spent it all." He offered a chagrined smile, amazed at his own candid admission.

"I'm not surprised." Arabella looked around at the cast and crew gathering around the stage. "Casper, would you lead us in a closing prayer?"

For the first time, Paul wondered if she would ever call on him to lead one of these group prayers. He hadn't prayed aloud in a group since college. But maybe Arabella couldn't get her head around asking Jesus to lead them in prayer. *Break this bread for us, will you? Turn this water into wine, maybe?* He couldn't blame her.

Paul was hearing murmurs about where to go for supper. He spoke before thinking as Tildy rolled a prop wall off the stage.

"You joining us for food after?" She hadn't been part of the after-rehearsal dinners before. He didn't recall her being around at the end of many previous rehearsals.

Looking over her shoulder as she rolled past him, Tildy tipped her head to the side. "I will if you tell me what you were about to say before Arabella called that last scene."

Recoiling, Paul reacted to the forwardness of that proposal. Or maybe he was anticipating the discomfort of trying to decide how much to tell her. Once again, he was left speechless, a half grin on his face like he was hoping she was at least half joking.

More than a dozen cast and crew gathered in the lobby once the stage was cleared. Jesus, at least the actor playing him, was not exempt from the latter task. Just as he didn't exempt himself from eating out with his new friends. He had to ignore the shrinking of his bank account to do the latter, but he counted it a good investment, given how few people he knew around town these days.

Paul waited for the group to gather and negotiate a location. He stood with his hands in his jeans pockets, shoulder to shoulder with Jesus. And he wondered whether it would be better for him to have a quiet meal with his mostly invisible guest.

"I would like you to go to dinner with them. I think you'll be glad you did. And having a good meal will help you later."

After staring at Jesus for too long, Paul responded to someone polling the group for venue preferences. Jared waited with his phone ready to call.

"I'll go anywhere. Whatever people want." Paul muttered that into the blend of answers.

He was adding and subtracting what Jesus had just said to him, managing not to stare at the man in the robe. Before he could find the bottom line to those sums, Tildy pushed through the auditorium door, accompanied by Arabella. Arabella had a husband and kids and had not joined the supper gatherings after most rehearsals. At least the ones Paul attended.

He waved at Tildy before realizing the two ladies were deep in conversation. He got no response from her.

"You'll get to talk to her. Don't worry. I have a message I want you to give her before dinner is over."

Again, Paul didn't get time to untangle all that, interrupted by travel arrangements once Jared confirmed availability of a large table at a popular pizza place. Two of the college guys asked Paul for a ride. He was pretty sure they were small enough to squeeze in. He hadn't given many rides in his stepdad's little car.

As they dispersed on the sidewalk out front, the low sun still shining over the trees around the parking lot, Tildy waved at Paul. "See you there. You owe me an answer." Her grin was friendly enough, but that didn't soothe his nerves.

Jesus followed Tildy with his eyes as if he might rather ride with her. Maybe she had a better car.

"You were awesome tonight, dude." Julian folded himself into the front seat next to Paul, his gangly legs nearly touching the glove compartment.

"Thanks. You were on target as well." Paul checked the rearview mirror. He wondered what difference it would make to Adam that he was sitting next to Jesus in the back.

Adam piped up. "You were more than just on target, Paul. You were inspired. I mean, that was one of the best performances I've ever seen ... ever."

Blushing, Paul slowly shook his head. He didn't want to say it was because of Jesus any more than he wanted to thank his agent and the Academy and all the little people who made him what he was today.

"Tell them as much as you feel comfortable telling. Use your imagination." Jesus delayed Paul's answer with this input, but it was welcome assistance.

"I really felt like I was getting to know the character. And, of course, I was inspired because he's so inspiring. I think I got into the story a lot better today. Some of it just came to me while I was on stage."

"Literal inspiration." Julian nodded somberly as if he recognized the phenomenon or had at least heard of it.

"I guess I took it more seriously today. I mean, it's a responsibility. We all have a responsibility if we're gonna tell this story. It's ..." Paul laughed. "The greatest story ever told."

Jesus was the only passenger who laughed. He was the only one old enough to remember that movie.

"Wait. Isn't that the name of a movie or something? What was it about?"

Paul chuckled. It wasn't the first time these college kids had made him feel old. "Yeah, it was a Bible movie from the sixties. It's a classic. Pretty old style, but it had lots of really famous actors in it. Even John Wayne playing the Roman Centurion."

"Ah. So did you study all the Jesus movies to figure out how to play him?" Adam was leaning forward to get his head near the guys in the front seat, though Paul had no trouble hearing him in the tight car interior.

"No. I'm not that ambitious. I just happened to see that one with my mom a bunch of years ago. It's the kind of thing they play around Easter on the vintage movie channels."

"Probably wouldn't help to watch most of those old movies anyway." Julian scrunched his brow. "I don't see Jesus being anything like the stiffs they have playing him in those films. He was the most chill person in the world. He wouldn't be all uptight like he's having a mental breakdown or something."

Paul checked the rearview again. Jesus was grinning. The prospect of getting movie reviews from Jesus made Paul laugh.

"What's so funny?" Julian turned toward him with expectation in his eyes, ready for a good joke.

"Oh, I let my imagination run sometimes. I was just imagining Jesus as a critic looking at how he's portrayed in the movies." Paul glanced at Jesus. Was that a small lie, or just avoiding the truth?

"Would he be gentle, or would he turn their projector tables over?" Adam snickered at his own joke.

Jesus smiled. "Depends on the film."

Paul was ready to laugh at that reply but caught himself before reacting to the invisible Savior. And he wondered how serious that comment was. Hard to tell with Jesus smiling so much.

They arrived at the parking lot of the pizza place not far from the church. There were only a few spaces left. Paul hoped Jared was right about there being a table big enough for the crew. As he worried about that, stepping out of the car and releasing the captives in the back seat, Jesus shouldered into him.

"I want you to tell Adam something from me."

Caught by surprise, Paul almost reacted aloud. But he held his tongue and sent a silent inquiry. *"What am I supposed to say?"*

"Tell him it will be worth it for him to catch the thief he knows so well. That will make sense to him."

"Yeah, but ..."

"I always wanted to work on TV." Adam was next to Paul.

Paul uttered a small grunt when he saw the obvious opening. "Uh ... you ever see that old show, *To Catch a Thief?*"

Adam's face brightened, and his eyebrows rose to max altitude. "How did you know that was my favorite old show?"

"Really—I don't know if you'll believe this—it feels like ... Well, Jesus told me. Uh, I felt like I was supposed to tell you that it will be worth it for you to catch the thief you know well." Those words had to be wedged past a tightening throat and shaky nerves.

Adam stepped toward the restaurant, apparently deep in thought about Paul's odd comment. When he spoke, his voice was distant and reminiscent. "I met an old guy who was a production assistant on that show back in the day." He touched his bearded chin for a second. "He teaches at the college part time. Hmm. He said I should talk to him about getting into TV."

"I guess you should talk to him, then." Paul suppressed a giggle.

Adam wavered on his feet when he turned to blink at Paul.

"Are you guys coming?" Julian was ahead several paces, craning his neck at them. Both Adam and Paul laughed. It was hard to judge whose laugh was more awkward.

135

By the time they got to the door of the restaurant, Adam and Paul were several feet apart. Paul had fallen in next to Jesus. But Adam held the door open and addressed the man he could see. "What you said was amazing, Paul. Knowing about me and that show. I'm definitely gonna look that guy up. Thanks, man."

"Well, thank God, I guess."

"Yeah. Of course."

Jesus elbowed Paul and nodded. "Well done. You're a natural at this."

Chapter 22

Is That Chair Next to You Taken?

Paul tried not to stare at Jesus as they shuffled single file toward the back of the restaurant. But he couldn't stop his distracted blinking as he tried to absorb what had just happened. His preoccupation staggered him into a guy seated at a big round table.

"Oh, Sorry."

"No problem." The guy looked up at Paul and hesitated. He turned to the woman next to him. "Hey, does that guy look familiar?"

The woman, in her thirties probably, was examining Paul shamelessly as he slipped past. "You're on that show. You're the bartender on my show. I watch you every day. Or I did. Where did you go?" She had rotated as far as she could to her right and now spun left, speaking louder as Paul pulled away from their table.

"Uh, I came home. Family issues." He raised a hand apologetically.

"Oh, wow. You're from here?" Her voice rose in timbre as well as volume.

Paul noted an increasingly hostile glare from the guy with that woman. Before he would need to apologize to the guy again, he bailed out. "Uh, enjoy your meal." As he caught up to the crew from the play, he shook his head at himself for sounding like a waiter, a role he had performed in LA in real life.

"That woman recognized you?" Tildy was standing next to a long table that seemed to be their destination.

He hadn't seen her before that moment. "Oh. Yeah. Soap opera fan, I guess."

"That guy was getting jealous." Adam smirked at Paul. He hesitated as if waiting to see where Paul would sit.

Paul was locked in on Tildy.

"Just take a seat over there. She'll follow you." Jesus pointed briefly toward the far side of the table.

Was that just predictive seating assistance, or relationship advice? Jesus seemed to be preoccupied with Tildy as much as Paul was. He had said something about giving her a message, hadn't he? Would it be like what he had just done with Adam?

Out of the corner of his eye, Paul caught Jesus nodding as he slipped past Tildy and aimed for the seats he had indicated.

Paul followed Jesus. Tildy followed Paul. Adam didn't follow the two Jesuses, unable to get past Tildy. Then he was waylaid by Jared, who was asking him for something.

Paul knew he wouldn't get Tildy to himself this evening, but he was glad to leave Adam behind. He suspected the college student would have some questions that might sidetrack Paul's opportunity to get to know the attractive set designer.

"I'm not playing matchmaker between you and Tildy, Paul. Just making sure you get a chance to talk to her. She has something to tell you once you give her my message."

Paul ventured a squinty glance at Jesus, struggling not to drop any of the pieces his invisible friend was piling on.

Jesus urged him toward a chair with a toss of his head.

Whether by miraculous means or simple coincidence, a seat remained empty directly to Paul's right. Tildy sat on his left, and Adam found a spot close to Jared. Jesus, of course, took that empty seat.

Once seated, Tildy tried to get Paul's attention. "You seem chronically distracted."

He didn't know how much he had missed, and it was impossible to deny her observation. Paul made eye contact, which revealed a strangely intense set to Tildy's face, like his mother when she thought he was coming down with something.

"I'm okay. I mean, sorry. Uh, I gotta admit, I've had a very strange day. I'm still settling in."

"To what? What are you settling into?"

Raised voices back at the other end of the table delayed Paul's answer. A reprieve, really. He didn't want to tell the truth, but he was getting a feeling that Tildy had some serious questions. Why so interested? Was it attraction? Serious attraction?

"Can we just order as a group and divvy up the cost at the end? Make it easier for the wait staff?" Daria, the other assistant director, proposed that to the table, but she was looking at Jared. Clearly the role of assistant director included organizing dinner orders and payment. Daria was seated across the table from Jared. She lifted her phone and said something to him, probably proposing electronic means for collecting contributions from the crowd.

Paul played spectator to all this while still sorting what he would say to Tildy. By now, he had lost track of all the explanations he owed her. What was clear was that she was curious about his odd behavior. He assumed that wasn't some mothering instinct involving concern for his mental health. And he assumed, as he often did, that the young woman was attracted to him.

Jesus rubbed a hand on Paul's upper back. "Relax. Don't get ahead of yourself. Just be present in this moment. You'll be glad you were."

A promise from an agent, producer, or director might assuage Paul in lots of situations. But Jesus brought more. His touch seemed to warm Paul in a soothing way. Paul's shoulders relaxed, and his head cleared. A clutter of defenses seemed to get stuffed away in a cabinet somewhere. Maybe he would get them out later. For now, he was hungry. And he wanted to get to know Tildy. He was even willing to relay what Jesus had to say to her. In fact, Paul was pretty intrigued about that prospect by now.

The group negotiated salads and three large pizzas along with pitchers of soda. No beer or wine ordered while eating with a church group, obviously. Paul didn't complain.

He grabbed the initiative with Tildy as soon as the waiter arrived and Jared ordered. "Tell me about yourself, madam set designer." He leaned toward her with what he hoped was his friendly, not seductive, smile.

She paused briefly as if deciding how to take his question. "I don't do set design full time. I actually work in the Patricia Rayburn Museum downtown as the art curator. Doing set design is really an old passion—something I picked up way back in middle school."

"Wow, maybe even earlier than I picked up acting. So, Rayburn—that's a new museum? What's it like?"

"I suppose some would say it's a hodge-podge. I've been there less than a year, so I don't have to take the blame for that. Eclectic is the way we're referring to it in the marketing material. Part of my job is to shape the collections into distinct media and periods that constitute a stronger identity for the foundation."

"Foundation?"

"A not-for-profit organization runs it and employs me."

"Do they pay well? Not-for-profit can be sparse, I know."

"No, it's good. Enough for me, anyway. I just need enough to live on and to support my painting habit."

"Paint habit? You sniffing thinner or something?"

She scowled and bumped his elbow with hers. "*Painting.* Oil painting." She snorted. "Though I have to admit I do love the smell ..." She shook her head and laughed.

"Okay. I was just kidding, of course. What subjects do you paint?"

"Children, these days. I'm in a child-portrait phase. Especially kids from war zones. Mostly the Middle East."

"Oh, wow. I guess that makes for some dramatic subjects. Huh. So you curate art by day and create your own art by night. Which one is your superpower, and which one your alter ego?"

"Do I have to choose?"

"Well, I guess it's too tight in here for me to twist your arm." He contorted toward her, pretending to begin that maneuver.

"You could probably move that empty chair next to you if you're feeling crowded."

They both looked at the chair to Paul's right. They both looked at Jesus. When Paul turned back toward her, Tildy's face had changed.

Her eyes were anchored to the place setting in front of Jesus. "Strange. I'm ..." She snorted and shifted her gaze to Paul. "Oh ... nothing."

"I'll leave that chair there." He spoke low and even, a small suspicion rising that Jesus and Tildy were conspiring about something, somehow. He glanced at the man on his right and recognized the warm smile. This one was aimed at Tildy, like she was an old friend. But maybe everybody was an old friend of Jesus's.

"We have a history, Tildy and I."

That comment from Jesus froze Paul, leaving him staring in the wrong direction. One of the women in the cast was seated next to Jesus. She reached for her long brown hair and tugged it back over her shoulder, then straightened her pale blue sweater.

"Uh, sorry. Distracted. Didn't mean to stare."

She shrugged it off, probably aware that Paul wasn't exactly staring at her. But he was getting a reputation as a space case.

He cleared his throat and turned back to Tildy. She probably missed some of Paul's interaction with that young woman, whose name he had forgotten.

Tildy seemed to be studying her own plate, almost in a posture of prayer. "You ever feel like Jesus is really ... really close by?" She looked up at Paul as if emerging from a short nap, responding to a dream she had.

Letting his eyes wander toward where Jesus's left hand was resting on the table and no farther, Paul answered honestly. "I didn't used to feel that. But today ..."

Chapter 23

Having an Unexpected First Conversation with Tildy

Large transparent salad bowls were delivered to three spots on the long table. There were sixteen people eating together according to those charged with keeping track of such things. Paul was preoccupied with keeping track of how much he'd already said to Tildy as folks took turns dishing tossed salad.

He dished for Tildy as well as himself. "Say when. Any special requests?"

"Can you get me one of those jalapeños?"

"If you insist. Onions too?"

"You think I'm loading up on pungent breath to repel unwanted advances?"

He shrugged. "Just asking."

Across the table from them sat Casper and a woman in her late forties who was probably his wife. That woman was in most of the crowd scenes of the play, not a named character like her husband.

Casper caught Paul's eye. "Paul, do you have any projects lined up after the play?"

Paul took a deep breath. The photographer for the romance novels had left a message on his phone this afternoon, but that didn't count. He wouldn't be doing that again. "No, nothing in the pipeline. Working as a barista near my apartment. I'm not sure how long I'll stay around."

"You're helping your mom out, right?"

As far as Paul had gathered, Casper was acquainted with his mom and stepdad, but he didn't know how well. This was a clearer window into that relationship than he had peered through before.

"She seems to be doing okay. I just wanted to spend some time with her. I didn't get to stick around after the funeral, so I'm making up for some lost time ... with Mom, anyway."

"So sorry about your sister." Casper's wife had hound dog eyes and an expressive mouth. Words of sympathy from her were automatically multiplied.

"Thanks. It was a shock."

"What happened to your sister, if you don't mind me asking?"

Paul didn't mind Tildy asking, but he was stuck between addressing the people across the table or just sharing his story with Tildy right next to him. He offered a sideways purse of his lips to Casper and his wife and turned toward Tildy, hoping his body language was a sufficient *Excuse me.*

"My sister, Theresa, was a nurse up in Chicago. She worked with critical care patients, mostly. Comas, major traumas. She was assigned a patient who had an infection that hadn't been identified, and somehow she caught it. No one knows exactly how. The patient died of that infection, and then my sister did too. I haven't heard whether they ever figured out what it was." He wondered now whether his mom knew. Wouldn't she have told him?

"Oh no. How long ago was that?"

"Last fall. We had the funeral down here, but my mom was still in Chicago when I finally got away from the TV show. It all happened so fast. She was sort of in shock. I had to basically get her and bring her home."

"Your mom's not married?"

"She is, but her husband was recovering from heart surgery, so he couldn't fly. That left her on her own with Theresa's fiancé. That guy was devastated. I felt like I was leaving him in a wreck, but I didn't really know him. And he barely knew I existed, I guess." He was meandering, his story losing focus.

"So you had to get back to work after the funeral, but your mom wanted you to stick around?"

"Uh, yeah. Did I say that?"

"Not exactly. I was raised by my grandmother. That's what she would have wanted in a situation like that."

"Oh. So you lost your parents?"

"My mom. My dad's still alive, and both my grandmas are alive, but my maternal grandmother was the one who raised me. My dad was out of the picture for a while in there."

"How long ago did your mom die?"

With her fork balanced between her fingers, Tildy rested her hand on the table. "About six years ago now. Yeah." She released a healthy sigh.

"Sorry. So sorry."

"I'm glad I found my dad and got back in contact with him before that. And my grandma carries on. Retiring soon. Hoping to move somewhere warm."

"Where were you raised?"

"Chicago suburbs, actually."

"Ah. Yeah. I visited Theresa up there once in a while. She went there for school—college and nursing school both."

"Oh. I went to Loyola for undergrad and U of Chicago for graduate school."

"Loyola. That was where she did nursing school."

"Huh. Small world is what we're supposed to say, I guess." She lifted her fork again and began to poke at the lettuce on her plate. "Your sister. Was she your only sibling?"

"She was at the time she died. And, for a while there, my mom acted like Theresa was an only child. They were very close." He set his fork down and reached for his water glass, realizing he had let a bitter tone into his story. "I had a brother. He died when I was still a teenager. Drugs."

"Oh. That's terrible. So now *you're* the only child?"

He nodded deeply, and Jesus resumed that gentle massage on Paul's shoulders.

Paul allowed his face to be drawn to his right, where the plate remained empty, but the chair remained occupied. He wondered at how quiet Jesus had been for the last few minutes.

Jesus answered gently. "This is your conversation. Yours and Tildy's. I'll get my chance before long."

Paul pretended he was stretching his neck and took a fuller look at Jesus, then turned back to Tildy and attempted a smile. He sensed that Tildy was with him, more than just next to him at the table. Were they connected by their family losses, or was there something more?

"You started to say something before about feeling like—like Jesus was ... close." Paul cut his volume in half, conscious of the people on all sides. A refill of the bread baskets had arrived, providing brief audio cover.

Tildy smiled in a sideways fashion. Did that mean she didn't want to talk about it? She was staring past him at Jesus's chair. "I know it sounds a little crazy, but sometimes I pretend Jesus is sitting next to me." She let her eyes coast from that supposedly empty chair right across Paul's face. Then she started to laugh, maybe a little hysterically. After a few seconds, she looked at him more squarely, but she abandoned an attempt to speak again and started laughing a little harder.

"Hey, how did you two get alcohol?" Jared, on the other side of Tildy, scowled teasingly at her and Paul.

Paul just shrugged. He wasn't sure what was going on.

Jesus elbowed him and lifted his eyebrows as if expecting something. Maybe something like recognition.

Paul absorbed the nonverbal message from Jesus for a second, then turned back to Tildy. That was when he got the joke. Here she was sitting next to *him*, the guy who was playing Jesus. She wasn't just pretending now, she was really sitting next to him. Even if he was just a pretend Jesus. He started to chuckle too, no longer just laughing at Tildy's reddened face and watering eyes. He was in on the joke. And probably in more deeply than she could imagine.

Paul ignored a buzzing on his phone. He assumed it was a text message, probably from his mother. He made a mental note to call her after supper.

After he and Tildy tumbled down from their humor, the first of the pizzas arrived. When all eyes turned toward the waiter delivering the pie, Jesus tugged at Paul's attention. "It won't be as easy as I would like, but you'll still have a chance to tell Tildy something for me."

Jared was orchestrating the food. He had enlisted Tildy to make space for the large pizza in front of her. That gave Paul a chance to look at Jesus.

"I'm glad to say whatever you want. But is it really something that's ... hard to tell her?"

"There's something else you need to do tonight. You need to answer your phone."

It was a newish phone, and Paul wasn't familiar with the settings for the ringtones. It was buzzing again. He had the ringer off, but the buzzing came through. He fished it out. It wasn't a text, it was a phone call.

He pushed his chair back, and the women on both sides of him raised questioning eyes. Paul glanced at the pale young woman with the blue sweater but focused on Tildy. "I have to take this." He was tempted to say Jesus had told him to take it, to justify interrupting the meal.

The phone stopped buzzing. It had been his mother. He could see he had missed two other calls from her. He hit the Call Back button.

"Paul. I'm so glad you called. I need you. Bob's in the emergency room. His heart's acting up. I thought I was gonna lose him there for a minute." She seemed to cover the phone. Maybe she was crying.

"Okay. Which hospital?"

"Saint Elizabeth's."

"Okay. Emergency department?"

"Yes, we're still here in emergency. Looks like we'll be here for a while. He has a private cubicle or whatever you call these little glass boxes." She sniffled hard. "Please get here as soon as you can."

Paul had wandered past the end of the table toward the fire exit. He said goodbye and touched the End Call button before turning back toward the table.

Tildy was looking at him. She seemed to know something. Maybe she was just reading his face.

"I have to go. My stepdad's in the emergency room. His heart." Paul slowed behind his chair.

Casper intercepted that news. "Bob? Is he okay?"

"I don't know. He had that surgery last year, you know. Mom said it scared her, whatever happened tonight. I have to go." He was addressing about half the table by now, but he turned to Tildy. "Can you walk out with me? I have something to tell you."

This was one of those moments when Paul was grateful for his acting experience. He knew how to act in an emergency. There was his bit part on a TV drama where he played the guy who had to call the police when someone was shot on the street. He knew how to act like he was calm in the middle of turmoil. Honestly, some of this turmoil was about cutting off his talk with Tildy, though most of the tension was about wanting to be there for his mom this time.

Tildy rose from her chair and led Paul toward the front door.

"Sorry, folks. Family emergency. See you all ... uh, tomorrow, probably." He was spontaneously implying he would be in church the next day, though he hadn't yet made that his habit.

A quartet of voices asked questions and said goodbye simultaneously.

Paul used the cacophony to justify not answering any of the questions. Instead, he caught up with Tildy, who was looking back at him, clearly concerned.

"Are you asking me to come with you?" She let him catch up to her as they approached the front door.

"No. I just had something I wanted to say before I took off, and I don't know when I'll get another chance." He glanced at Jesus and wondered why this was so urgent. Or was it urgent? Jesus had been cryptic about it so far.

Tildy just frowned in a curious way and stepped through the door when he held it open for her.

Jesus pressed right up next to Paul as they all three slowed down under a lamppost planted in the front sidewalk. The sun had set. Jesus reached a hand and put it on Tildy's shoulder even as he leaned into Paul.

She shivered visibly.

Paul recognized the sensation. "Remember how you asked me about feeling like Jesus is close?"

She nodded, letting her face drift to one side, almost facing Jesus directly.

"I've had that all day. I really believe I'm hearing from him ..." He stopped himself from admitting everything. "And he says he has a message for you."

Tildy froze with her tongue between her lips as if caught licking them. Her eyes expanded.

Jesus told Paul what to say, and he tried to deliver it in exactly the same tone, the exact words.

"He says that he wants to meet with you tonight. And you don't have to go into your closet because he knows it's too crowded." Paul was thinking about people who talked about a prayer closet. He assumed that's what Jesus was referring to.

Tildy's knees buckled, and she grabbed Paul's arm to keep from sitting on the pavement.

Another experience Paul recognized. "Whoa. You okay?"

She took a deep breath. "Okay? Uh, yeah. You said 'closet'?"

Paul looked at Jesus, who nodded.

"Wait." She froze. "Do you ... do ... do you see him? Are you seeing him ... now?" Her voice quivered disharmoniously.

Paul wanted to take a deep breath as he considered his answer, but he didn't find room for air in his lungs. He just nodded and glanced at Jesus.

"I knew it!" Tildy stomped one foot. "I knew there was something." She stared at Paul, squinting slightly. "Maybe I should go with you."

That wasn't what Paul expected her to say. And as much as he wanted her with him, he was pretty sure Jesus didn't.

He could see Jesus squeeze Tildy's shoulder again.

Again, she shivered.

"He's gonna meet with you. I guess near your closet or something." Paul was feeling the urgency of his mother's need now.

"Okay. You go. I—I wanna talk with you about this later."

"Yes. Of course. Text me your number." He recited his number, and she fumbled with her phone after extracting it from the pocket of her leather jacket.

"Okay. Thanks. See ya." Paul kissed her on the cheek before he realized what he was doing.

She dodged just a fraction of an inch, and he grunted what was meant as an apology.

He heard his phone buzz as he headed for his car. Hopefully a text from a new number.

Chapter 24

His Mother Needs Him Beside Her Again

Paul had to look up the hospital on his phone. He had never been to St. Elizabeth's before. The map on his phone knew the way. Letting the device guide him freed some bandwidth to review what had just happened with Tildy.

"I'm not even sure what that was." He took advantage of not needing to introduce the topic with Jesus.

"You did well, Paul. Just what I wanted you to say."

Paul, feeling his personal fuel level tap bottom, checked the car's gas gauge. It was fine.

"You didn't get any pizza."

Paul glanced at Jesus. "You couldn't help with that?"

"I tried, but not everyone was cooperating."

"Wait ..." Paul wanted to dig through the implications of that, but it threatened to be a deep hole. "No. Okay. Whatever. What I really want to know about is Tildy. I mean, not just know about her, which I would also like to know, but what happened between you and her."

"It wasn't a bad breakup or anything." Jesus sniffed a laugh. "But you'll have to ask her to tell you the story. I won't decide what you should know. She gets to do that."

"She gets to decide?"

"Of course she does. About all kinds of things."

"Oh. I know that. But what were you saying? You had some kind of thing with her some time ago? Not a bad breakup?"

"That part about the breakup was a joke. But apparently not a very good one, given the need for me to explain."

"Uh, well, I guess I did know that part was a joke. But ..." He had lost track of what he was asking.

"Ask her yourself. She'll tell you as much as she wants you to know."

"About closets and all that?"

"Mm-hmm." Jesus nodded, but his lips were sealed.

As they made the turn onto the major road on which the hospital was located, Paul adjusted his thoughts toward what was happening with his mom and Bob. "Is he gonna be okay?" Not having to explain who he was asking about might make him lazy, but Paul wasn't ready to apologize for that.

"He has stabilized. I'm not going to tell you how all this turns out."

"Why not?"

"Because you also get to decide."

"Decide what?"

"Decide what you're willing to do. Then we'll see what the results are."

"You're holding out on me?"

"You are free to choose for yourself. I can help you when the moment arrives, but sometimes it's better to do your lines extemporaneously. You work well that way, Paul."

"Really? You think I should get on live TV or something? Or improv theater?"

"Hmm. Maybe not that. I'm not talking about career choices, though I'm glad to help with that too. No, right now I'm talking about life choices. And some are best taken in the middle of the situation. You need more than facts to decide all kinds of things. You need to keep an open spirit and trust in your intuitions."

"Trust in myself? That hasn't worked out so well lately." He slowed at the last major cross street before the hospital.

"Actually, you've *ignored* your instincts at some crucial junctures. That's contributed to some trouble. With Amber and others."

"So, I ..." He was prone to ask questions whenever Jesus said these things, but this time he didn't feel like finishing the query. Something in what Jesus was saying sounded familiar.

"There is a moment just before you give in to a temptation when something inside you questions whether giving in is worth it. And whether you have a choice. Whether you might be able to resist."

"That's you?"

"No, that's you. The real you. The authentic Paul. The one that I designed." He tipped his head slightly. "Since I designed you, you might see some similarities between us." He stretched his biggest grin but then sobered a little. "Your authentic self can resist. The part that cannot so easily resist is the part trying to please others, trying to rely on the opinions of others."

Paul was shaking his head as he pulled into the hospital driveway. Not arguing. Not even challenging. Just waiting for it to settle. He shook his head without intention. Maybe he was just slowing down to allow the fresh rain of what Jesus was saying to sink in past the chaff and the dried weeds. Into the parched ground.

"For now, let's focus on getting Bob out of the hospital." Jesus glanced at Paul but kept his eyes forward as if on a mission.

Paul felt like the driver for Jesus's mission. Even as he mechanically laid down one foot in front of the other from the parking lot toward the Emergency Department sign, Paul was available for whatever Jesus was planning. Paul was here to discover, not to create.

Was Bob well enough to go home? Was that what Jesus meant by getting Bob out of the hospital? Was Jesus against hospitals?

"No. I'm against death. I'm against sickness. And I'm all for healing and resurrection."

"Yeah, I've heard about that." It was half joke, half automatic response. To some extent, Paul had gotten used to having Jesus around. Visible. Talking and treading out these mysterious and fascinating pathways. He took a deep breath and stepped through the heavy glass door marked Emergency.

Paul spotted the reception desk once he entered the waiting room. The attendant had just returned to her chair behind the high counter. "Robert Ellis?"

The tall woman with her dark hair pulled back tight and silver reading glasses halfway down her nose, checked a computer screen. "He's in bay twelve." She pointed to tall double doors with lots of red print on white metal signs.

Paul thanked her and headed for the door on the right. In the wide corridor inside that door, he scanned the bays nearest him. Eighteen was on his right, number one was on his left. Bob was somewhere in between.

Jesus appeared to wait for Paul to discover this before heading straight to a glass-enclosed room with a curtain pulled over the inside of the sliding door.

Paul didn't even ask, just veered into line with Jesus until he saw the number next to that cubical. He knocked on the plaster doorframe below the number twelve. There was a six-inch gap between the door and the wall, but the full-length curtain concealed the occupants of the room.

"Come in." His mother's voice wavered just a little, like she had strained it earlier in the evening. "Oh, Paul. I'm so glad you're here." She stepped toward him and spoke in a subdued tone.

Bob seemed to be asleep or at least resting, his eyes closed. His glasses were scooched up a bit too high on his nose, so Paul could see his eyes under the frames.

"Is he okay?"

"Another heart attack. We just got the blood test results back. He's stable. Nothing on the heart monitor to worry about now, but it took something out of him." She tipped her head and looked at her husband with heavy sympathy.

"What about you? You doing okay? What do you need?" He took her hand in his and tried to discern the look on her face. Weary, probably. Though exhausted in a way that wasn't familiar. Of course, he hadn't been there when Theresa was in the hospital, or Bob the time before that. This weariness was different than the resigned huddle she had assumed during Theresa's funeral. But at that point it was too late. There was no reason to even raise her head.

Mom's head was raised now, though maybe with some effort. She shook it at him. "No, I don't need anything. I had a coffee a little while ago. Seems like it might be a late night. They just confirmed he'll have to stay over, but finding a room usually takes a while."

His mom was over sixty, and Bob was older. Paul didn't know how much older. He could hear his mom's veteran wisdom through her weariness. This was what you faced when you got older. Knowing how long it took to get a heart patient into a hospital room was something that came with age.

Paul patted her shoulder and slipped his arm around her. They turned together to look at Bob. His eyes were open slightly, looking at them under his glasses.

Mom stepped to the bedside and settled his glasses onto his nose so he could use the lenses. "How do you feel, dear?"

"Not too good. I feel like I need to go to the hospital."

"Well, you're in the right place then." Mom folded her arms and stood with her stomach pressed against the railing of his bed.

That comment about the hospital recalled to Paul what Jesus had been saying on the way here about getting Bob out. Apparently Jesus hadn't been talking about taking Bob home tonight. What then?

Jesus slid up next to Paul. "He needs healing from the trauma of the heart attack and from the long-term problem with his heart. I could do that."

Turning to face him directly, too tired to pretend Jesus wasn't there, Paul managed to think his reply instead of speaking. *"Okay. Go ahead. Take care of that, then."*

"Sure. I'll walk you through it."

"Walk me through ... what? Delivering a message?" He had a handle on that little favor Jesus had requested a few times now. What did Jesus have to say to his old stepdad?

"Be healed. That would be the basic message."

Noticing his mother turned toward him now, Paul stared past Jesus's shoulder, pretending to study the whiteboard mounted on the pale green wall next to him. The name of the nurse had been wiped off and replaced with another, but the pen had skipped and most of the letters were illegible. About as illegible as what Jesus was saying to Paul.

"I heal people, Paul. You know that part of my story."

"So, like, comfort? Like, giving him comfort? Relief from the pain or something?"

"How are you doing, Paul? How was play practice? Exhausting?"

He turned toward his mom. "It was pretty intense. I guess I put more energy into it today."

"Well, that's good, isn't it?" She leaned toward him but apparently decided to stay next to Bob instead.

Paul couldn't tell what that aborted move was about, but he was busy figuring out if Jesus was serious. Or maybe just how he was being serious. It was probably just Paul who wished Jesus was joking. "Uh, did you call anyone from church? Like, to get them to pray for Bob?"

"Oh, no. It's late now. I'll call tomorrow morning."

Paul looked at the clock. It wasn't eight o'clock yet, but it was probably too late to catch anyone in the church office, assuming that's where you'd call for a thing like this. "Well, I told some folks at the restaurant before I left."

"Oh. How was dinner?"

Paul shrugged. He didn't want his mom to feel guilty for starving him. "It was good. Gigio's pizza."

"Oh. I thought I smelled something."

Jesus had slipped away from Paul and was leaning over Bob's bed opposite Paul's mom. That was strange, but Jesus could hover over Bob if he wanted, as far as Paul was concerned. He watched for a second to see if Jesus would do some kind of healing thing.

Instead, the Savior looked at Paul. "You could go to the other side and lay a hand on his shoulder like this."

At exactly that moment, Bob turned his head toward Jesus's hand. But he didn't say anything.

While trying to measure the coincidence between Jesus's touch and Bob turning toward it, Paul drifted toward where his mom stood. He was curious to see what Jesus would do.

"I told you what I would do. The question is, what are *you* willing to do?" Jesus kept his hand on Bob's shoulder and ushered Paul to the opposite side of the bed with his eyes.

Paul squeezed past his mom. "How are you feeling, Bob?" He set his hand on Bob's shoulder like Jesus was doing. Not exactly a mirror image. But close.

"I'm okay. A little pressure along here. I guess that's the strain from the heart attack."

"Tell him you'd like to pray for that pressure to go away."

Paul had to force himself not to stare at the invisible man. He adopted the role of the dutiful stepson instead and aimed a concerned nod at his stepdad. Concerned enough to pray for him? Maybe a heart attack was cause for desperate measures.

"Ask him." Jesus nodded at Bob.

Paul sighed. "Hey, do you mind if I pray for you, Bob?"

Bob tipped his head back a little more, examining Paul through the bottom section of his glasses. Reading the fine print, perhaps.

Mom intervened. "Well, that's nice of you, Paul, but I can call the church in the morning. There'll be someone in the office before the first service starts." She was standing directly across from Jesus, trying to talk Paul out of praying.

"I'll just give it a little prayer." He looked at Jesus. *"But you have to tell me what to say."*

"Okay, but you have to put some feeling into it. Bob is in pain. He's not fully recovered, and that itself is putting a strain on him. Stress from pain could make things worse."

Paul swallowed hard. Listening to Jesus, you'd think something important was depending on Paul. He didn't like that feeling. This was completely unfamiliar territory.

"Just say, 'Thank you, Father, for Bob, and for preserving his life. Now, in the name of Jesus, I tell chest pain to go away.'"

"I am not going to say that. That doesn't even sound like a legit prayer."

"Legit? Really? Who decides which prayers are legit and which ones aren't?"

Paul's initial answer was that his mom would decide. She would certainly have an opinion.

"She actually won't mind. She watches people on TV who pray like this."

"She does? I didn't know she watched ... praying stuff on TV."

"Trust me. Just say it, and trust me."

Paul nodded for Jesus to go ahead and feed him the line again. Then he did his best to imitate the words and the tone. What else could he do? When he finished, he glanced at his mom.

"Did you learn that in California?" She was leaning into him.

Paul had not been attending church in California—something he was regretting today. And he hadn't been watching anyone pray like that on TV either. "Uh, no. I've just been thinking a lot about Jesus, you know. Thinking about how he acted and thinking about doing things I learned from ... uh, studying him."

"You mean for your part in the play?"

He shrugged slightly. "That, and ... and for faith and for life, really." He sighed again. "I can use the help, to be honest."

She nodded slowly. "Sure. We can all use some help."

Paul was distracted from his mother by his stepdad scooting himself up in the bed with surprising vigor.

Bob had a silly grin on his face. "Well, I feel better. That pressure went away right when you said what you did."

"What? It did? Really?" Paul's voice cracked.

Bob laughed.

So did Jesus.

Chapter 25

Uncomfortable in This Hospital or Any Hospital

Playing God was definitely a thing Paul would never do. Not even a Morgan-Freeman-voiceover God. And certainly he would never fool around with anybody's health. If he had thought his prayer would actually impact Bob's health in some way, he would have kept his mouth shut. He wasn't qualified to mess around with anyone's heart. What was Jesus thinking?

Paul emerged from these thoughts to see Jesus smiling at him. Perhaps he was amused by this line of contention. He seemed to be waiting for something.

They were alone now, outside the emergency room bay in which Bob was being examined by a physician's assistant. Part protocol and part simply making room, Paul was clearly expected to leave during the exam. Mom had stayed.

"I don't feel comfortable with what just happened." To Paul, this qualified as a mature way to complain to Jesus. Doing so inaudibly was further evidence he was handling it well. His head was bowed as if meditating.

Jesus stood up straight, facing Paul. "You're not used to that kind of praying, but it worked."

"What about that? How is it even possible that what I did in there made a difference? It wasn't me, really. It was you, right?"

"We worked together. And it worked because you were assuming you couldn't do anything. You were relying on me. Because you could see me, you believed you should follow my instructions, leaving the results to me. You were obedient. We healed him together."

Paul was leaning close enough to the gap in the sliding door that he could hear some of the proceedings inside the bay. He heard laughter. Bob and the physician's assistant were laughing together, but not Mom.

"I don't understand all that, but I guess everything about being here is uncomfortable." Paul noted a second furtive glance from a young woman at the nearest nurses' station.

"Right. Hospitals are generally uncomfortable places. What happened to Theresa added to that discomfort for you."

Theresa had worked in a hospital in Chicago, of course. And their mom was with her when she died in that same hospital. Paul had found his mom arranging for Theresa's transport and burial when he finally arrived. The living woman he found there was like a bad rendition of his mother. A B-list actress who played his mother in some made-for-TV drama.

Right now he listened at that opening to the emergency room bay as his mom asked a question. Her voice sounded brighter than when Paul had first arrived tonight, but he couldn't catch the details of her question.

At Theresa's hospital, Paul had located Mom by her voice. A nurse had sent him on a maze quest toward the administrative office where his mother was signing papers. He was in the middle of trying to decide if he'd made a wrong turn when he heard her voice. A dried and cracked version of her voice, like one of those varnished Renaissance paintings with veiny fissures on the surface.

Mom's look had been no better than her sound. When he knocked and pushed through the half-opened door, he immediately noticed that her hair had lost its usual buoyancy. Her face was drooping too. Only her eyes brightened at his arrival. And that very briefly before she burst into tears and surged out of that chair and into his arms.

When Pete had died, Paul was not yet fully grown. And Theresa was there to comfort Mom. But in that hospital administrator's office after Theresa died, Mom leaned her whole weight into Paul as he wrapped his arms around her diminished frame.

Clearly the loss of her daughter had robbed her of the will to eat. What about the will to live?

Gazing into his mother's eyes when they had pulled out of that first desperate hug, Paul thought he saw hostility beneath her grief. Was it hostility toward him? That question dogged him the whole time he followed his mother around, making transportation arrangements and cleaning up Theresa's house.

Meeting with Theresa's fiancé was almost as painful as that first sight of his mom. Of course Phil had spent time with Paul's mom. They had suffered together, each building their own hostility toward the sickness robbing them of the person they loved most in the world. But Phil nearly collapsed when Paul's mother informed him that the funeral and burial would be back in Theresa's hometown. At the time, Paul had the impression that Phil would have fought that decision if he hadn't been so weighed down with his loss.

Paul envied Phil for being able to be there at the end. Before Theresa died. But that envy probably had more to do with a desire for a place free from guilt—the guilt Paul was feeling for not getting there sooner.

"Well, none of us expected her to go so fast." His mom wasn't even looking at him as they sat in an airport coffee shop waiting for their flight home, Theresa's final flight home. Mom's proffered excuse felt halfhearted.

Spending so much of his time listening to people say things they didn't mean, mere words in a script, might have tainted Paul's ability to believe even the words of his mother. Did she really not blame him?

He blamed himself. He had delayed flying to Chicago twice. Once he met with his agent to go over an offer for a car commercial. Some trendy new vehicle that wanted a nontraditional couple filmed popping the hatchback in order to hike in pristine wilderness. The second delay had been about Stefany. She and Paul had been busy with filming the soap, their schedules not always synched. He felt like he had been neglecting her. Assuming

Theresa would recover, he delayed his flight one more day to be with his girlfriend. A romantic dinner at home.

That was the night Theresa died. Paul was sipping champagne by candlelight while his mother watched her only daughter breathing her last. When he discovered the multiple messages about the decision to disconnect life support, he had crashed to the bathroom floor, shattering his phone's screen and breaking a finger.

His splinted finger was there as a constant reminder. It spoke cruelly and persistently throughout the whole visit to Chicago and then back home. Its pain, its reminder, carried through the funeral and the moment he told his mom he had to get back to LA. The splint and medical tape testified that he had missed her calls when his mom needed him most.

So here he was in a hospital again. This time he arrived before anyone died. His mother was stressed but not hollowed out. Still she couldn't have recovered from that lonely loss in a Chicago hospital. How did she find the courage to go to another hospital after that?

When the physician's assistant pulled the door open and slipped past, Paul passed through the opening and pushed through the curtain. "Well, what's the verdict?"

"The physician's assistant was encouraged by what he saw, but they still want him to stay overnight."

"That seems reasonable. Do they have a room for you yet?"

Again, Mom answered for Bob. "Not yet, but they're working on it."

"Probably making sure the mint is on the pillow and the wine is chilled." Paul rounded the bed to the side where his mother stood smiling weakly.

Bob laughed. "Well, this isn't LA. No wine, I'm thinking."

"Maybe a six-pack?" Paul was glad to joke with Bob. It was the best part of their relationship.

Bob's laugh came as a low chuckle that started a coughing fit.

"Take it easy on him, kiddo." Mom patted Paul's shoulder and slid in closer to Bob, who wiped at his mouth as he finished coughing.

"Staying the night doesn't sound like a bad idea." Bob rearranged the wires for the EKG, which ran under the blue hospital gown. "One day with all these things attached is tolerable." He lifted his right arm, which had an IV port and a thin tube running up to a plastic bag of clear liquid.

Paul noticed Jesus taking a seat on the lid of the laundry bin by the door. He assumed Jesus wasn't tired. Ghosts don't get tired, do they?

"I'm not a ghost, and I'm not tired. Just settling in for a bit."

Settling in was what Paul would do, then. "Well, I'll wait around until they get your room ready."

"Oh, you don't have to do that on a Saturday night. You must have better things to do." Bob's round face grinned optimistically.

Paul could only imagine what Bob thought he did on a Saturday night. Bob probably wasn't thinking of Paul spending the last few hours of the day hanging out with Jesus. But Paul couldn't blame him for that. Last Saturday, Paul was drinking with Roger and testing the prospects of taking a shapely blonde home with him. Better to be here with his mom and his stepdad. And Jesus.

"He can stay a bit, can't you Paul?" His mom said that with sedate confidence.

Paul acknowledged his mother's assertion with a nod. "So what were you doing when it started? Or is that embarrassing?"

Bob chuckled again, and Mom scoured Paul with another warning stare.

Keeping his grin on, Bob said, "Oh, just helping in the kitchen. Getting supper ready. We've been cooking together lately. Not doing too bad at that, are we, dear?"

Mom gave half a shrug. "It's hard when you've been doing things on your own for a long time, but we get along pretty well in the kitchen."

"Is that because Bob is willing to be the sous-chef?"

"Sous-chef?" Mom gave a little headshake, still glowering.

"Fancy restaurants have the head chef and the sous-chef. The sous-chef is the second in command." Paul glanced at Jesus, who seemed thoroughly content with this mundane conversation.

"Oh, that sounds about right." Bob kept his chuckle brief and light this time.

Paul had never been tempted to think of Bob as a dad replacement. The dad role was tainted for him anyway. And Bob was always avuncular in their interactions, with no effort to father Paul as a young adult. But Bob had a daughter from his previous marriage, so he knew something about being a dad.

"Did you talk to Sandra?" Paul looked at his mom.

"You know, I should call her and tell her it's okay. Thanks for the reminder."

"Call in here. I wanna talk to her too. Then she'll believe I'm really not dying ... this time." Bob's smile didn't leave despite a bit of grim humor.

"I can go take a walk and come back." Paul opened the door as his mom poked at her phone.

"Okay, dear. See you in a bit."

As he stepped into the broad corridor outside bay twelve, Paul wondered if a close observer would notice the curtain moving twice as he and Jesus both exited the room. He was back to considering those invisible man movies he had seen.

Jesus bumped shoulders with him as they headed to the big double doors out to the waiting room. "I'd like you to talk to someone for me out in the waiting room."

After a brief check with the man close at his side, Paul asked a silly question. "Are you serious?"

Jesus grinned. "Always."

Chapter 26

Reason to Believe a Little Bit More

As the tall wooden door swung closed behind him, Paul noticed an older man sitting alone in a wheelchair on the opposite side of the waiting room. The guy held something to his face—probably an ice pack. Turning to Jesus, Paul confirmed he had found their next target.

"You knew it was him without me even telling you." They walked side by side past the TV, which was blaring a police drama into the mostly empty place.

"What am I supposed to do?" Barely hesitating at that old man as he swept his eyes around the room, Paul noted that his approach was undetected. He was as invisible as Jesus behind the ice pack held against the man's face.

"Pull out your phone and sit down over there. You can answer texts from Roger and Tildy."

Paul nearly grunted his surprise before adjusting his path toward an armchair ten feet away from the old man. Was Jesus advocating a ruse?

"You have real text messages waiting. Not a ruse."

"But you want me to talk to that old guy, right?"

"He'll be more receptive if you don't look like you're here on a mission even if you are."

The next pause in Paul's brain came over the news that Tildy had texted him. That sent questions in an entirely different direction.

Paul quickly dispatched Roger's message, a request for a wingman as he ventured to a neighborhood club. **"My stepdad is in emergency room. Staying with my mom for a bit. He's gonna be OK."** It was a good excuse.

Sitting back, he crossed his right leg on his opposite knee and read Tildy's second message, after using her initial message to add her number to his contacts list.

"How is your stepdad?"

Well, not exactly romantic, but she had taken initiative. It was something.

"He's doing better. Staying overnight in hospital. I'll wait here til he gets room."

She texted back almost immediately. **"Good news."**

"Maybe we can talk later when he gets settled."

"Call me if it's not past eleven."

That was generous. She must be a night owl like he used to be before his current coffee shop job.

"Will do."

Nothing more from Tildy after that. Stefany was one of those texters who couldn't let him have the last word. Paul had even played around with that to see how far she would go. Once he counted eleven replies after the conversation was really over. Not that he ever pointed that out to her.

Jesus was sitting next to Paul and looking at the man in the wheelchair. "Okay, he's noticed you. And he would be open to you saying something."

"Really? Should you be telling me this?"

"You're good at reading people, Paul. If you had been paying attention to him instead of focused on your phone, you would have figured it out yourself. You were just otherwise occupied."

While Paul scowled at Jesus, sitting to his left, the old man sat up a bit and looked squarely at him with his one uncovered eye.

Paul stopped scowling and adopted a stranger's smile instead. "What are you in for?" Paul had never been in a jail scene, so he was using a cliché line from some anonymous play or film.

The old man had a ruddy face, deeply lined. His eye was hooded, his bushy eyebrow half-gray and half-black. He pulled the ice pack away from his other eye, revealing a purplish swelling where wrinkles gave way to an unnatural plumpness. "Got robbed."

"Oh. That looks painful. Have you talked to the police?"

"Yeah. It happened just up the street. There's always cops around the hospital this time of night, I suppose. They said I should come in here."

"What did the robbers get, if you don't mind me asking?"

"Just my watch and my wallet." He shrugged. "Wasn't a great watch. Don't think they knew what they were doing." He shook his head. "But I don't look forward to getting all that stuff in my wallet replaced. And the billfold was a gift from my daughter years ago."

"Tell him you'll go find his wallet for him." Jesus delivered that proposal while still looking at the old gentleman.

"What—?" Paul slammed on his brakes and cleared his throat to cover that escaped word. He was still learning that arguing with Jesus was senseless, something he might have figured out before seeing him. He looked long and hard at the old man instead of Jesus. What did he have to lose? "I know this is gonna sound crazy, but I have this feeling I can find your wallet. I think it's lying on the ground not far from where you got robbed."

"How would you know that? You're not ..." The old man had rested his arm on his leg, the ice pack dangling. He seemed to be examining Paul more closely. Hopefully Paul didn't look like the assailant.

Jesus kept Paul on track. "It'll just take a few minutes. Text your mother and then get going." He gave those instructions like the commander of some kind of unit, maybe a police unit that recovered wallets. Or was it a superhero cadre with x-ray vision, etc.?

"I've had a very unusual day." Paul stood, hoping to explain himself. "And I'm actually starting to believe that Jesus is talking to me. I know that sounds crazy, but if I find your wallet, then you and I can both believe ... at least a little more." Not his best speech, but not bad for an ad-lib.

The old man just stared, dumbstruck.

"I'm Paul, by the way." Paul reached a hand for a shake.

The old man complied. "Ivan."

"Okay, Ivan. I'll meet you back here in a few minutes, or find you in one of the rooms."

Ivan shook his head slowly but didn't say more.

Paul pulled out his phone and texted his mom. **"I need to run out and get something. Will be back in a few minutes."**

"OK."

The speed of her response implied the phone call with Sandra was over. That accelerated his feet as Paul followed Jesus to the exit.

"Which way?"

Jesus gestured to the right. "We can walk. It's not far. And it's a nice evening."

He was right. The temperature hadn't dropped since that afternoon, at least not much. A southerly breeze was bringing warmer air, perhaps.

"So, do you do this sort of thing often?" Paul didn't bother with telepathic communication or touching his ear to pretend he was on the phone. There was no one near the hospital entrance when they stepped out.

"Finding things for people?"

"Yeah, I guess."

"You can always ask me when something gets lost. You're allowed."

"That's one of your included services? No extra charge?"

"Indeed. And, in this case, it will be just like what you said. Both you and Ivan will be inspired to believe in me a bit more."

"Does that frustrate you? That you have to do tricks like this to get us to believe?"

Jesus was walking loosely, his arms swinging like he was doing his daily exercise, walking with his friend. "I don't think of it as a trick. This will be a great help to Ivan. I'm glad to help him any way I can."

"But you can do anything, right?"

"I am appearing to you like this, Paul, as a sort of intervention, as I said. It's not my normal mode these days. The current plan is for you and my other followers to do things like this with my leading. I really am inside you. Always with you. And I can do the same things I did when I walked on the earth in a mortal body."

"Mortal body?"

Jesus gestured to his right and continued to lead the way, now nearly a block from the hospital entrance. "I am here in bodily form. Not a ghost. But this is a resurrection body." He briefly disappeared and then came back. "It has special powers, but it is still a body."

Paul felt like he had gotten off track, but he appreciated that Jesus answered even his tangential questions. "So you want us to help people by ... what? By asking you where to find an old man's wallet?"

"You can at least ask."

"But sometimes you'll say no?"

"There will be times when you won't have the physical resources to provide help. Other times when you won't have the spiritual resources, such as faith. And you can't be in more than one place at a time. So prayers are answered accordingly. I don't think of it as my Father and I refusing to recover a man's wallet."

Starting to regret that he hadn't at least tried to understand more about the Bible and theology, Paul just shook his head. He was disappointed in himself. Not for his current confusion, but for his lifelong apathy.

"Don't let past shortcomings slow you down. Set your sights on what is ahead of you, and determine to follow my lead. That's all you need to do, Paul."

"Sounds simple." Paul followed Jesus up a long driveway next to an industrial building. Some kind of light manufacturing or storage place. It was a blocky building with very few windows. "You're leading me down a dark alley."

"You trust me?"

"Almost."

Jesus laughed. "Very honest. And something to build on." He strode confidently toward a dumpster next to that building.

"I thought you showed me that it was on the ground?"

"I did put that thought into your head. The robber tried to throw it in the dumpster but missed."

"Huh." Paul followed like a kid going to his first haircut. Not certain it was safe, but having no easy options for escape.

Jesus pointed to the corner of a large dumpster with dark sides and a lighter lid. There on the ground was a square object just barely visible on the black asphalt.

"Wow. You did it."

"I've done better miracles than this." Jesus grinned as Paul stood up and held the wallet in front of his face.

He wouldn't be able to confirm any of the contents in the dark, but he was glad to find there were still items in the old leather billfold.

The walk back to the hospital seemed quicker, but Paul didn't suspect that was miraculous. They were talking about a couple times when Paul tried to get involved in a church group only to be discouraged by one thing or another.

"I don't blame you for being discouraged now and again, but you will have to find an imperfect group of believers. The perfect ones are all in heaven with my Father." That was Jesus's final word on that subject.

They pushed through the revolving door into the emergency room entryway, nodding to a security guard now posted by the inner door. Paul realized he was holding Ivan's wallet, a stolen item, in his hand as he greeted the guard.

"Not cool." He pocketed the wallet.

Jesus laughed at him. Or maybe just near him.

They found Ivan in bay ten, not far from where a nurse and an orderly were preparing to move Bob to a hospital room. Paul waved at his mom through the open bay door and raised one finger to indicate he would be back soon. There was no space for him in there anyway.

He and Jesus paused outside the bay where Ivan was being examined by that same physician's assistant. The two men in that room stopped talking and looked curiously at Paul.

Paul spoke through the slim opening in the sliding door. "I found your wallet, Ivan. I actually didn't check what's left in there though. Let me know if you need some cash. I assume there's none of that." Paul was riffing again. The part about the cash was probably cover for the really remarkable thing that was happening. He pushed through the opening and held out the wallet.

"How in the—" Ivan reached up and took the wallet. "You really did find it." He scowled at Paul for a few seconds before cracking open the billfold. "Credit cards and cash are all gone. Still have my driver's license though."

"Well, that saves some trouble."

"It sure does."

"How did you find it?" The physician's assistant was batting his eyes, trying to catch up.

"Uh, well, I know it sounds crazy, but I really believe Jesus told me where to find it."

"Huh." The young PA just froze.

"Hard to argue with success." Ivan chuckled.

"Yeah, exactly. Well, blessings." Paul backed toward the open door.

"Uh, yeah. Blessings." Ivan waved his wallet at Paul ... and Jesus.

Chapter 27

A Day and a Night to Remember

After exiting Ivan's emergency room bay with a gaping audience behind him, Paul found Bob halfway into the corridor. The nurse had apparently been called away for something, and the orderly was talking with Mom and Bob.

"Oh, I'm sure they sent some rich plastic surgery patient packing so they could give you the room. Priorities, you know." The husky guy with one hand on the bar at the head of Bob's bed joked.

"How do you know I'm not some rich guy in here for plastic surgery?" Bob joked right back.

"Tummy tuck, maybe?" Paul wedged into the conversation. He had met a few rich plastic surgery patients.

"I was thinking breast enhancement." Bob looked at Paul and clutched his chest playfully.

"Behave yourself, old man." Mom swatted at him, landing her slap on the railing nearest her.

When the orderly got the go-ahead, Paul stood aside as Bob was rolled into the broad corridor. Paul's mind was rolling off toward what Tildy was doing this evening. Was she still with the crew at the restaurant? He checked a wall clock and guessed dinner was over. Was she doing something with Jesus? Something about her closet? He checked Jesus for clues, assuming he had read that question on Paul's mind.

With a *Don't bet on it* grin, Jesus just watched as Bob was rolled away, Mom striding along next to him.

Paul sped up to catch his mom. Together, they fell behind the mobile bed and followed the orderly, who was still joking around with Bob.

Mom spoke to Paul in a confidential tone. "You know, this is the opposite of what it was like with Theresa. I couldn't be in the room with her. There was no joking around. No signs of life, really."

Paul slipped his right arm around her shoulders. "Theresa's death was so shocking. Having to go through it like that was torture." He had heard lots of details from her before, but he didn't begrudge his mom reminding him. Really, she was celebrating how much better this experience was for her.

"Did you get enough supper? I probably interrupted it, huh?"

"I'm fine. What happened to *your* dinner?"

"Bob collapsed to the floor before anyone arrived. I was able to text them before the ambulance got there."

"So is there a fine meal just sitting on the stove?"

"Hmm. Yeah, I suppose there is."

"Want me to go over to your place and clean things up?"

Mom looked at him like she was wondering where the joke was, but her examination seemed to find his offer serious. "Okay. Assuming I'm staying here, which I'm not assuming yet. I'll let you know if I need you to do that. No sense in all that food going to waste."

"Right."

Jesus patted Paul on the back. He surely knew that his presence, visible to Paul, influenced the generosity of the offer. Mom and Bob's house was farther away, but not as risky as searching for a stolen wallet. Jesus and Paul exchanged a smile.

"I must say, you seem pretty cheerful this evening." His mom tilted her head back to study Paul's face.

He couldn't tell if she'd seen him smiling at his invisible friend. "It has been a very strange day, but I think all together, it's been one of my best days in a long, long time."

"Really? What's that about?"

"Playing Jesus. I'm really feeling like I'm getting to know ... to know more about him." Maybe that counted as chickening out. Paul resisted a visual check-in to discern what Jesus thought about it.

"Well, I did hope taking that part in the play would help you out spiritually. I don't suppose I kept that a secret."

Actually Paul hadn't thought of it in those terms. It felt more like it was about his mom trying to keep him around for a while, at least through Easter. At this point, he had no plans one way or the other. His agent had no news about returning to the soap opera, and the car commercial was still on hold.

"Talk to Casper about a regional theater role when you get a chance." Jesus did that thing where his voice joined in among Paul's thoughts as if it belonged there.

Paul did a double take that included trying to imagine what Casper might know.

"He has connections. And he knows about something coming up."

Paul stole another glance at Jesus before they all squeezed onto the elevator. The ancient rabbi wasn't offering more details.

"Have you looked around here for, like, some kind of theater company? I'm sure there's something. Don't know if you can make any money at it." His mom's voice wasn't quite as comfortable inside Paul's head as Jesus's, but, then, she wasn't speaking into his head. She was talking to the blurry reflection of the five of them in the elevator doors.

Paul nodded as a sort of placeholder.

The orderly interrupted. "We're out this door." He turned his head and nodded behind him toward the back of the elevator. It opened as soon as the elevator stopped.

Addressing Jesus instead of his mother, Paul kept his conversation internal. *"Is my mom overhearing our conversation? Is she, like, hearing you, sort of?"*

"Yes. 'Sort of' is right. She's like everyone else. You hear my voice, but you discount it as a stray thought—your own thought or maybe even the devil tempting you."

"Tempting me to do regional theater?" Paul just now noted how odd it was to hear words such as "regional theater" in Jesus's voice.

"Tempting you to stick around for a while."

Paul nodded. He had no idea whether it was more likely the devil would tempt him to stick around or to go back to the West Coast. But that was beside the point. It was probably even beside the point that was *already* beside the point.

"*If I were to stick around, would it help my mom? And maybe fix things between us?*" Paul and Jesus were following Mom, who was walking alongside the bed again, talking to Bob.

"That's one of those questions that can only be answered in partnership with the people involved, the people who will have to do the work. You and your mother, in this case."

"*So you don't know, or you're just not saying?*"

"I do know. I see the end from the beginning. But telling you the end is not going to help you. If I say things are going to work out, you might be tempted to just relax and wait for them to work themselves out. Recovering trust between you and your mother will require work. Do the work, Paul. It will be worth it."

"*So you're telling me to stick around here?*"

"No, I'm telling you to work on your relationship with your mother. How you do that is up to you. Obviously there are advantages to sticking around as you try."

Paul nearly missed the turn into the hospital room, focused for a moment on Jesus's sandaled feet. He was still fascinated with the authentic touches. How old were those sandals, for example?

Jesus chuckled as Paul looped back to follow the small caravan into the room.

Apart from the sound of Jesus chuckling, the floor was quiet. It must be near nine o'clock by now. When did visiting hours end?

"Soon." Jesus was clearly well informed about hospital policies as well as what was going on inside Paul's head.

"Here we are." The orderly, named Benny according to his name tag, parked Bob's bed and looked up at the door where a nurse had followed them in. "I'll leave you in these capable hands. Have a good night, folks."

"You too."

"Bless you, Benny." Jesus had a glint of affection in his eye as he watched the orderly walk past him.

To Paul, it appeared that Jesus liked everyone.

"Yes, I do."

Chapter 28

A Chance to Follow Up with Himself

Paul patted Bob on his beefy shoulder and gave his mom a long hug during an overhead announcement about the end of visiting hours. He should be leaving anyway. Bob needed to get his rest.

"I'll stay the night." Mom was looking at Bob. "I'll feel better staying close. This recliner looks pretty good."

"So you want me to stop by and clean up your dinner?"

"If you wouldn't mind."

"Of course not. You gonna loan me a key?"

"There's one behind the delivery box on the porch. You have to reach down in that crack behind it. It's in a little metal box. That was Bob's idea."

That it wasn't his mom's idea to conceal the spare key in a dark and damp crack was no surprise. Paul suspected his mom had never retrieved the key from there. "Got it."

On the way out the door, Jesus pronounced a sort of blessing over Bob and his continued recovery. Paul joined him with a silent amen. Maybe he could become the kind of person who would pray with Bob before leaving, but he wasn't ready for that role yet.

"You will grow in your faith, Paul. If you give it a chance."

"Give it a chance, or give *you* a chance?" Paul said that aloud but didn't see anyone who would judge him for talking to himself.

He and Jesus got on the elevator, Jesus laughing appreciatively.

"Here's a question. Should I call Tildy now, or wait till I get to my mom's house?"

"I would wait. You can use the speaker phone while you clean the kitchen."

"Great. Glad I asked."

"Me too."

On the way to his mom's house, they discussed the merits of Paul's various acting roles. Jesus demonstrated intimate knowledge of all of them but didn't seem to have strong opinions about most.

"What about modeling? I know that book cover thing was a mistake." Paul pulled away from an intersection under a new green light.

"It was, but you don't have to keep beating yourself up about it."

"Is that what I was doing?"

"You keep thinking about it so you can clarify that you know it was wrong. It's one of those things you do to win over the audience inside your head."

Paul released a bellowing laugh. "Don't hold back there, Dr. Freud. I can take the hard truth." His laughter died an early death. "But you're serious, of course. I know I do that. I, like, rehearse things for an audience that I imagine in my head."

"Most people just consider that thinking, but you have an increased ability to separate yourself from your thoughts. Distance where not everyone can find distance."

"That comes from acting?"

"Your acting benefits from that distance. How else could you say a line like, 'Buddy, you do that again, and I'll hunt you down and feed you your own heart'?"

Choking on a laugh and a gasp that crashed in his throat, Paul had to wrestle the car back into the center of the lane. "You remember that line? Huh. I remember that line. What the— That was in college. That was, like, eight years ago. And the play was entirely forgettable." He pounded on the steering wheel once. "*Ha.*"

"One act. Mercifully short. And well forgotten. But you and I remember."

"Yes." Paul shook his head. "And you're reminding me of it to show how I can say total nonsense with a straight face?"

"Yes. It's also a window on the internal separation that can cause you trouble. Remember what I was saying about sympathy for yourself? Or self-empathy, if you like."

"Uh, okay. We're back on that. I guess we never settled it."

"It will take some work and some time to sort it. You might consider a counselor."

"Yeah. I was never able to stick with that, but lots of the people I know in LA ... well, you know, of course."

"It can be helpful. Your church will have a list of recommended counselors."

"My church? Is that what it is now?"

"That's up to you, of course."

"Hmm. So I can act because I can sort of ignore my feelings? Like, set aside what I know is true in order to do a part?"

"Yes. Acting is a form of storytelling. I'm in favor of that, as you might have noticed. So I'm not saying it's inherently problematic, just that the ease with which you do it is indicative of a thing or two you could benefit from examining."

Paul stared into the dome of light preceding the car for a few seconds. "I really can't find anything wrong in what you're saying, but I gotta say that I never expected any of this. You showing up and the stuff you're saying." He glanced at Jesus in the passenger seat.

"Fortunately you are able to process events and words well after you experience them. You can think on these things for a long time. And you can consult me along the way. I'm not going anywhere."

"You keep saying that." He took a deep breath. "I guess I believe it, sort of. Are you going invisible right at midnight, then?"

"Sure. Central time zone."

Paul laughed. "Just wondering."

"No problem."

When they arrived at his mom's house, Paul parked in the driveway. The little car was back home. The neighbors were less likely to be suspicious of him in this vehicle. The house had never really felt like Paul's home. He was away at college when his mom and Bob moved here. They were already thinking ahead to retirement, finding a single-story home ready for their old age. Now it seemed that old age had arrived. At least the first crashing waves of it.

Paul pulled the painted wooden delivery box away from the brick wall and found an inch-wide crack between the porch and the bricks. He had already anticipated the eeriness of sticking his fingers into a dark crack in the night, but it was early in the year, and most of the crawling things he feared in cracks would still be dormant. He hoped.

The black metal box was less than two inches below the surface, but that didn't mean Paul wouldn't have nightmares about his hand being grabbed by a subterranean beast later tonight. For now, he survived, and he managed to get the metal box opened and the front door unlocked without incident. He flipped on a light switch just inside the door. His first attempt lit the porch. He turned that off and hit the second switch, which gave him lamp-light in the living room.

"Smells like food in here."

"It was going to be a beautiful dinner. Indian food."

"Indian food? My mom makes Indian food?"

"One of her friends, Mrs. Gupta, is Indian."

"Ah, yes. I've heard her mention Mrs. Gupta. But that's risky. Making Indian food for someone who's gonna know whether you got it right."

"Your mother is brave."

"*Ha.* Well, yes, I can see that. She's been through a lot. And she just keeps going on."

"Yes, she does." Jesus followed Paul into the kitchen.

As Paul had guessed, the stove was covered with pots and pans, four of them, lids on and burners off. He wasn't sure about the health of preserving the food now, but he'd leave that to his mom to work out.

"Where did she get the naan bread?" He lifted a linen towel to examine the stack of flat Indian bread. Then he spotted the plastic bag it must have come in.

"A new store just half a mile from here."

"I would have been shocked if she made her own naan. I knew a woman in LA ... Well, you know about Kavitha."

"Yes. I know her well."

That reminded Paul of his other agenda for this evening. "Okay to call Tildy now?"

"Go ahead and give her a try."

That sounded a bit noncommittal, but Paul was starting to understand that even Jesus had rules he chose to follow.

"You gonna help me put this stuff away?" He wasn't sure if he was teasing or not. Would Tildy hear Jesus banging pots in the background even if she couldn't see him the way Paul could?

Well, he would just call her and find out.

Chapter 29

Getting More of the Story from Tildy

"Paul. How is everything?"

"Bob is settled into a hospital room. Do you know Bob?"

"No. And I don't think I've met your mother either."

"Okay. Well, he's not feeling too bad now, but there was no argument about whether he should stay the night. Mom's staying with him."

"Huh. Okay. And what are you doing now?"

Paul had just clattered the lid of the largest pan on the stone countertop. "I'm cleaning up the dinner they were preparing when Bob hit the floor."

"Oh. They were right in the middle of cooking?"

"Yes. They had invited people over. Apparently they cook together. I suspect Bob is strictly the assistant."

"The sous-chef, huh?"

Paul laughed. "Yes. I tried that word on Mom and Bob, but they acted like they'd never heard the term."

"Is it a generational thing?"

"I don't know." Paul was watching Jesus effortlessly locate storage bags and containers. Clearly he had been in this kitchen before. Or something. "Uh, so what about you? Did that message from Jesus make sense?"

"Yes. It really did."

"Something about your closet?"

"*Ha.* Yeah. That's a very long story, but it meant a lot to me to hear that part especially. There's no way you could know about that, so I knew it really was from Jesus." She paused. A long pause.

"Have you ever heard of anything like that before?"

"Well, yes, actually. I have sort of a history." Another breather. "Though I gotta say, hearing Jesus's words through you was a wake-up call."

"A wake-up about cleaning your closet?" When he said that, Paul had no idea if this was even something he should be joking about. But Jesus was laughing quietly.

"When I was a girl ..." Tildy hesitated for two seconds. "I've never told anyone about this. Not since I was a kid. Most people would think I'm totally insane."

"Uh, well, I'm in the process of rethinking my definition of sane, actually. Maybe you can help me out with that."

Jesus had stopped his storage tasks and laid one hand on the counter, smiling sagely at Paul.

That was when Paul became aware that Jesus was hearing both ends of this conversation. He was, of course, well aware of what both people were doing right now.

Tildy was telling her story. "Well, I had this experience. Really a series of experiences when I was eleven years old. I really believed I was hearing Jesus speaking to me." She hesitated again. "And even appearing to me."

Paul stood blinking at the sink and the bowls stacked in it, a multicolored stack. He raised his eyes to check on Jesus. Right then, he was wearing the biggest smile Paul had seen on him yet.

"Jesus is smiling, like, really big right now."

"Oh ..." Tildy fell silent.

"Uh ... well ... like, I guess you know now what I meant about redefining what sane is these days. Really just today."

"Yeah. So ... can you still ...?" Tildy's voice faded as if she was drifting away from the phone.

Paul wasn't focused on her disjointed reply. He was focused on absorbing the satisfied shine on Jesus's face. Then he revisited what Tildy had just told him. "But you said that you actually saw him? Like, more than once? In your house?"

Tildy was quiet, but Paul could hear her breathing even over the speaker phone. "I did. But you believe me, don't you? The same thing is happening to you."

"Yes." He snickered. "Yes, the same thing is happening to me. And I do believe you."

"Wow. How long ...?"

"Jesus is making a one-day appearance. Just for me."

Tipping his head to the side, Jesus seemed to imply an amendment was needed.

Paul guessed what it was and interrupted the first word of Tildy's reply. "But not just for me. He's been doing and saying things for other people too."

"Like, for me?"

"Yes. And Bob. Apparently Bob's feeling much better after Jesus and I put our hands on him and sort of prayed."

"I prayed for my grandma's heart arrhythmia back in the day."

"Really? So this is a thing?"

Tildy laughed freely, taking a long moment to compose herself with a high-pitched sigh at the end. "I guess it is a thing, though I remember him telling me the visibility part was unusual. He was really adamant that he would go invisible but *not go away*."

For Paul, this felt like discovering someone else had seen the UFO hovering over his neighborhood. Here was someone who had been through this before him. Though her experience somehow involved a closet.

"Wait. So you met with him in your closet?"

Tildy laughed some more. She might have even been crying a little. She sniffled as she collected herself again. "It was a joke, really. That movie, *Monsters Inc.*, was pretty new back then. And he sort of pretended to come out of my closet. Though I knew, even at age eleven, that Jesus wasn't, like, lurking in my closet."

"He does seem to like a joke."

"Huh. Definitely. But lots of it was serious too." She drew a deep breath. "I did go into my closet after that, to be alone and try to be aware of him still with me even if I couldn't see him. There were a few times in my life when I thought I heard him giving me directions. Like, suggestions for what I could do for someone or for what I needed for myself."

"I guess it's hard to remember he's still there when you can't see him." Paul was thinking about what lay ahead for him.

"Yeah. Of course. I have kinda gotten ... deaf to his voice, I guess. That's why your words about him meeting with me outside my closet were really helpful."

"Oh. So did you do it? Did you meet with him, like, before I called?"

"I guess I did, in a way. I sat on the floor in my bedroom on this soft furry rug I got when I was still in middle school, and I talked to him. Out loud. And I guess I believed he was with me more than I've been sensing recently."

"Hmm. But you're going to church. You haven't given that up."

"I am at the church. But I gotta admit, I chose this one because of the stage productions. Not so much because I saw it as a way to stay connected with Jesus. Really, my connection with him was very private. It didn't depend so much on church. Though my dad and I did start attending church when we first got back together. He's more into it now than I am, really."

"Your dad is? I guess that's good. Did it come from Jesus appearing to you?"

"I think it did. I was more interested in church than I would have been if Jesus didn't come creeping out of my closet those times. And that got me asking my dad about going to church. He wasn't going back then."

Paul continued his cleaning, trying to keep the banging and clattering to a minimum. "Creeping? Huh, I'm trying to imagine ... I mean, you saw him more than one day?"

"It was an everyday thing for several days. But not all day. He didn't go to school with me, really. Mostly just met me at home. Though he did sneak out once or twice."

"But not just one visit for one day?"

"Right." Tildy was silent for a second. "Is that how it is for you? You said for one day only, didn't you?"

Studying Jesus with a bit more suspicion, Paul was testing whether he really wanted this visit to go on and on. "Yeah. He said he would never leave me, and he might show up this way again later. But this is a one-day deal."

Jesus reached up and clasped Paul's shoulder with one hand. The effect of that touch was deep calm. Was there something magical in his touch? Well, this was Jesus in his mother's kitchen. Magical seemed not too far a stretch.

"Miraculous. I don't do magic," Jesus gently corrected Paul.

Paul turned to the phone, wondering if Tildy had heard that. But she was probably just silently waiting for him.

She spoke up before he could think of what to say next. "He didn't tell me he would show up again later, but I'm not surprised he gave you a message for me. It always felt like he was reaching out. And not just reaching out to me."

"An intervention." Paul probably interrupted her. "That's what he called it for me."

"Oh, really? What's that about?" She made a small noise. "No, you don't have to tell me about that."

Paul took a deep breath as he sprayed out a large avocado-green bowl. "I can't say I fully understand that part. Not yet, anyway. I sure do need some kind of help, but maybe there were a lot of reasons I needed an intervention."

"Well, me too. And Bob, probably."

"Huh. Yeah. And there have been a few others today." Paul opened the dishwasher and slid the bottom rack out. "I guess I'm not the only one who needed a word from Jesus."

"I suppose intervention is his thing." Tildy sounded wistful. Maybe tired.

"Yeah. I kinda wish you could come over and see him with me."

Jesus shook his head slowly.

Paul didn't wait for Tildy to reply. "But I know I have to go through some of this with him one-on-one."

Her voice was resigned. "And I probably wouldn't be able to see him anyway. No, you go ahead. Get all you can out of this day." Then her volume intensified. "But you have to promise to tell me everything."

"Everything?"

"Okay, not everything. But ..."

"I would love to debrief this with you. I need someone to believe me so I can even start to figure out what this is about."

"Yeah. I know what you mean."

"Well, okay ..."

"Yeah. Well, have a good night, Paul." She paused. "You too, Jesus."

Chapter 30

What Exactly is this an Intervention For?

"She's right, you know. Intervention is what I do. My Father sent me into the world to intervene where no one else could."

"That must have been, like, a huge burden. Knowing only *you* could do it." Paul was running a damp cloth over the counter. Fortunately his mom and Bob weren't messy cooks.

"I had help. My Father was with me every moment of every day."

"So then you ... you would go off to pray. Like, I remember you doing that even before the garden scene."

Jesus chuckled.

Paul assumed that was about him calling it a scene. He didn't bother to apologize. Not with Jesus chuckling so easily like that.

"Going away to be alone with my Father was important during my mortal life. Knowing he was with me didn't prevent the masses of people around me from distracting my attention. To truly be here as a human being, I had to give up the capacity I have now to be aware of infinite inputs simultaneously."

"You sound like a supercomputer or something."

"My Father does think I'm super."

Paul stopped with the foot pedal on the garbage can pressed, the lid standing open and his palm full of dried spices and crumbs.

"I know you think that was corny." Jesus tilted a grin at him.

"I wasn't going to say that."

"You were thinking it."

Paul laughed. "What do you care? You can have a corny relationship with your dad if you want." His laughter died hard.

Jesus was watching like a doctor or nurse monitoring a patient. Or maybe more like a loved one attending the hospital bed.

"Your dad is alive. He can be reached, if you're determined to do it."

Bailey was a common name. Searching for Warren Bailey had produced millions of hits in Paul's web browser. Adding his dad's middle name narrowed that down to mere thousands. Or tens of thousands, maybe. "Does my mom know where he is?"

"She doesn't know exactly, but she has information that would further narrow the options."

"Why don't *you* just tell me where he is?"

"That would violate your dad's freedom."

"He doesn't want me to find him?"

"Apparently."

Paul scowled at that odd response. Then he adjusted his aim. "What would be the benefit of me finding him? I mean, for me. The part you can tell me about."

"Right. You need some closure, Paul. You have some questions. He's the one who should answer those. Your identity has a lot to do with where you come from, the people you come from. Understanding yourself is important. Contact with your dad, extensive contact with him, will help you."

"Help me get over ... to get past the losses?"

Jesus sighed. "Connecting with your dad won't erase the pain of him leaving when you were just a boy. You won't get over that by seeing him or even getting to know him."

"I remember him, sort of." Paul pictured a wiry man with long limbs, dark hair in waves around a triangular head. His forehead was square, his hairline straight across. His eyebrows were dark like Paul's, his eyes like Paul's too. And Paul could always remember his dad laughing. Joking.

"That makes it harder, in a way." Jesus spoke pensively.

"What does?"

"Recalling him as humorous and carefree. If your dad was so happy, why did he leave you?" Jesus shrugged. "That's your question, not mine."

For Paul, having someone tell him what questions resided in his head was like having a stranger reach into his dresser and pull out a T-shirt Paul had forgotten about. A shirt with some memory attached.

"Like the band shirt your mom let you buy with your birthday money when you were thirteen."

"That's not still in my drawer, is it?"

"No. And it wouldn't fit you anyway."

"Huh. But I know what you mean. I don't even keep up with that band anymore, but the shirt was symbolic. It was my choice. My mom let me make my own choice." He looked around the kitchen. His mom's kitchen. Two more containers to fit into the fridge, then he was done.

Jesus opened the fridge door as Paul carried the two plastic containers, heavy with leftovers from a meal no one ate.

Stopping to look down at those laden containers, Paul said, "I just realized how hungry I am."

"Why don't you warm up some of that?"

"Is it safe?" He had been thinking his mom would have to figure that out when she got home.

"Are you asking for my educated medical opinion, or are you relying on my extensive experience with leftovers, like with the loaves and fish?"

Maybe his hunger was dulling Paul's wits. He barely laughed at the reference, but he did figure out that Jesus wouldn't suggest eating leftovers if they were dangerous. The lamb shank and spicy potatoes looked enticing. Some broccoli masala was in the fridge too. At least the broccoli seemed safe. The potatoes too. He would have to take Jesus's word on the lamb shank. Jesus knew something about lambs, of course.

That thought started Jesus laughing big and long.

His laughter was contagious. Paul snorted as he assembled a plate of the leftovers for the microwave. The sound of humming electronics filling in when Jesus's laughter diminished.

The dinner smelled better once freshly warmed. Paul had run the hood vent for fifteen minutes after Tildy hung up to clear out some of the lingering odors. A spritz of citrus air freshener had helped. His awakened hunger overpowered the stale smell that remained.

Seated at the table with his meal set before him, Paul lifted his fork and knife but hesitated. Jesus was seated across the broad dining table with the bare surface in front of him. "It doesn't feel right eating with you just watching like this."

"You did it before."

"I was trying to convince myself that you weren't real before."

"You believe in me now. Tildy helped."

Paul nodded, still debating eating while Jesus went hungry, so to speak.

"Okay, I'll join you." Instantly an identical place setting and meal appeared in front of Jesus. Then he reached a hand across the table. "Shall we give thanks?"

Jesus had demonstrated fading out and fading back in. He had done a few other miraculous things too. But that dinner materializing out of nowhere was stunning. Paul was literally stunned. He reached for Jesus's hand in slow motion.

And Jesus prayed. "Thank you, Father, for providing this meal and for providing the companionship across this table. Please bless this food to our good health. Amen."

Paul's mom had taught him to end with "In Jesus's name, Amen," but he could understand why Jesus didn't do it that way.

Jesus laughed with his lips closed around a bite of food, lifting his eyes to watch Paul cut a slice off the lamb shank.

The food had cooled to easy eating temperature. The spicing was perfect. Paul admired his mother's progress as a chef. Maybe Bob had something to do with that. Paul had grown up with frozen meals out of plastic bags, at least for most nights.

"She was working. It was hard for your mom to do everything."

"Dad made sure of that."

"She recovered. And she tapped her ability to succeed in business. You kids were taken care of."

"Financially, at least. That's true." Paul chewed and swallowed. "I guess we might not have been better off if my dad stuck around. He kept losing his jobs."

"Yes. He had a hard time holding down a job, though he was a good salesman when he stuck with it."

"A salesman?"

"I know you think of him as more of a handyman and construction worker, but that was just what he fell back on when he got fired from the sales jobs. More people were willing to take chances with him for less visible positions." Jesus chewed and swallowed, then sipped from the water glass that had arrived with the miracle plate.

"I blame him for what happened to Pete, of course."

"Yes. Because of the addiction and the abandonment. Addiction *is* something that gets passed on from generation to generation. But blaming your dad doesn't make you happy. It certainly adds nothing to his life. He has suffered much over Pete's death."

"I didn't talk to him at the funeral."

"He saw you there."

The food was good, but Paul probably wasn't enjoying it for all it was worth.

"That bitter taste doesn't come from the food, Paul. It comes from refusing to let your father go. Refusing to release him from obligations he clearly did not fulfill. He won't be able to do anything to free you from your bitterness over the losses."

"There's that word again."

"Losses. Yes. There were things *my* Father and I granted you and your family that were stolen away by your enemy. Losses that felt like being robbed or having your house burn down."

Paul nodded, continuing to eat his late supper out of habit now more than hunger. Maybe watching Jesus eat kept him going despite a waning appetite. A buzz on his phone distracted him and delayed an approaching funk.

It was his mom. **"How's it going? We're settling down for the night here."**

"Going fine. Eating some of your leftovers."

"Oh, that's good. They won't all go to waste."

Paul thought about assuring her that Jesus was helping with that, but it occurred to him that he didn't know exactly how this worked. Was Jesus just pretending to eat pretend food?

Jesus tossed a piece of broccoli onto Paul's plate.

Paul examined it from a safe distance and then examined Jesus. What distance would be safe from him? He stabbed the bright green vegetable with his fork and popped it into his mouth. It was the same as what was on his plate, just as Jesus's miracle had implied. An identical meal to share with Paul.

But where did that food come from? If Paul went to the fridge, would he find more of the food missing from the containers than when he put them in there? And the plate? Was the miracle a matter of transporting the plate from the cupboard, or was it the creation of a new one?

Jesus chuckled and sipped his water. He wasn't answering Paul's questions, though he seemed to be monitoring them.

"Not gonna let me in on all your secrets?"

"What's the fun of that? Discovery is a great motivator."

Paul scowled at that oblique answer as he said good night to his mom via text message. She proposed he spend the night at her house, but he wanted to sleep in his own organic bed and wake up in his apartment tomorrow so he could walk to work from there.

Jesus set down his fork, lifting his water glass again. "I'm still with you either way."

Chapter 31

In Search of the Way to Escape

Together, they put their dishes in the dishwasher, and Jesus grabbed a rag to wipe the table down.

"I know where you could get a job. You're a good worker."

Jesus chuckled. "I'll keep that in mind. I've had a few offers."

"Temptations?"

"Working with you at the coffee shop is tempting. Not in a bad way."

"Not like the devil saying you should throw yourself off a tower?" Again, Paul was riffing, not paying attention to where his reference might lead. At that moment, he was turning off lights and leading the way out of the house. He picked up the black metal box from the sideboard before turning off the last of the lights.

Jesus exited to the porch as Paul dealt with the hardware. "The devil has no temptations for me these days. He was never very persuasive."

"So was it a real temptation?"

"Of course. But there are degrees of weakness in the face of temptation. That there is an alternative to what God wants doesn't mean we have to follow that other path. Still, we have our choices."

"I'm not doing any more romance covers."

"One temptation taken down."

"Not sleeping with Amber again."

"Good. You know what you want. Don't let the devil tell you otherwise."

A hollow growl in Paul's chest seemed to imply there might have been something wrong with the lamb.

"It's not the lamb." Jesus was walking next to Paul toward the waiting car.

"What? My indigestion?"

"What if it's not indigestion?"

"What do you mean?"

"Well, we were talking about temptations and the devil. There are indeed devils tempting you away from my path. And there are some you've become accustomed to keeping around."

"Not just sleeping with Amber or Stefany?"

"There are many kinds of temptations, not only sexual ones. Those physical satisfactions met a need for belonging and for emotional comfort. They fed you in ways that will never satisfy. They are just symptoms of enemies with whom you need to contend."

Paul slid into the driver's seat as Jesus mirrored him. Before he started the car, he looked at Jesus for a second. "Is this gonna get depressing?"

"It doesn't have to be. The only reason to talk about temptations, and the powers the enemy has in your life, is to get free from them."

"Powers? You said *powers*, didn't you?" Paul knew Jesus had said that, he just wasn't sure of its significance.

"Ask your questions, Paul. Never stop asking. There is no subject out of bounds for you and me."

The streets were quiet in this neighborhood. There would be more traffic near Paul's place. The nighttime tranquility of this residential area was good for contemplating the words of the impossible man sitting in his passenger seat.

"So, what happens if I, like, give in to temptations?"

"You lose touch with me and my Father, to some extent."

"Like, separated?"

"Not in the eternal sense, though your temporal actions can have eternal consequences, of course."

"But separated, like, off the path?"

"That's a good way to think of it. You still belong to the party even if you wander away from us."

"Party?"

"I was thinking of the pioneers traveling west in the history of this nation. Like in the play you did in eighth grade."

"Whoa. That was a long time ago. My first starring role."

"Before you even knew you wanted to be an actor."

"Yeah. I just did it because Susan Jaworski was the female lead."

"Your first kiss."

Paul could feel himself blush. He was thirteen again. A lonely and angry adolescent. Aspiring to be with Susan Jaworski had filled a void. "Dad was gone. Pete was starting to get in trouble."

"Yes. You began to think of them together, two of a kind, around that time."

Taking a deep breath as they slowed at a stop sign, Paul glanced toward Jesus. "Is this still about temptation?"

"Yes. And the power of giving in to it."

"I only kissed her. That was pretty innocent, wasn't it?"

"As I said, not all temptations are of a sexual nature."

"Listening to some preachers, you would think every temptation is about that."

"You don't listen much to those preachers."

Waggling his head side to side, Paul granted the point. Maybe he was just avoiding the actual point Jesus was making. "What *is* the point?"

"You've been holding on to resentments toward your father for a long time, as well as resentment against Peter." Jesus sounded more formal, more distant than Paul had experienced him during this extraordinary day. Maybe the spell was wearing off. Jesus was fading. Going away.

"I will never leave you." Suddenly his voice was closer, his very real breath warming Paul's neck.

Paul shivered, though it wasn't so cold out. The car seemed to be driving itself, like a horse returning to its barn after wandering free for a while. Paul was grateful for the autopilot, especially if Jesus was departing.

"I will never leave you."

As if suddenly aware that someone had climbed into his car at the last stoplight, Paul snapped his head to the right.

Jesus was there. Right there. That close. He was looking at Paul. Not laughing. Serious. And attentive.

"Stop. Paul, stop!"

A second of confusion intervened between that warning and hitting the brake pedal. Paul narrowly missed rear ending an SUV at the last stoplight before his turn. He swore and shook his head. Clearly having Jesus there was a distraction. A handicap.

"I will never leave you."

The little clock on the dash said it was past ten. That was pretty close to the actual time, as far as Paul could recall. Jesus would be going—at least invisible—in less than two hours. Midnight. Witching hour.

"I will never leave you."

When Paul stopped next to an available parking spot a block from his apartment, he turned to look at Jesus. That last repeated assurance was delivered with intimate feeling. But Paul was feeling closed in. Like bodies pressed against him on a crowded train, the car seemed crowded.

His hands started to shake, and he canceled his parallel parking attempt twice before finally slowing to a bump against the curb. He scraped the rear tire along the concrete for a second as he attempted to straighten the car. How long had he been struggling to get into this parking place? It seemed longer than the three minutes the clock on the dash was claiming.

"Let's get you home." Jesus opened the passenger door and spoke like a designated driver after a late night of drinking. But he was getting out of the wrong side of the car for that.

Paul delayed his exit with that banal observation. Obvious. Senseless. So stupid. How could he be so stupid?

Jesus was next to the driver's door now. He caught it as Paul tried to swing it fully open. A large black sedan slid past, missing the car door by less than a foot.

"What's wrong with me? What's happening?" It was a silly question to ask after an entire day of hallucinations. What *else* was happening to him?

"Let's get you home." Was Jesus reciting the same lines because he was losing interest? Just saying what was expected of him?

Instead of answering Paul's thoughts with words, as he had been doing all day, Jesus took his arm and guided him around the car and onto the sidewalk. The car door got closed at some point in that transition. Paul hadn't been paying attention.

He was feeling a bit off. That lamb was definitely bad. He should tell his mom so she wouldn't eat any of it. Paul looked at Jesus to see if he might have gotten food poisoning too. But that seemed unlikely, given that Jesus was only a figment of his imagination. Imaginary visitors don't get food poisoning. Paul was pretty sure he could find that in the instruction book that should have come with this day of delusions.

Before long, they were pacing side by side up the wide walkway toward the glass doors on the front of Paul's building. The building that was temporarily his home, rather. Not his. Not his for long.

The lobby was quiet, the stairway empty. That was just as well. Whatever Paul was suffering from might be contagious. Or at least embarrassing. Contagious embarrassment. Why did he feel as if he had been drinking? He didn't even have wine with dinner.

"Almost there. You'll feel better soon." Jesus was still playing the role of friend of the inebriated. Was he expecting Paul to be sick? Was that how he could promise Paul would feel better? That seemed increasingly likely as they climbed the stairs.

"No. None of that. I command all sickness to back away." This time Jesus seemed to be upset at Paul's thoughts, aiming a rebuke right at them.

Rebuke? What did that remind him of?

Jesus took the key from Paul's hand and unlocked the door. Did he really need a key? If he was real, couldn't he, like, zap the door lock or something?

No answer from the man in the long robe who was flipping on the lights.

As soon as he got inside the apartment, Paul turned toward the restroom. But Jesus hung on to him.

"No need for that. You are not going to be sick."

"The lamb ..."

"It was fine. This is about something else."

"Huh? Like what?"

"Spirit of confusion, I command you to back down and let go of Paul's mind."

Paul blinked as some kind of film was ripped away from his thoughts. The room got brighter. His breathing was easier. He hadn't even noticed he was having trouble breathing before that. Then his nausea made a strong comeback.

"None of that. No sickness. Go away." Jesus was leading Paul to his couch at the same time as he was telling somebody—or something—to go away.

"You cannot do this. This is not up to you." Paul allowed those words to come up through his throat much the same way he had expected his supper to exit.

"Silence. You will not speak unless I tell you to."

Paul would be quiet. Jesus sounded like he meant business. But something inside Paul was expanding, like a sudden swelling just below his heart.

"I want you to renounce your bitterness against your father, Paul. For all the wrongs he committed against you, let go of your bitterness."

"But ... but what he did was ... was so ..." Paul's words lodged in the back of his mouth. That swelling in his chest joined them there, escaping in a burst of sobs. His heart exploded upward and came out in wailing tears.

Jesus had his hand on Paul's near shoulder. At some point, he had seated himself next to Paul on the couch.

To Paul, it felt as if they had been here all evening, on the couch just like this. He couldn't remember what had happened before.

"Do it, Paul. Renounce the bitterness."

Paul's head was turning left to right and back, a broad negation. A spasm of disbelief. Whatever was happening to him was entirely unbelievable. Even more unbelievable than Jesus sitting on the couch next to him.

"Let go of the bitterness. Will you let it go?"

"I—I guess. I mean, I guess I do want to. I just ..."

"Say the words after me."

Paul wasn't looking at Jesus, he was staring at the glass coffee table. A picture filled his mind—the heavy glass broken and bloody against the tan rug.

"No violence. No threats. Paul is safe."

Having Jesus interacting with Paul's thoughts had become normal at some point in the day. It seemed very handy at this point. That bloody image startled Paul. He hunkered down, his breath slowing, his mind clearing. "I do. I want to. I will renounce my bitterness."

"Repeat after me."

Paul followed Jesus one phrase at a time. "I let go of my bitterness ... toward my father ... for the wrongs he committed ... against me and my family."

Something had settled onto the room like a warm vapor. A sweet, living cloud.

"And I accept total forgiveness ... for my years of bitterness ... by the loving mercy of God." Paul exhaled for longer than normal, longer than physically possible. The air going out was not so sweet as the atmosphere filling the room.

"I give you peace. I give you joy. I release you from accusation. From accusing and from being accused." Jesus sounded more ... Jesus-like there on the couch. This was more of the sort of thing

199

Paul would have expected from him, if he had expected anything from a visible and audible Jesus.

"I am still here. I will never leave you."

Just then, in that moment, both statements seemed entirely true.

Chapter 32

One More Round of Cleaning up Leftovers

Laboriously turning his head toward the kitchen, Paul checked that it wasn't yet midnight. Not even eleven yet. How long had he been on the couch with Jesus? They had started there early in the day, but lots of other things had happened since then.

Jesus came back into the room with a glass of water. When he had left, Paul couldn't say. He handed the glass to Paul and sat at the other end of the couch again.

When Jesus sat down, Paul stared at him instead of sipping from the glass in his hand. Jesus was no longer in costume. He was dressed similarly to Paul. Maybe even in something out of Paul's closet.

"Don't worry, I didn't steal your clothes."

"Oh, it's okay. I don't mind." Paul could say that honestly because he wasn't sure what was happening. It was hard to object to what he didn't understand.

"It's a trick."

"What?"

"Switching into these clothes. It's meant to make you feel a bit more comfortable with me. With me being real. With me being current. Being here. Not just some ancient historical character you play onstage."

"Okay." Paul remembered the glass of water. He drank sloppily, dribbling water down his beard.

"Do you understand what just happened here?"

Paul gulped and wiped at his beard with his free hand. "You mean before you changed clothes?"

"Yes." Jesus chuckled. "Before that."

"I ..." Paul slowed to consider what to say. What did he understand? What he had started to say, he really *didn't* understand.

Jesus helped him out. Again. "The bitterness had been residing in you so long that it took hold of you. A spiritual hold. Bitterness allowed a spirit to get into your life. Your pain opened a door. Your resentment left the door open. And an enemy took advantage."

"That was ... that was an enemy?" It was a weird thing to say, but not as weird as what he was thinking. *Wait for Jesus to say it ... the d-word.*

"Yes. A demon. A spirit that works for the accuser."

"Uh ..." Instead of reiterating or clarifying, Paul paused. He nodded. He was noticing an ache in his chest, but he clung to his belief that he was too young to have a heart attack.

"Peace. I release healing into that torn place in Paul's heart."

Paul waited as that torn place absorbed new warmth that soothed it until it disappeared. "Then ..." He stopped this time because of the long list of questions queuing up in his head. His head felt good, actually. Clear. He knew what the questions were, at least.

"Yes. You're more yourself now."

"I was ... less myself?"

"You were. The pain was real, and it was your pain, but your enemy took it and tainted it and made it something of his own. He never creates, he only distorts and corrupts. It's like the difference between a brand-new bolt and one that's so rusty you can hardly recognize it as metal."

"Rusted? Corrupted? Like, not real anymore?"

"A different kind of real, but certainly not as it was intended to be. Not authentically yours. It was a sort of joint project between you and the spirit of bitterness. You allowed it to distort your original contribution."

"My pain? That was mine?"

"Of course. It isn't possible to lose your father the way you did without pain. If it had been painless to you, that would have been inauthentic from the start."

Authenticity was a commodity Paul recognized. Directors looked for it in acting. At its core, acting had to be authentic to be believable and impactful. The trick was that it was *not* real. It was acting.

"That accounts for some of the confusion. It's easy to get tangled up in that conundrum."

"Conundrum? Like ... like a paradox?"

"Yes. Acting feels like faking authenticity sometimes. Sometimes it feels real."

"You know this ...?"

"I know you, Paul. I know you from the inside out. I know how this is for you." He paused. "I know lots of other actors, of course. And I have shared in their experiences as well, even when I have to do so from a distance. I am a present observer of you and everyone around you. All I ask is that you let me be a participant and not *just* an observer."

"Oh. Huh. Okay. I mean, are you asking?"

Jesus smiled. "I asked you before, when you were fourteen. You heard the good news in the clearest presentation of your young life, and you accepted me as participant. No longer distant. You invited me into your heart. You were inviting me into your experience. Your whole life. Every aspect of it. And I never left."

A trembling sensation from deep in Paul's chest—even below that, deep in his gut—prevented him from speaking. A sudden urge to get up and run out of the apartment locked his brain as he struggled to control his limbs.

"Abandonment spirit, go. Get out." Jesus spoke evenly and firmly.

The part of Paul that wanted to run out the door seemed to do just that. And in doing so, it seemed to stop being part of him. Not something he had lost. Not something he would miss. Not anymore.

"I bless Paul with peace and fulfillment. No regret. No loss where abandonment has gone away."

"Huh." Paul was in control of his voice just enough to grunt one syllable.

"I will never leave you."

Adjusting his gaze without turning his head all the way, Paul assessed the man sitting next to him. Something of a hipster with his long hair and beard, his cotton button-up shirt open at the throat to show his dark green T-shirt beneath. Was Jesus wearing a Paul costume?

Jesus smiled.

Paul began to laugh hysterically. Literally hysterically. He wasn't making it happen. He didn't even feel like he was letting it happen. The laughter was happening without his cooperation, maybe without his consent. But then he decided to consent. Why fight it? Slurping to keep from drooling from the corners of his mouth, Paul accepted another tide of hilarity, though he couldn't say what was funny. Maybe it wasn't funny. Maybe it was just free. He was just free. Free to laugh. Free to be silly. Free to release. To be released, really. His inner space was free space. Open.

Was it unoccupied?

"Be filled with my Spirit." Jesus had leaned toward Paul and had placed his hand on the middle of Paul's chest. "Be filled."

The laughter continued, but it went deeper. Some tunnel far below anything he had felt before—at least so it seemed in the moment—was being filled by Jesus. Paul hoped whatever Jesus was filling it with wouldn't leave. He seemed to be leaking.

"Think of it as a river. It comes from me. It need never dry up. I will never leave you."

They were back to that. But this time, the promise of Jesus's ongoing presence eased his mind into an even greater level of awareness. His laughter slowed, and his breathing began to return to a sustainable pace. Would this stream of bubbling life really be available later? When Jesus went invisible?

"If you want it to be."

"Why would I not want it?"

Jesus took a deep breath, as if he had answered that question before. Had Paul ever asked anything like it?

"This living water comes from me. It lives, it thrives, because you freely open yourself to its flow. I will never stop sending it, just as I will never leave you. But you are free to ignore my presence. You are free to avoid the flow of my life-giving river."

As much as Paul grasped the truth of what Jesus was saying, grasped it with a grip that felt familiar and certain, he wondered why he had missed this before. "Did I just miss it? Did they tell me? Did anyone tell me?"

"Remember Rosemary?"

"My professor?"

"She also attended the church you were part of in those college days."

"Sure. Of course. I remember her."

"Remember that class in acting she taught at the church? She took you aside. She asked your permission to place her hand in the middle of your chest."

"Uh, maybe."

"She looked you in the eyes and placed her hand on your diaphragm. And she told you that you could live out of your core if you wanted to. That you could act from that place if you wanted to. And she said that *living* from that well would make it much easier to *perform* from there. You asked her about it after, and she explained that she was talking about living out of my presence."

"Oh. I—I guess I didn't get it."

"No. You didn't comprehend. You didn't grasp it. Not that time nor many other times when a living freedom was offered to you. There were hindrances."

"Hindrances? In-inside me?" Paul was thinking of those recently vacating entities that had been less visible than Jesus. But they seemed just as real in the moments when they left.

"Yes. The strategy of the enemy is to occupy deep spaces in the lives of my people. Things like bitterness give him permission. His presence makes it hard to live out of your true core. It makes it hard to believe. Hard to comprehend. Hard to accept."

"So, what Rosemary was saying was not just about acting. She was, like, connecting to my faith?"

"Everyone has an authentic self even if they haven't given their lives to me. But my presence gives you opportunity to access and protect that authentic self. If you're willing to pay the price."

"The price? Like, getting rid of the bitterness and that?"

"Like being willing to let down your guard, including renouncing the protection those spirits offer."

"Protection from what?"

"Your bitterness toward your father was a defense. It was intended to protect you from that kind of abandonment happening again. As if it were up to you. That's one of the lies."

"I guess there are a lot of lies."

"Yes. They breathe lies. Your enemy cannot survive without them."

"Uh, was there actually more than one of those ... things?"

Jesus nodded. "The bitterness was the strongest. The others were rattled loose by its departure. We've been doing a bit of clean up ... of some more leftovers."

Paul raised his eyebrows. Finally, a subject he knew something about.

Jesus smiled at that thought.

Chapter 33

As the Clock Creeps Closer to Midnight

Above his kitchen table, a white-faced analog clock reminded Paul that his Jesus adventure was about to end.

"Maybe this day is ending, but there are other adventures for you and I. New ones available every day." Jesus had one leg crossed at a ninety-degree angle, an arm stretched along the back of the couch. He faced Paul with a lowered gaze that included sympathy as well as promise.

"Do I have to do anything? Like, accept something the way I did at the beginning?"

"You can accept me into your life every day. You can start your day with acceptance. Not just an abstract acceptance, but a commitment to do whatever I have for you that particular day."

"Like, sort of dedicating my day to you?"

"Exactly."

"But what if I screw up? I mean, there are still gonna be temptations, right?"

"Falling to temptation doesn't disqualify you from dedicating your days to me any more than you get disqualified from being an actor by missing a cue or inverting a line. Just get up and try again, like with everything else."

As simple as it was, that sort of persistence sounded exhausting.

"Don't let the length of this day taint the possibilities. You're tired now. You need rest. But, in the morning, you can hand the new day over to me. Plan on doing it. But wait until it arrives to receive the grace and strength to actually do it each day. I always show up exactly on time."

"You never miss your cues?"

He chuckled. "Never."

Paul looked at Jesus beneath heavy lids for a few seconds. "So, is this like that movie where if I stay up all night, you won't go away? Or is midnight definite?" With so little energy left, Paul wasn't even sure which answer he wanted. Maybe it wasn't even a serious question.

"No. Let's stick with midnight, Cinderella."

"*Ha.* There's a role I never even tried out for."

"Prince Charming was more your style."

"But he was always this fake guy. Like, too untouchable." Here was a subject Paul could dig into even this far into the night.

"Whenever you think of yourself as someone's rescuer, you actually distance yourself from them as well as from your true self."

"Wait. Is this about Prince Charming?"

Jesus laughed from deep in his chest. He was subdued a bit, perhaps, but he showed no signs of being tired. At least not nearly as tired as Paul. "I did a little turn there while your head was spinning."

"Huh. Oh, yeah. I guess you did." Paul listened to the sound of his own breath through his nose for two seconds. "Well, I guess I do tend to sort of see myself as a Prince-Charming type. I know a couple women have said that to me, called me something like that."

"Seven women."

"What?"

"Over your life, seven women have called you Prince Charming or something very close to that."

"You ... You're, like, keeping track?"

"Does it sound obsessive?" Jesus shrugged and adopted a look of mock innocence.

Paul snorted laughter through his nose. "Uh, well, I don't think I should judge."

"That's a good policy." Jesus leaned back as if relaxing a bit more. "I just bring this up because it's a pattern you should address. You and I can take it up as an ongoing project in the days ahead."

"So you have this whole fix-up agend— uh, *project* for me, then?"

"You may look a bit like me, but you are not me. And you won't be given the task of fixing anyone. But *I* have taken on the task of fixing *everyone*. As much as they're willing to be fixed."

"Didn't you just do that to me? I mean, wasn't what happened here"—he indicated the couch—"Wasn't that getting fixed up?"

"Yes. And you don't have to worry. It won't always be so intense as that."

"Huh." Paul had to pause to figure out if this conversation had left the tracks at some point. "Okay, so I don't have to be Prince Charming, saving the poor maiden. I definitely don't have to be anyone's savior. Nobody's fixer. But what about you? I mean, me and you?"

"You mean working together?"

"Yeah. Like, it seemed like you gave me things to say today that helped people. A few times, actually."

"Yes. That is your role. To cooperate with my efforts to help others. But notice how little you actually know about what was, or is, going on in the lives of people you touched today. You didn't have to take responsibility for a lot of details. You were just doing your part. Just do what I ask you to do, and you'll be part of my salvation in the lives of many people. Even more than you can be aware of."

"Are you talking about doing that through acting, or more than that?"

"I can use your talents, but leave that to me. Take the roles and jobs I put before you and resist the ones your enemy wants to ensnare you with. Then let me direct you along the way, day to day."

"No big, grand plan?"

"It's okay to plan, but don't get hung up on the long term and lose sight of what's directly before you."

"My next job?"

"Talk to Casper, remember?"

"Yeah, now I remember. I wasn't remembering it until you said that again."

"You can always ask me for reminders. I'm always ready."

"Like one of those digital assistants? Hey, Jesus, what's the weather today?"

Jesus laughed. "Oh, you don't have to disconnect any of your digital assistants on account of me."

"Huh. Okay." Paul checked the clock. Only fifteen more minutes. "If I wasn't so tired, this would be nerve racking." His stomach churned a little. Probably not spoiled lamb shanks. Nerves. But how could he be nervous about his life going back to normal? It wasn't like he'd been longing for Jesus to show up and now had to face the end of his dream.

"You may not have understood that this was what you wanted, Paul, but you were longing for something like this. A connection. The ultimate connection."

Paul just nodded at his guest. It occurred to him that listening might be the best way to use the last fragment of their time.

Jesus's words slowed as if to allow for Paul's weariness. "You have been looking for connection all your life, as most people do. The connection that will satisfy is the one my Father provides with him and with me through the Spirit. But you have often settled for alternatives that are much better supported by the world around you. Even after you asked me into your life, you still lived in a culture that didn't expect me to do anything because they don't believe I'm real."

A memory about discovering at age five that Santa Claus was not real briefly poked its head above the fog.

"Ho! Ho! Ho!" Jesus did his Santa imitation from deep in his belly, slender belly though it was.

Paul's more genuine laugh was a tired version.

Chapter 34

The Moment When the Two Become One

Paul had slipped down the couch until his head rested on the back cushion and his knees were pressed against the coffee table. Under normal circumstances, this would have proven it was past his bedtime. He did have work tomorrow after all. As he looked at Jesus, he noted the next day was Sunday. He was working this Sunday. He had agreed to sub for one of the college kids who went home to visit his parents this weekend. So Paul was *not* going to church tomorrow. Should he call in sick and go to church instead of work? Would that be twisted?

Jesus met him in the middle of this bleary meander. "Don't worry, Paul. You won't lose your faith because you work one Sunday. But you can be less available for taking a Sunday shift next time."

"Okay." He was willing to agree to anything. Even Jesus leaving, if he really needed to do that.

"Not leaving. Going invisible. Remaining inside you where you can only see me with the eyes of your heart."

Paul pictured a heart emoji with eyes on it. He couldn't recall actually seeing such a thing before. Maybe he could copyright it.

Jesus looked at the clock. "It's time."

"Oh. Okay." Paul pressed his hands into the seat cushion and forced himself to sit up with his lower back against the back of the couch. "So, what are you gonna do?"

"Go back inside where I belong." Jesus gestured toward Paul's chest.

A scene from *Alien* seized Paul by the throat. A little bit of terror and a twitter of hysterical laughter locked up his response.

211

Smiling broadly, Jesus shook his head. Perhaps he didn't want to dignify those odd thoughts with even a joke. Maybe the time for joking was over.

Paul took a deep breath. Jesus was closer. He had slid across the couch cushion without Paul noticing. For one second, Paul felt like there were two of him or two of Jesus sitting on the couch. He shook his head much like Jesus had a second before.

They were elbow to elbow now, but the feeling of Jesus's arm against his was not like any other human contact. It was cold and hot at the same time. Paul began to shake. Not shivering. Not trembling, exactly. Just ... shaking.

Jesus seemed to be fading at the same time as he was glowing more brightly. As if he were being transformed into pure light, Paul felt like he could see into or even through the shining man next to him.

Like northern lights radiating from Paul's own eyes, that glow from Jesus seemed to be infecting him, invading him. They were still two. They were pressed together shoulder to shoulder. They were glowing together.

"I will never leave you." Jesus's voice came from outside and inside at the same time. Then it was like Paul was saying it. "I will never leave you." Was that Jesus using Paul's voice?

That thought shook Paul more violently.

Then there were bells. Midnight?

Were there really bells at midnight? He couldn't recall hearing them before. It wasn't New Year's Eve. But the ringing became a humming, and that seemed to reside inside his head. Contained there. Vibrating his eardrums from within.

He could no longer see Jesus, but he could feel him as clearly as he could feel his own skin. Jesus was not gone, but he was no longer visible. He was with Paul. He was inside Paul.

Jesus inside. Jesus on board. Paul started to laugh at that nutty notion. *Jesus on board.* His laughter expanded and intensified. Two voices. Two men laughing. Jesus was still with him. He had not left Paul.

I will never leave you.

It was like an idea with its own illumination included. The words came to him from within, but they didn't come from himself. Not his own voice. Not even his memory of Jesus saying it over and over.

I will never leave you.

Paul's dad had gone away. His big brother had burned his own life to the ground. The enemy had robbed Paul of his big sister. They were all gone.

But Jesus would never leave him.

Maybe Paul just fell asleep. Maybe he passed out there on the couch.

Chapter 35

Back to Normal on the Morning After

Paul scrunched his eyes shut tight. His phone was talking to him. Calling to him. Yelling at him. It was his alarm. Morning. Time to get up.

Reflected sunshine off the building across the street slipped beneath the shades on the windows at his feet. When did he lie down on the couch? Why was he sleeping out here?

His alarm continued to honk at him. He had to roll to his side to extricate his phone from his front pocket. How had he managed to sleep on top of that slab of metal and glass for so many hours? He tapped the screen and glared at the one who dared wake him at this hour.

Did he have a hangover? No. No drinking he could recall. But, then, that might be a really bad sign. He turned his head toward the window. It was brighter than he expected. Spring was springing itself on him as it seemed to do in the Midwest, where its arrival really mattered.

Relaxing the twist of his neck, Paul had to decide what had happened. What did he think about what had happened? He pictured being a guy who awoke with verve and enthusiasm after spending a day with Jesus.

But was it real? Had he really ...?

In that moment, he knew he had an option. A real option. He could pretend it didn't even happen. He could perhaps acknowledge that he had *thought* it was actually happening at the time. But, on later reflection, he could decide it was a strange sort of short-term insanity. Or not really insanity. More like his imagination running away with him. Kind of a funny experiment, really. An experiment in acting, of course.

Then there was the other choice. Not the bouncy guy with the big gleaming grin, his personality transformed because he had met Jesus. That wasn't real. That wasn't a real option for Paul, not the authentic version of himself that Jesus had been talking about.

He *had* been talking about that. Paul could recall the conversation late in the night. It was real.

Now what?

"Well, I could get off this couch and go to work." Saying that aloud seemed to break the seal off the day. He was really awake. He was really starting the day that came after Jesus's visible and audible visit.

Swinging his feet to the floor, he kicked his shoes aside in the process. Staring down at his brown leather shoes reminded him of the leather sandals Jesus wore. An authentic Jesus costume if ever there was one. Paul laughed at that assessment, and his laugh seemed to echo as if it were dubbed over a prerecorded track of him laughing. Him or someone else.

"Are you there? Really there?"

He thought he could hear the answer, at least inside his head. *"I am here. I will never leave you."*

"That's good. That's very good." He rocked forward and stood, only lightly knocking his shins on the coffee table. "Wake up, Paul."

"Wake up, my friend." Jesus would say that. That was him. His character. His line.

Smiling on the way to the bathroom, Paul imagined being a mellow version of that smiley enthusiast he was picturing before. This guy, this version of the smiling guy, would be consistent with his character. His authentic character.

"Is it okay to play a part if the part I'm playing is my authentic self?"

"More than okay. Real progress, I would call it." Was that just what he wished Jesus would say to him? It was pretty convincing. At least convincing to himself. Who else would he need to convince?

He thought of Tildy when he paused in front of the bathroom mirror, but he lost his hold on her when he recalled seeing Jesus in that same mirror the previous morning. "Wow! *Ha!*"

He completed his visit to the bathroom accompanied by his own laugh track. By the time he finished drying his hands, he suspected he might actually turn into the guy with the bright smile and a sunny outlook on life.

"Would that be so terrible?"

"Huh?" He wasn't ready yet to take questions.

Paul stumbled into the kitchen and poured a glass of filtered water, noting the pitcher was almost empty. With one hand, he placed the pitcher under the faucet and turned it on. With the other, he took a long drink.

After a gasp, he said, "Hanging out with Jesus for a whole day seems to make one extremely thirsty." He used his documentary-narrator voice. He laughed another of those reinforced laughs. He and his friend both being entertained by his humor.

"But you don't always have to be funny."

That was a simple statement, but it felt profound. Was it something he didn't know already? Something he really needed to hear? When did he get the idea he had to be funny? Well, it was early. That was probably the answer. Probably? No, definitely. When he was little, and his dad was angry, yelling, moody. When his mom was doing the victim thing, silent and drippy. Little Paul had discovered that making them laugh was gold.

"Dang, that is profound. Too profound to come out of my own imagination." He waited for someone to contradict him. Maybe he should have been waiting for applause. The invisible friend he was addressing now didn't contradict that early developmental insight.

"Early developmental insight." He could do the narrator voice deeper. More Morgan Freeman. Hmm. Maybe some future in that.

"In playing God?"

"No, but definitely in playing Jesus."

He chuckled through his shower and getting dressed. The humor ended when he looked at the clock. Why had it taken him so long to get ready? He was late. He swore and then apologized to his invisible audience. That was when he started thinking about having an invisible audience that he had actually met.

Leaving his building, he immediately realized he should have worn a jacket. But it was too late now. He picked up his pace and continued toward the coffee shop.

Back to that audience—maybe he had performed for an invisible audience for as long as he had felt the need to be funny. But it wasn't always clear who that audience was. Not his dad or his mom, necessarily. Though not *not* them, probably.

He was walking too slowly. He stretched his legs and picked up speed again. It was brisk and damp in the early morning. Not quite foggy, but close. He swung his arms to get his circulation going and to battle the chill that was penetrating his cotton button-up shirt. *"Am I gonna be in trouble?"*

"Apologize before Chester says anything."

"Chester? Oh, yeah. He's covering this morning. Hard to keep track of everyone's schedule."

As he approached the shop, Paul reviewed that brief conversation. Had Jesus just reminded him of who the Sunday morning manager was? Maybe Paul was just accessing that data from some backup disk inside his head. Unless Jesus was still with him.

Yes. He was. And that was cool.

He knocked on the glass door of the coffee shop.

David, a pale young man with messy hair under his uniform cap, was in the dining area arranging chairs. He pointed his finger at Paul like it was a gun and pulled the imaginary trigger.

Paul, of course, acted out being shot. Grasping his chest like a silent film star, he raised the back of his hand to his forehead in wounded grief.

David opened the door laughing. "Wow, I really get my money's worth with you, I see."

David and Paul had only worked together once before. The younger guy was strictly weekends, and Paul was mostly weekdays. Paul grinned, a little embarrassed. He had been quick to ham it up, but he was late to work.

He spotted Chester coming out of the kitchen, talking to a woman behind him who had a familiar voice.

"Sorry, Chester. Apologies for being late."

A brief cloud crossed the older man's round face, and he paused to scratch at his short-cropped Afro beneath his green baseball cap. "Our Daily Grind" was stitched in gold letters on that uniform cap. Paul's hat was presumably on a hook in the break room. He never took it home, afraid he would forget it.

"Oh, I'll let it pass. I know you usually don't do Sundays." Chester pursed his lips.

"Partying late last night, no doubt." David was back at the chair arranging.

"Had to see my stepdad in the emergency room and clean up some things for my mom, actually." Paul would leave out the late-night talk with Jesus.

"Oh. Is he okay?"

"Yeah." Paul was next to Chester now, on his way past him toward the break room. "Heart attack. But he was feeling okay when they got him into a room last night."

"You good to be here?" Chester had turned his round torso to follow Paul.

Paul stopped. "Sure. I'm good. Thanks for asking. Just a bit groggy."

"Nothing a tall mocha won't fix." David was heading toward the counter now, a green linen towel in one hand.

"Check the dumpster to make sure the lid is closed, will you?" Chester bypassed David's joke and sent him away.

"You want me to restock cups and lids up front?" Paul gestured toward the dispensers he could see across the counter.

"Yep, as soon as you suit up and clock in." Chester might have been a football coach or maybe just a player in the past. Paul couldn't exactly recall the gossip he had heard, but "suiting up" reinforced a faint recollection.

Paul resisted a joke about getting his pads and helmet and congratulated himself for that as he stepped around the counter and down the hall. "Is someone else getting the bathrooms?" He noticed a paper napkin trapped in the bottom corner of the men's room door."

"No. You can do that after the cups." Chester collected the small prop-up blackboard from where it leaned next to the front door. He lifted it as if it needed updating, not like he was ready to put it outside. It was still forty-five minutes till opening.

Paul had his marching orders, just like he wanted. *Give me a script, give me direction, then let me do it.* That was how he worked best in acting and in jobs like this.

He waved at Kirti when she looked up from the tray stack she was attending to, but he lost sight of her and refrained from saying anything as he stepped down the hall. The terra-cotta tile floor seemed clean. The night crew had done a good job of that.

He grasped the brass handle of the break room door, the only door in the place not on a tight spring. It swung easily, revealing Angela wiping at her nose with a tan recycled napkin.

"You okay?"

"Oh, you don't wanna hear about my problems."

"Actually, I do. But I got in late, so I need to get busy first. I'll look for you later." The energy with which he said all that felt like someone else's energy. Angela was a nice kid, but Paul didn't find her attractive at all. And he usually reserved such attentiveness for more attractive young women.

He missed most of her response while punching his time-card—her reaction positive and maybe a little surprised.

He marveled at his own generosity. Not just curiosity. Not flirting. Real interest. He grinned at her in lieu of a verbal response that might have missed some nuance in what she had said. And he grabbed his hat, checking for the label inside to confirm. Clean aprons hung next to the lineup of caps, and he lifted one without bumping into Angela, hunkered in the corner next to them.

"I have no idea what's going on with you, but I have a feeling everything's gonna be okay. Just a feeling. We can talk later." He looped the apron over his head and adjusted his cap.

She was silent. Probably in shock.

Maybe Paul should be shocked himself. Was this that smiley churchy guy he was imagining earlier? Had someone abducted the real Paul? Or was this guy the real one? He restrained himself from patting her on the shoulder, a conscious choice that earned another internal congratulations, and he headed back toward the front of the store.

Kirti greeted him. "Slumming it with the Sunday crew, I see."

"Wait, I thought this was a promotion." He feigned shock and disillusionment. He was always acting. Especially at work.

She laughed at him. Kirti's dark eyes, ruby lips, and caramel skin were nothing like Paul's mom's, but her voice and her maternal concern for her coworkers brought his mother to mind. He said a silent prayer for his mom and Bob as he listened to Kirti's laughter.

When he passed her, on his way toward the small storeroom, he recalled the thought about not needing to be funny. He wondered how his joking affected his relationship with his mother. That was more than he wanted to think about during a coffee shop shift. "Later." He said it under his breath as he grabbed a big plastic bag containing two stacks of cups. Smalls. Then one of mediums and another of talls.

It was honest work. He could focus on it while he was doing it. That would be okay, wouldn't it? Or should he be looking for some therapy time with Jesus? Maybe as he cleaned the bathrooms?

"Feel free to do either, both, or neither." Again, he could imagine Jesus saying that.

Paul hauled his bulky but light load out to the counter area where Kirti was checking the napkins. He could hear Chester joking with someone by the back door. Probably the bakery delivery. They were right on time.

Considering that last bit of imagined advice from Jesus, Paul wondered if a single day of seeing Jesus was enough for him to be confident of what Jesus might say. Well, a day of seeing and hearing.

"That, and all those Bible studies. And, of course, there's the play."

He used the sharp scissors from under the counter to slice away the tops of the three plastic bags. He tipped each stack of smalls into the dispenser, carefully pushing one stack and then another from outside the plastic bag. He managed to fill the nearly empty dispensers without touching the fresh cups. He turned to the next bag and started the same process for the mediums.

"You could just wash your hands and do it twice as fast." Kirti propped her hands on her hips and cocked an eyebrow at him.

Paul had been using a method he was taught in LA. Different coffee shop. "Habit." He shrugged at Kirti. "But that's a good reminder." He went to the sink after dispensing his second cup tower.

Kirti started filling the tall cups. She was wearing the thin plastic gloves she used for food prep. Those didn't work well for handling the coffee cups, making slips and drops more likely.

Paul decided not to tease her about the hypocrisy of telling him to clean up while she used gloves. He didn't have to make fun of everything. He could just wash his hands and get back to work.

"Let's see those." When he finished, Kirti held out her hands like a kindergarten teacher ready for inspection.

Paul showed her his still-damp hands, which she examined front and back.

"Okay, that'll do."

"Thanks, Mom."

"You're welcome, junior."

Paul guessed that Kirti was ten years older than him. Was she flirting, or just having fun with what could be the boring part of the job? The fast fulfillment of perpetual orders was captivating. Talking to customers was sometimes sensitive, rarely boring. This was, perhaps, a good time for jokes.

He left stocking the front to Kirti and grabbed a pair of those gloves for cleaning the bathrooms. At least the men's. Angela had the door to the women's propped open and was carrying a bottle of spray cleaner and a roll of light brown paper towel through the door.

Once he gathered his cleaning supplies, Paul let the men's room door swing closed behind him. He was feeling the need for a moment of privacy. Privacy with Jesus.

"Is this an inappropriate place to talk to you?" He knew the answer, really. He was just apologizing in a subtle way.

"I'll never leave you. Not even in here."

Chapter 36

Is There a Future in Sticking Around?

The Friday before Palm Sunday, four days before the play was to open, the cast and crew put on a performance for some of the Christian school kids and the church staff. A dress rehearsal with an audience was how Paul pictured it. The lighting wasn't quite right since this performance was a matinee, but it was an opportunity to put everything together in front of a friendly crowd.

After the performance, Paul was wiping away makeup with a small round sponge when Casper joined him in front of the dressing room mirrors.

"How many churches even have a dressing room?" Paul let his thoughts leak out once Casper stood shoulder to shoulder with him.

"Probably not many. This church takes its dramatic productions very seriously."

"Yes, they do."

"Which is good for you and me." Casper looked at Paul in the mirror. "Do you have a job lined up after this?"

Paul hesitated over wondering if Casper was getting paid, but that seemed unlikely, given that Paul was playing Jesus for free. "Uh, no. My agent isn't finding anything in the area. Not right away. There's a possibility of a part in a cable TV series that's being shot in a rural part of the state. Darrowville? That's nearby, isn't it?"

"Never heard of it."

"Very small town, apparently."

"What about theater? Would you do a theater production?"

Not until Casper asked that question did Paul remember that Jesus had said to check with him about his next job. Or something like that.

"I would do theater. You know of something?"

"It's not Broadway. It's not even off Broadway. But it's a paying gig."

"But do I have to wear a chicken costume and hand out flyers?"

Casper wheezed a high and lengthy laugh. "I'm guessing this is the voice of experience I'm hearing."

"Desperate times."

"How do you feel about banditry?" Casper wiped at the line where the makeup met his collar, his chin and his grin stretched high.

"Well, I think I would do the chicken suit again before resorting to crime."

This time Casper's laugh was squeezed, his neck stretched and his lips closed. He lowered his bearded chin and looked directly at Paul, not at his reflection. "There's a local community theater production about a legendary bandit from this area. They're starting auditions for the lead the Monday after Easter. It's a part much too young for me, or I'd be going for it."

"It pays?"

"It does. A decent weekly wage once rehearsals begin."

"Sounds like it might be good timing for me."

"I thought it would be."

"I haven't decided on staying around."

"This might give you reason to." Casper paused his self-administered unmasking to examine Paul again for a moment. "Another reason, perhaps."

Was he referring to Paul's original reason for coming home—to spend some time with his mother? Or was he thinking of something else? Someone else?

As if hearing her cue, Tildy knocked on the dressing room door, which stood open a few inches. "Are you still decent?"

"I don't think that's an appropriate question to ask of Jesus." Casper arched his eyebrows in mock disapproval.

"What makes you think I was talking to him?" Tildy, one hand pressed to the doorpost, leaned her cheek on the back of her hand.

"My wife, for one thing?"

"Thing?" Paul was not yet entirely comfortable with Tildy, as in not knowing how to even think about their relationship. Humor was, of course, his refuge in uncertainty.

"Now don't you tell her I called her a thing."

"Tell who?" Pamela, Casper's wife, didn't miss her cue either.

"*Ha*. I've been set up." Casper shook his head at himself in the mirror.

After a scowl at her husband, Pamela addressed Tildy and Paul. "Are you two joining us for one last cast dinner before opening night?"

"One last gasp." Casper was removing his eye makeup now.

"Actually, that's why I came by. I have to work tonight after the museum closes. We're putting the finishing touches on that exhibit that opens tomorrow." Tildy had stepped aside to allow Pamela easy access to the dressing room. The older woman was pulling off her long black wig and checking her makeup.

Paul wondered if Pamela was considering keeping the dramatic makeup for dinner. He looked at Tildy. "Well, thanks for telling me." He paused, not sure what more to say. He was torn between sadness that she wouldn't be joining them versus satisfaction that she felt she should tell him specifically that she couldn't make it. They had eaten dinner together the previous Sunday, just the two of them. But they had not called it a date.

She and Paul said simple goodbyes, and Tildy left the dressing room with a small smile and a wave. Oddly, it seemed like something of an early milestone. Didn't the whole exchange imply that she thought they were in a relationship, even if only in the early stages? Why else come to tell Paul she wasn't eating dinner with the crew? Otherwise she could have just told Jared or some of the stage crew. Surely telling the fake Jesus wasn't part of her crew responsibility.

These speculations reminded him of middle school. Did she like him? Did she *like* like him? Check this box if you do ...

The next time he saw her was at church on Palm Sunday. They had talked briefly on the phone Saturday, Paul checking in on the new installation at the museum. It was a workday for her. Tildy had invited him to see the new exhibit with her on this Sunday.

Check this box.

Before the start of the second morning service in the massive auditorium, Tildy surprised him by apparently searching him out. She greeted him somewhat breathlessly. "I've been looking all over for you. The boy playing Jesus for the kid's pageant got chicken pox. They want you to fill in for him."

That his first instinct was to believe her probably said something about how interested he was in pleasing her. Apparently irrationally so. After two heart beats—fairly heavy ones—he laughed. "*Ha*. It would've probably been more convincing if you'd said he had strep throat. I don't think kids are getting chicken pox these days."

She sniffed a laugh through her nose and took over his seat after he stood and shifted over one from the aisle. "What would I know about current childhood illnesses?"

"A little less than I do, it would seem."

She was still laughing. "Did you play a doctor on TV or something?"

He bypassed the opportunity for an off-color joke. He was behaving himself with Tildy. "Not even a doctor on TV." He adopted a chagrined smile and shook his head.

The rise of music from the stage interrupted their banter. This church had an extensive children's ministry as well as a dedication to art and drama. The pageant reenacting the Palm Sunday procession was well-choreographed and only cute because of the small actors in their small costumes, not because of the usual childish breakdowns of script or decorum. No tears were shed among the little ones as far as Paul could tell.

But a few of the adults were wiping at their cheeks during the joyful celebration of the coming of the peaceful king. As Paul allowed that joy to well up inside him, he sensed the presence he had been attending to on and off for the past week. He could almost feel Jesus rubbing shoulders with him, enjoying the pageant right here with Paul and Tildy.

At the end of the service, Paul did a mental check-in on his Sunday to-do list. Meeting Tildy at the museum was the grand finale as far as he had planned. That was late in the afternoon. Here they were at 11:45, shuffling out of the auditorium. Paul contemplated stretching for a chance to spend more of the day with her. The crowded lobby wasn't the best setting for sensitive negotiations, but he edged toward the opportunity. "So we're getting together at three, right?"

"I'm counting on it. Were you planning to meet me outside the front door of the museum? It looks like rain, maybe."

"Uh, yeah. I'll park across the street." This wasn't going as he had hoped.

She puffed her cheeks and looked around at the crowd where they stood near the coffee bar.

"What are you doing between now and three o'clock?" He tried to sound like it was idle curiosity.

"Oh, just lunch and maybe some light housework and laundry."

"Ah. The three Ls. Hard to beat that combination." He scanned the crowd briefly. "Or we could do the lunch part together, at least. And, you know, just go to the museum together ... whenever."

"Yeah? You wanna make a day of it?"

"I do, actually. Even if laundry is included."

"Hmm. Don't get ahead of yourself, dude." She crossed her arms tightly over her chest. There was a girlish glint in her eyes and a curvy grin on her lips.

"No problem. I wasn't really devoted to the laundry angle, I gotta say."

"Not surprised."

They went to lunch at that same pizza place as the night of Jesus's visit. Paul claimed the place owed him a pizza. "Or maybe not this place particularly, but the universe in general."

"The pizza universe?" She spoke over her shoulder at him as they followed a waitress to a table for two.

"Something like that." As attractive as Tildy was to him in every way, Paul still felt awkward around her. He figured part of that was their almost-shared experience of seeing Jesus. But he also assumed it had something to do with dating a church lady. He hadn't done that before. Not since youth group. And those girls were no ladies. *Ba dump bump.*

In college, he didn't intentionally avoid dating women from the student ministry or from church. It just worked out that way. Mostly he dated other drama majors, and those women didn't attend church. Not his church, anyway.

After ordering their pizza and salads, Paul fiddled with his silverware and let his eyes wander around the room. In the vacuum reminiscent of many early dates, Paul realized there was one thing he wanted to talk about more than anything else. "So any more insight since that message from ... Jesus?" He tried an apologetic grin in case an apology was his next move.

Tildy laughed. Then, as she began to cycle down, she started laughing even harder. "I just realized how much of a relief it is to have someone ask me that question who really understands." She paused to catch her breath. "You know? I mean, understands what it's like to really be with him."

Paul relaxed the apology off his face and waded into his own relief at what Tildy was describing. Yes. Someone who could relate.

And that's what they did at lunch that Palm Sunday. They talked again about what it was like to see and hear Jesus, and what it was like after he went invisible. The struggles. The surprises. And the continued wonder of knowing he is always near. Occasionally they had to lower their voices, assuming people around them wouldn't understand. Or that they *would* understand and ask to be moved to a more distant table.

Much of the conversation felt like Paul getting things into the open that had only lived inside his head. Things he didn't say at their first dinner. Getting them out of there with Tildy and Jesus was the great provision of that lunch. Even better than the pizza.

The museum exhibit was interesting and even inspiring. When he and Tildy stood in front of a portrait of a little girl with strands of stray hair falling over her face, he recalled Tildy's art. "One of yours?" He grinned.

"Funny you should say that. This was one of the pieces that inspired me. We've had this on display for as long as I've worked here."

"So much emotion."

She looked at the portrait and then at Paul. "You feel that?"

"I guess I do. I mean, it was something"—he lowered his voice—"that Jesus said about me. Being able to feel what other people are feeling."

"Even in a portrait?" She didn't sound doubtful, more impressed.

He didn't want to claim too much. "Maybe I'm sensing what the painter was feeling. Or maybe what I'm really feeling is what it means to you." He knew instantly that this last speculation was true.

Tildy shivered, then turned toward him. She nodded silently with the slightest smile playing around her eyes. And maybe a hint of recognition.

Chapter 37

The Power of the Resurrection Lives On

Opening night for the play was Tuesday. That was so early in the week that it felt to Paul like another dress rehearsal. Maybe that was good for him, relieving some of the pressure. He had gotten used to doing small parts in bigger productions, even if the production was just daytime TV. But playing Jesus was a lot of responsibility, and he felt the weight of it whenever he stopped to think about it. Fortunately, when he was in the middle of performing, he wasn't thinking about it.

"Good work, everyone." Arabella said that at the end of the first night. She had said it after rehearsals too. "Good work."

A good show. That's what Paul was thinking, though he noted no one said it that way.

"You were so inspiring." The young woman who played Mary Magdalene sounded like one of those LA fan girls he knew.

"I was inspired. Inspired by the whole cast and crew. And, of course, inspired by Jesus." As literally true as that statement was, Paul guessed it sounded like an empty religious cliché. He couldn't control that, and he didn't apologize for saying it the way he did.

The shows on Wednesday and Thursday went well. Attendance was good, though not sold out either night. Paul could only wonder if Greg Swanson had accepted his invite. There were a few folks from work who'd found out about his starring role too.

Irma came to him after the performance on Thursday to congratulate and thank him. "I hardly stopped crying through the whole thing. It was so amazing. I never believed ... so ... much, that Jesus is real ... as I do tonight."

"Wow. Thanks. I mean … I don't know what to say. I guess you and I both got a chance this year to really see the meaning behind all this." He gestured toward the stage. He wasn't sure she knew what he meant, really.

When the Friday performance ended, Paul went for late-night tacos with Tildy and some of the cast.

Maybe the tacos were a bad idea just before bed. He dreamt a lot that night. One dream seemed to go on and on. He was on stage. He was playing Jesus. But he had left his costume at the coffee shop. The only possible solution seemed to be going on stage with no clothes. Surely it would be inappropriate for Jesus to wear jeans and a T-shirt. Naked Jesus was more authentic according to the logic of the dream.

In the dream, Paul repeatedly questioned whether this was right. It didn't feel right, being up there in front of the church with no clothes on. Part of the time it was just a rehearsal. That wasn't so bad, at least in the dream. But much of the time it was him naked in front of a packed house.

He was ready to turn and run from the stage by the time they got to the part where he was supposed to be agonizing in prayer while his disciples slept. The dream added new tension to that very powerful scene. Why did the disciples get to have clothes? That was so unfair. Couldn't Jesus just wear a disciple costume?

While standing naked in front of the religious leaders, Paul saw someone in the stage crowd who looked familiar. But then he was gone, and Paul thought he might have imagined him. For whatever reason, Paul did get to wear the modest loin cloth that was his costume on the cross. But the resurrection scene was back to naked Jesus.

Paul was humiliated as he stepped out of the tomb. In the dream version of the play, he had to do some elaborate hand gestures—something like sign language. And he tried to find refuge in focusing on those moves and not on his lack of clothes.

Then, much to everyone's surprise, the real Jesus showed up. And he, too, was naked. And he was not ashamed. He was not afraid of what people would think. He had no fear of messing up those elaborate hand gestures either, because he had invented them.

Paul woke on Saturday morning achy and barely more rested than when he'd lain down to sleep. Another Saturday without work brought to mind the time with Jesus. The usual mundane chores around his apartment and trips to stores felt different as he imagined Jesus with him. It wasn't the same, but somehow it emphasized how real the experience two weeks ago had been.

That night, Tildy met him immediately after the final full production. "That was wonderful. I got chills so many times." She lowered her voice. "It was almost like seeing him again." She rested a hand on his arm and leaned in close where Paul stood outside the dressing room.

That was when he decided to blame her for his naked Jesus dream. She was the one who had asked if he was still decent when she came to the dressing room the previous week. Or maybe Casper was to blame for teasing about the inappropriateness of her question.

That crosswind of thoughts slowed his response. Paul realized he was just staring at her and smiling. "Oh, sorry. I was drifting there. It's been an exhausting week."

"Tomorrow should be easier, though."

The Easter service would be packed with lots of other elements. Paul's role involved no lines, just a reenactment of the resurrection scene. He was expecting much less intensity.

"What about after? Can you join us for Easter dinner?" He had asked her earlier in the week, and Tildy had to check on something. He wasn't sure what.

"Yes. Just ... It's just Easter dinner with some people from the church?" She let go of his arm and leaned back a little.

"Yeah. My mom invites a few folks she knows who don't have family in the area. It's really just these two older women and me this year." He snickered at her. "It's not a meet-my-family sort of meal."

"Huh. Yeah. I was kind of wondering." Her lowered eyes and diminished volume hinted at her embarrassment.

Paul pushed past it. "So, are you coming?"

"Sure. Thanks for inviting me. Tell your mom thanks. Should I bring something?"

"No. She told me not to. She's got it covered. Bob is back in the kitchen, apparently. The two of them have it under control."

By the next morning, Paul was more excited about having Tildy with them for Easter dinner than about the big production at church. Two services rerunning the scene in which he came out of the tomb. No problem.

As with many churches, Community Fellowship was packed on Easter morning. Paul didn't have a seat in the auditorium, hanging around backstage for both services instead. He had to stay in makeup and costume. That was just fine for him. It had been a long week. Backstage, he was able to focus on finishing strong with playing Jesus.

The first service ran smoothly. That was no surprise. But Paul was caught off guard at the effect of the combined resurrection celebration. The passion play had been a dramatic production. A show. An inspiring show, hopefully. But it wasn't the same as a morning worship service. And the congregation seemed to be fully primed this Easter morning.

As he stood in front of the tomb with his hands raised—no elaborate hand gestures required, and a full costume provided—he felt a chill rush through him as the whole auditorium erupted in cheers. That hadn't happened during the evening play performances. Not so enthusiastically, at least. A handful of *amens* and vigorous applause had been the standard response.

After that surprise during the first service, Paul's expectations elevated for that resurrection moment in the second service. And maybe he was feeling relaxed by the fact that it was almost over. As he stooped low through the mouth of the tomb, careful not to knock himself unconscious and ruin the triumph of the scene, he felt a rich reservoir of joy internally and sensed the same from the people in the congregation.

But something happened in that final celebratory moment when he stood tall and raised his hands toward the gathered congregation. Paul was not alone in the spotlight. He knew he wasn't there by himself pretending to be Jesus. He was with Jesus.

That realization melted his knees and lightened his head. At the same time, he felt himself being propped up. Supported. Lifted, even. If he had levitated off the stage, he would have hardly been surprised.

Like a crowd at a football game cheering a last-second winning touchdown, the crowd exploded, and Paul felt himself exploding with it. Instead of the simple, satisfied smile he and Arabella had worked out for his silent acting in this final scene, Paul laughed out loud. Not that anyone could hear him with the great din the congregation raised.

He laughed. And Jesus seemed to be right there laughing with him.

In the electric excitement of that moment, Paul was thinking, *"Where do I go from here?"*

Through the roar of the crowd, past the sound of his own laughter, Paul thought he heard an answer. *I will never leave you.*

Where would Jesus go from here? Where would Paul go from here? Wherever it was, they would go together.

Chapter 38

The Problem with Witnessing an Unspeakable Miracle

After the second service on Easter Sunday, Paul was still at church half an hour past the benediction, finally getting out of costume. Even in street clothes, he had to press through a crowd that milled in the backstage area. But when he finally broke clear, Tildy was there waiting for him.

"Well, I guess the mob didn't carry you away on their shoulders. You're still here."

"That's 'cause I told them I owe it all to the fantastic set designer. The mob is out looking for *you* even as we speak." He faked a vigilant glance left and right in search of the crowd in question.

"*Ha ha.* Thanks." Tildy grinned at his joke and waited as Paul nodded his acceptance of more compliments from a clutch of people in the lobby.

"I hope they're celebrating Jesus and not just a good show." He spoke close to Tildy's ear, noting an array of earrings in a rainbow of colors.

"I think so. I felt like Jesus was right there. Like he was sort of invited in by all the praise." She made eye contact even as they navigated through the people chatting and shuffling toward the exits.

"I felt him. I felt him up there with me. I think he was holding me up. Keeping me from collapsing." Paul kept his voice local while nodding his gratitude for another comment from a passerby.

He could see Tildy struggling, her face shifting from bright amazement to brief frowns and furrowed brows. He assumed she was regretting the awkward setting for something she wanted to say. Eventually, Tildy just laughed and shook her head. They would surely get a chance to talk later.

They took their separate cars and met again in the driveway of his mom's house. An old tan sedan Paul didn't recognize was already parked in the drive.

"I guess they usually have a bigger crowd. I think Bob's heart attack interfered with the invitations this year." Paul waited as Tildy closed her car door. She was holding a cardboard tube about two feet long. "What's that?"

"A gift. Something I drew. You can look at it later. Maybe put it in your car so you don't forget to take it home."

He took the tube from her hand. "Okay. Wow. That makes me curious."

"Yeah. But it's just between you and me. Not something to share with everyone in there." She gestured toward the front of the Cape Cod style house.

"Right. Just boosting my curiosity even more, but I'll wait." He opened the passenger door and slipped the tube onto the floor in front of the seat. This time he locked the car, now that it contained something valuable.

Tildy was carrying a bottle of sparkling juice in her other hand. A bottle that matched the one in Paul's hand. "I guess you interpreted your mother's instructions not to bring anything exactly the same way I did." She laughed at their twin bottles as they paused by the narrow sidewalk toward the front door.

Bob surprised Paul with a jolly greeting at the door. Paul had been picturing him sitting sedately at the kitchen island or maybe at the dining room table. But the hale version of Bob that welcomed them dumbfounded Paul.

"Hello. Thank you for inviting me." Tildy handed Bob her bottle, beating Paul to it.

"Oh, we're glad to have you. A small crowd this year. The more the merrier." Bob took the bottle from Paul and mutely compared them. "Good thing I'm not driving today." He hoisted the nonalcoholic beverages head-high and laughed.

As Bob headed toward the kitchen, Paul hung his sports coat on the rack near the front closet. Tildy kept her sweater on.

His mother arrived in the living room as Tildy was smoothing the front of her pale-yellow dress with small white flowers on it. "Hello, Tildy. I don't think we've met." Mom was wearing the light blue dress and shoes Paul had seen at the service this morning. She had a red-and-white checkered apron over it.

"Pleased to meet you. Thank you so much for having me over. All my family is up in the Chicago area."

"Oh, Paul mentioned something about that." The corners of her mouth twitched in a way that Paul suspected Tildy wouldn't notice. For his mom, and for him to a lesser extent, the mention of Chicago always brought Theresa to mind.

It was around this time of year that Paul had last seen his sister in Chicago, in fact. Not exactly Easter weekend, but close. That twitch in his mother's mouth and glitch in her holiday cheer awakened regret in Paul. He had thought of that last visit with Theresa many times since, wishing he had made more of it. He had gone out one night with some old friends who had moved to Evanston. At the time, leaving his sister at home that one evening seemed trivial.

"Have you met Marian Ross? Or Peggy Merrill?" Mom extended a hand toward two elderly women who were shuffling in from the direction of the kitchen.

Paul assumed the older folks had been gathered in there instead of the living room because Mom and Bob were putting final touches on the meal.

"Have a seat out here while I get the meal on the table, will you?" Mom seemed a bit distracted, but probably just by the usual hostess obligations.

"Can I help you?" Tildy stopped herself midstride toward the couch, making the offer before Mom completed her escape.

"Oh, no. I have just the last little bit to do. Almost ready. That service went longer than I expected. And all the afters, you know."

Paul did know. He was the reason for the delay of this meal, and he hoped nothing had been ruined. He was just settling down and listening to Tildy interview the two older women when his mother exclaimed something from around the corner. He tuned in to what she was saying.

"How is that even possible?"

Perhaps it was endemic to being the youngest kid, but Paul wondered if he had done something wrong. He hadn't been in his mother's kitchen since the night of Bob's emergency room visit, but he had been all over it that night. Him and Jesus. He looked at Bob, who had stopped his rocking chair and furrowed his brow.

"Paul, do you mind coming to help me? I do need something." His mom appeared in the dining room doorway.

"Oh, sure."

Tildy shifted in her seat but settled back into listening to an extended answer from Mrs. Ross.

"What's up? Is something wrong?" He hustled into the kitchen behind his mom, ready to apologize.

"Well, I wouldn't say it's wrong, but did you bring a plate over here the other day when you were here? Do you have a set of plates just like mine? I don't remember."

"No. I came here straight from the hospital. I ate some food, but I only used your plates."

She led him to the cupboard behind the kitchen island. "I don't know if I'm forgetting something, but it just doesn't make sense." She was more hunched over than Paul remembered, as if the burden of this new trouble was compounding the weight of her years. "I was thinking we could just use the good regular dishes since there's just the six of us. It's a setting for eight. I'm sure it's a setting for eight. But there are nine dinner plates."

As he monitored the concern on his mother's face, the significance of what she was saying dropped on Paul like sudden rain. And he started to laugh. Once he started, he couldn't stop. Though he wanted to stop, because he didn't want to explain why he was laughing. He didn't want to explain where that ninth plate came from. Maybe he was a bit hysterical. His hunger at the end of a stressful pair of church services probably didn't help.

Tildy appeared in the dining room, a worried look on her face. Which confirmed for Paul that he was chortling like a nut.

Bob appeared next. "Okay, you have us curious. What's going on in here?"

Mom threw her hands in the air. "Paul's laughing at me for losing my marbles, I guess. I could have sworn this was a set of eight plates, but now there's nine."

"Well, clearly they're reproducing when we're not looking." Bob chuckled.

Tildy snorted at that. "But wouldn't those be *smaller* plates?"

Paul shook his head at her, wondering if he could get her to help him somehow. His hilarity was cooling under a dampening tension about what to tell everyone. The other two guests had also arrived to join in on the joke. Surely he couldn't admit what had happened. No one would believe him if he did. No one besides Tildy, of course.

"Maybe someone else brought a plate of something, and they had the same design." Tildy was looking at one of the dinner plates.

Paul imagined she was looking at exactly the same plate Jesus had eaten off of. The same plate the invisible man had produced out of thin air. The ninth plate. The heavy ceramic set, a toasted gray color with a gold band around the rim, didn't look very common to him. The proposal that someone who had the same set had left one here seemed almost as unlikely as the real story.

But he couldn't do it. He couldn't tell the real story. He just shrugged. "That's not one of mine. My plates aren't nearly this nice."

"Well, I guess I know that." His mom shook her head. "I gave you my chipped old plates." She sighed hard through her nose, and that was the end of it from her. Shrugging was all anyone could offer at that point.

When Paul and Tildy drifted toward the dining room table as Bob and Mom carried in the last few serving dishes, Tildy smiled at him as if sharing in the humor and the mystery. But he couldn't resist wincing in a guilty way.

Tildy furrowed her brow in question.

"I'll tell you later."

She half squinted one eye and nodded. She looked like a woman who might have found the culprit, but Paul knew she couldn't guess the nature of his crime.

It was a pleasant and well-prepared meal, marred only by occasional fits of laughter that Paul sometimes managed to disguise as clearing his throat or choking on a drink of sparkling grape juice.

By the end of the meal, Tildy was looking at him suspiciously, and he was feeling guilty about withholding the secret of the miraculous plate.

Chapter 39

Jesus as Seen by a Local Artist

Even though they had driven separately, Paul gathered his jacket and prepared to leave at the same time as Tildy. He was tired. Ready to kick back for the rest of the day. But his top priority was finally telling someone the plate story.

They said grateful goodbyes to his mom and Bob, and to the other guests, then headed out the front door into the cool sunshine of early April. When they were far enough from the front of the house, Paul attracted Tildy's curiosity with a wide-eyed smile.

"What?" She pushed a braid out of her face.

"I have to tell you what happened with the plates."

She looked back toward the house and lowered her voice. "So you *do* know where it came from."

He nodded deeply. "Do you have a few minutes?"

"Sure. I wanna hear this story that you couldn't tell your mother."

"I know. So maybe we could go to the park over here on Pearson? Just back the way we came in."

"Yeah, that's okay with me. I'll follow you there."

The grassy residential park took up one block bounded by streets lined with houses. They both found street parking and met on the sidewalk under a budding fruit tree that Paul couldn't identify. Crab apple, possibly.

"Busy place." Tildy wore a pair of round sunglasses with black plastic rims. It was a good look for her. The wind tossed her sunny skirt and swung her braids gently.

"Yeah. I guess it's where you go after Easter dinner. We're so trendy."

"Indeed. But stop stalling, and tell me what happened."

They sauntered shoulder to shoulder along the straight sidewalk, and Paul told the story of him and Jesus cleaning up his mom's kitchen.

Tildy smiled during that part of the story. "I'm trying to remember. I guess he did help me with little things in the kitchen, but it wasn't like I had to clean up the whole place when I was eleven." She shook her head and let her eyes fade toward her memories.

But Paul was still approaching the big reveal. "So I said something about feeling strange that he had to just watch me while I ate. He was sitting across the table from me, and he sort of held his hands aside, and this whole place setting—complete with lamb shank and potatoes and all—just showed up." He grinned at Tildy as she did the calculation with a gaping mouth.

"Wait. He, like, just zapped that plate out of thin air?" Her voice hit a high note Paul hadn't heard from her before.

He was back to laughing. This time there was no reason for restraint, and he didn't feel so guilty anymore.

Tildy was still shaking her head at his story. "Oh, my. I see why you couldn't tell your mother. No way would she believe that."

"Right? Like I would say, 'Well, you know, Mom, that's probably the plate Jesus materialized out of thin air the other day when he ate lamb shank with me.'" His laughter took a goofier turn, and he had to stop walking for a few seconds.

Tildy put a hand on his shoulder as if she feared he would collapse.

But Paul was getting a grip on himself. "I guess it's even funnier because I knew I could tell you, and you would believe me. It wouldn't be so humorous if I had to keep that whole thing to myself."

Nodding and sniffing another laugh, Tildy turned briskly toward him. She sobered a little. "You know, he could have, like, just magically transported a plate out of the cupboard to the table. It didn't have to be a whole new plate."

Paul nodded deeply again. "Yeah, that's right. Maybe he did it this way on purpose. Maybe he did it so ... so I could tell my mom what happened." He wondered now if he had missed an opportunity. Was that what Jesus had in mind?

"I don't know. I'm with you—I don't think she would have believed you. I mean, I told my grandma about Jesus touching her and healing her heart palpitations, but she just acted as if she didn't hear me say it. She couldn't accept that explanation even if there wasn't another one available."

"Oh. Huh. You didn't tell me about her reaction before."

"I haven't told you everything."

"That's good to know. Apparently I need to ask better questions."

Tildy twisted her shoulders left and then right, her thin white sweater catching the breeze briefly. "Well, I gotta take some of the blame. I'm pretty slow about sharing all that happened with me and Jesus. I'm much more used to *not* telling."

"Sure. Understood." They turned at the second corner and walked back into the sun. "I definitely get it. I do."

"I don't know how much wisdom it takes to figure out what to say to people who are unlikely to believe you, but I don't seem to have that much myself."

"Well, maybe we can help each other with that."

She turned toward him and took a peek over her sunglasses, which had slipped a bit. "Are you planning on sticking around for a while, then?"

"I'm gonna give it a try for at least the full six months of my lease. I'm auditioning for a community theater gig tomorrow that would pay better than the coffee shop and justify sticking around. Justify it financially, that is."

"There are other sorts of justifications."

"Yes. There are." They walked in silence for a few seconds. "What was in that tube you gave me?"

"You'll have to see for yourself." They were headed back toward their cars.

"Did you say it was a drawing you did?"

Tildy just smiled. Maybe it was a nervous smile. What was in that plain cardboard tube that made her nervous?

Within a couple minutes, they were back near Paul's loaner car. "Okay if I look at the drawing now?"

She hesitated. "Sure."

"You were thinking I would look at it alone."

"Yes. But I'm willing to take the chance."

"Huh. I hope I can get to it before I die of curiosity."

She stood back on the sidewalk as he pulled out his keys and went to manually unlock the passenger door. It was warm in the car, a little greenhouse parked by the curb. He lifted the tube, which was now the temperature of a living person. He watched Tildy even as he twisted the top off.

She laughed. "The other end is already opened."

Paul flipped the tube to confirm her claim. Still, he held the cap in his hand as he peeked. White paper. He stuck two fingers inside to get a grip. Careful not to smudge or rip it, he tugged and tugged again until heavy paper extended past the mouth of the tube. He glanced at Tildy again as he pulled the paper free.

She pushed her sunglasses up and crossed her arms over her chest. She looked away, and he did too, sorry to make her uncomfortable. But maybe she had done that to herself, risking whatever she feared by doing whatever this rolled-up drawing represented.

Tucking the empty tube under his arm, he found the edge of the drawing and unrolled it, his hands shaking a little.

Tildy stepped up and took the tube and the cap from him, a bit brusquely. He attributed that to her nerves, obvious in her every movement.

It was a drawing in pencil or charcoal. Dark lines on textured white paper. A person. A hand. A face. Two faces. He held the drawing at arm's length, speechless. His throat closed down, and he forced his breathing to slow.

"It's him." The words came in a rough whisper.

"Is it? Is that what he looked like for you too?"

"Exactly." Paul forced a laugh. "Though I can't say I recognize this other guy."

Tildy grunted a laugh and let her arms drop. The cap fell on the ground, and she bent quickly to pick it up, tottering in the grass on her thin white high-heeled sandals. "I was afraid he might have looked different to you."

Shaking his head, Paul continued to study the image of two men with long dark hair and beards. The image of Paul was probably from one of his publicity photos online. And Jesus was from a recent visit.

Tildy's voice was warm and close. "It would be okay, of course, if he looked different. He explained that to me way back when. He told me he could appear any way he wanted. Glorified body or something." She was nearly leaning on Paul's shoulder, looking at the double portrait with him.

"Yeah, I can imagine him saying that." He looked at Tildy. She had pulled her sunglasses off at some point. "How did you remember him so clearly?"

"I couldn't forget." She tipped her head briefly to the side. "And I did a drawing of him when I was twelve. One of my best drawings up to that point. I pulled that out to make this one, so that helped a lot."

"Sure. Of course." He let the drawing roll back onto itself, a broad white tube held in one hand. His hand was still shaking. Part of what shook him was the pose of the two men. The closeness. The friendly lean of the real Jesus toward the man caught by him merely playing Jesus.

He was still trying to regulate his breathing. To settle his fluttering heart. "Thank you. This is priceless. Literally priceless."

She glanced at him. "Good. Don't sell it."

He wrapped an arm around her shoulders. "Never. Not even when you become world famous."

"Okay. You just wait for that day."

"I will. I will wait." Did she know he was talking about something else?

245

She seemed to be examining his eyes in search of an answer. In search of certainty.

"Were you thinking I was going away soon when you drew this for me?"

She blinked rapidly. "Maybe."

He nodded. "Thanks." He tightened his grip on her shoulders. "I plan to stick around for a while. For more than financial reasons."

She met his eyes. "Good."

You might also like:

Seeing Jesus Series: https://www.amazon.com/dp/B074CGZ26F

Keep On Asking, Book 1 of The Prayer Rider Series: https://www.amazon.com/dp/B0B1CHX4QY

Sophie Ramos Series: https://www.amazon.com/dp/B08NGWQWF5

Get Up, Eleanor: https://www.amazon.com/dp/B08B1LN3VK

Alice's Friendship Bench: https://www.amazon.com/dp/B09F1CVXVK

Small Lives: https://www.amazon.com/dp/B08HGTSXNT

Subscribe to my newsletter here www.jeffreymcclainjones.com/subscribe-1to know what I am working on now.

Checkout my website at https://www.jeffreymcclainjones.com for all my other books.

Printed in Great Britain
by Amazon

34412415R00138